Praise for the Immortals Series
by Alyson Noël

"*Evermore* is addictive. When I wasn't reading, I was thinking about how I could sneak away to read some more. I couldn't put it down. I dreamt about this book. And when I was finished, I couldn't get it out of my head. This book was simply breathtaking." —*Teens Read Too*

"Teen angst and the paranormal make a combustible mix as Noël utilizes typical themes and gives them a dangerous and eerie twist. Getting hooked on this new series, The Immortals, is guaranteed."
—*Romantic Times BOOKreviews* (4 stars)

"*Evermore* will thrill many teen fantasy–suspense readers, especially fans of Stephenie Meyer's Twilight series. . . . Noël creates a cast of recognizably diverse teens in a realistic high school setting, along with just the right tension to make Ever's discovery of her own immortality—should she choose it—exciting and credible."
—*Booklist*

"Readers who enjoy the works of P.C. Cast and Stephenie Meyer will love this outstanding paranormal teen-lit thriller."
—*Midwest Book Review*

"Get ready for a wild ride that is filled with twisting paths and mystery, love, and fantasy. . . . The writing style, story, and characters are a bit like Meyer's and Marr's popular books, but written with a new twist and voice. And after reading the book, you too will probably want your own Damen, even if it means making the ultimate sacrifice."
—*The Book Queen* (5 stars)

"I found myself unwilling to put the book down, even though I had to at some points, because I wanted to know what was going to happen. . . . Ever was so real and her emotions were so believable that it was a little creepy. It's like Alyson Noël is actually a grieving, love-struck teenager. She got Ever completely perfect. And by perfect, I mean delightfully flawed and deep."

—The Frenetic Reader

"Evermore is a wonderful book that I believe would be a lovely addition to any library . . . a book that fans of Stephenie Meyer and Melissa Marr should add to their collections. Definitely engaging and will catch your attention the minute you open to the first page!"

—Mind of a Bibliophile

"Alyson Noël creates a great picture of each and every character in the book. I am a fan of the Twilight series and I recommend this book to those who like the series as well. It is a very quick read, with all the interesting twists and turns."

—Flamingnet book reviews

"I loved this book. It really keeps your attention throughout the story, because the puzzle gets pieced together bit by bit, but you don't know exactly what happened until the end. . . . I would definitely recommend this to my friends."

—Portsmouth Teen Book Review

"This is the first installment of the Immortals series. Ms. Noël pens a well-detailed story that makes it easy for the reader to visualize both the characters and the world around them. Evermore has a familiar theme that attracts readers, but inside this book you'll find that the author has added some unique details that sets it apart."

—Darque Reviews

"*Evermore*'s suspense, eerie mystery, and strange magic were interestingly entertaining. . . . I found Ever to be a character I could really respect. . . . Recommended."   —*The Bookworm*

"Beautiful main characters, tense budding romance, a dark secret, mysterious immortals—what more could you ask from this modern gothic romance?"   —*Justine* magazine

"*Evermore* was a great way to lighten my reading load this winter and provided me with a creative, magical story that I really enjoyed. This is the first in a series for Noël and I think she may have a hit on her hands. . . . *Evermore* has good and evil, likable characters, vivid descriptions, and a good story."   —*Planet Books*

"I fell into it easily, and loved the world Noël created. . . . The fact that Ever had psychic powers was truly interesting. They flowed neatly through the book and I felt Ever's pain. . . . Trust me, this book was really good. I couldn't put it down. Alyson Noël created an amazing new world, and after this book I am so curious to see where it heads because, honestly, I have no idea."
       —*Reading Keeps You Sane*

"Ever is an easy character to like. I really felt for her because of all she lost and what she struggled with daily. . . . *Evermore* was a really fast, engaging read with some great characters. It is the first in a series, so I'm eager to see if we will learn more about Ever, Damen, and friends in the next one. . . . It's sure to be a great read."
       —*Ninja* reviews

"The writing here is clear, the story well defined, and narrator Ever has an engaging voice that teens should enjoy."
       —*January Magazine*

"When I got a copy of *Evermore*, I sat down to read it, intending to read only a chapter or two. Instead, I blazed through the first hundred pages before I knew it . . . and then I didn't want to put the book down. Except I couldn't keep my eyes open any longer. So I picked it up the next morning and finished it. Now I can't wait . . . to see what happens next." —*Blog Critics Magazine*

"This young adult novel ponders immortal love and the knowledge that 'revenge weakens and love strengthens.' Fans of the Twilight series should love it." —*Orange Coast*

"Noël writes an emotional, thoughtful book that made me cry in a couple of places. *Evermore* was an easy novel to get sucked into, and I wanted to get back to it as soon as possible. If you love Stephenie Meyer, you will LOVE this book." —*Night Owl Romance*

"*Evermore* is a fresh and original work that . . . branches out and explores new ground. Definitely recommended." —*Cool Moms Rule!*

"I totally LOVE Alyson Noël's *Evermore*. . . . Noël has delivered a deliciously fresh new series that will be the next new thing. . . . Every teen and even adults everywhere will be hooked and waiting for more. . . . This is a keeper and a book that you have to go out and buy right now because if you don't you will be missing out. People will be asking if you have been living under a rock if you don't give *Evermore* a try, and that is just not acceptable." —*Talk About My Favorite Authors*

also by alyson noël

Evermore

Cruel Summer

Saving Zoë

Kiss & Blog

Laguna Cove

Fly Me to the Moon

Art Geeks and Prom Queens

Faking 19

blue moon

blue moon

alyson noël

st. martin's griffin ✠ new york

This is a work of fiction. All of the characters, organizations, and events portrayed in this novel are either products of the author's imagination or are used fictitiously.

BLUE MOON. Copyright © 2009 by Alyson Noël. All rights reserved. Printed in the United States of America. For information, address St. Martin's Press, 175 Fifth Avenue, New York, N.Y. 10010.

www.stmartins.com

Library of Congress Cataloging-in-Publication Data

Noël, Alyson.
    Blue moon : the Immortals / Alyson Noël.—1st ed.
        p. cm.
    Summary: Eager to learn everything she can about her new abilities as an Immortal, Ever turns to her beloved Damen to show her the way, but just as her powers are increasing, his are in decline, and as she searches for a way to save him, she finds herself with a wrenching choice to make.
    ISBN-13: 978-0-312-53276-5
    ISBN-10: 0-312-53276-8
    [1. Psychic ability—Fiction.   2. Immortality—Fiction.   3. Supernatural—Fiction. 4. Death—Fiction.]   I. Title.
    PZ7.N67185Bl 2009
    [Fic]—dc22

                                                                    2009010679

10   9   8   7   6   5   4   3   2

For Jessica Brody,

who's so freaking gifted, in so many ways, it's not even fair!

acknowledgments

Big, huge, sparkly thanks to: my awesome editor, Rose Hilliard, whose enthusiasm, insight, and shared fondness for exclamation marks make me glad she's on my team, along with Matthew Shear, Katy Hershberger, and everyone else on the St. Martin's crew; Bill Contardi, who's everything I could ask for in an agent and more; Patrick O'Malley Mahoney and Jolynn "Snarky" Benn, my two BFFs who are always ready to celebrate once the manuscript is finished; my mom, who's been stalking the YA aisles of her local bookstore for four straight years now; my amazing husband, Sandy, who's so dang good at so many things, I sometimes wonder if he's a secret immortal; and last, but not least, major *major* thanks to my fabulous readers—you guys are the absolute BEST and I couldn't do it without you!

Every man has his own destiny;

the only imperative

is to follow it, to accept it,

no matter where it leads him.

—Henry Miller

one

"Close your eyes and picture it. Can you see it?"

I nod, eyes closed.

"Imagine it right there before you. *See* its texture, shape, and color—got it?"

I smile, holding the image in my head.

"Good. Now reach out and touch it. *Feel* its contours with the tips of your fingers, *cradle* its weight in the palms of your hands, then combine all of your senses—sight, touch, smell, taste—can you taste it?"

I bite my lip and suppress a giggle.

"Perfect. Now combine that with feeling. *Believe* it exists right before you. Feel it, see it, touch it, taste it, accept it, *manifest* it!" he says.

So I do. I do all of those things. And when he groans, I open my eyes to see for myself.

"Ever." He shakes his head. "You were supposed to think of an *orange*. This isn't even close."

"Nope, nothing fruity about him." I laugh, smiling at each of my Damens—the replica I manifested before me, and the flesh and blood version beside me. Both of them equally tall, dark, and so devastatingly handsome they hardly seem real.

"What am I going to do with you?" the real Damen asks, attempting a disapproving gaze but failing miserably. His eyes always betray him, showing nothing but love.

"Hmmm . . ." I glance between my two boyfriends—one real, one conjured. "I guess you could just go ahead and kiss me. Or, if you're too busy, I'll ask him to stand in, I don't think he'd mind." I motion toward manifest Damen, laughing when he smiles and winks at me even though his edges are fading and soon he'll be gone.

But the real Damen doesn't laugh. He just shakes his head and says, "Ever, please. You need to be serious. There's so much to teach you."

"What's the rush?" I fluff my pillow and pat the space right beside me, hoping he'll move away from my desk and come join me. "I thought we had nothing *but* time?" I smile. And when he looks at me, my whole body grows warm and my breath halts in my throat, and I can't help but wonder if I'll ever get used to his amazing beauty—his smooth olive skin, brown shiny hair, perfect face, and lean sculpted body—the perfect dark yin to my pale blond yang. "I think you'll find me a very eager student," I say, my eyes meeting his—two dark wells of unfathomable depths.

"You're insatiable," he whispers, shaking his head and moving beside me, as drawn to me as I am to him.

"Just trying to make up for lost time," I murmur, always so eager for these moments, the times when it's just us, and I don't have to share him with anyone else. Even knowing we have all of eternity laid out before us doesn't make me any less greedy.

He leans in to kiss me, forgoing our lesson. All thoughts of manifesting, remote viewing, telepathy—all of that psychic business replaced by something far more immediate, as he pushes me back against a pile of pillows and covers my body with his, the two of us merging like crumbled vines seeking the sun.

His fingers snake under my top, sliding along my stomach to the edge of my bra as I close my eyes and whisper, "I love you." Words I once kept to myself. But after saying it the first time, I've barely said anything else.

Hearing his soft muffled groan as he releases the clasp on my bra, so effortlessly, so perfectly, nothing awkward or fumbling about it.

Every move he makes is so graceful, so perfect, so—

Maybe too perfect.

"What's wrong?" he asks, as I push him away. His breath coming in short shallow gasps as his eyes seek mine, their surrounding skin tense and constricted in the way I've grown used to.

"Nothing's wrong." I turn my back and adjust my top, glad I completed the lesson on shielding my thoughts since it's the only thing that allows me to lie.

He sighs and moves away, denying me the tingle of his touch and the heat of his gaze as he paces before me. And when he finally stops and faces me, I press my lips together, knowing what's next. We've been here before.

"Ever, I'm not trying to rush you or anything. Really, I'm not," he says, his face creased with concern. "But at some point you're going to have to get over this and accept who I am. I can manifest anything you desire, send telepathic thoughts and images whenever we're apart, whisk you away to Summerland at a moment's notice. But the one thing I can't ever do is change the past. It just is."

I stare at the floor, feeling small, needy, and completely ashamed. Hating that I'm so incapable of hiding my jealousies and insecurities, hating that they're so transparent and clearly displayed. Because no matter what sort of psychic shield I create, it's no use. He's had six hundred years to study human behavior (to study *my* behavior), versus my sixteen.

"Just—just give me a little more time to get used to all this," I say, picking at a frayed seam on my pillowcase. "It's only been a few weeks." I shrug, remembering how I killed his ex-wife, told him I loved him, and sealed my immortal fate, less than three weeks ago.

He looks at me, his lips pressed together, his eyes tinged with doubt. And even though we're merely a few feet apart, the space that divides us is so heavy and fraught—it feels like an ocean.

"I'm referring to *this* lifetime," I say, my voice quickening, rising, hoping to fill up the void and lighten the mood. "And since I can't recall any of the others, it's all I have. I just need a little more *time*, okay?" I smile nervously, my lips feeling clumsy and loose as I hold them in place, exhaling in relief when he sits down beside me, lifts his fingers to my forehead, and seeks the space where my scar used to be.

"Well, that's one thing we'll never run out of." He sighs, trailing his fingers along the curve of my jaw as he leans in to kiss me, his lips making a series of stops from my forehead, to my nose, to my mouth.

And just when I think he's about to kiss me again, he squeezes my hand and moves away. Heading straight for the door and leaving a beautiful red tulip behind in his place.

two

Even though Damen can sense the exact moment my aunt Sabine turns onto our street and approaches the drive, that's not why he left.

He left because of me.

Because of the simple fact that he's been after me for hundreds of years, seeking me out in all of my incarnations, just so we could be together.

Only we never got *together*.

Which means *it* never happened.

Apparently every time we were about to take the next step and consummate our love, his ex-wife Drina managed to show up and kill me.

But now that I've killed her, eliminated her with one well-placed though admittedly feeble swipe to her rather compromised heart chakra, there's absolutely nothing or no one blocking our way.

Except me.

Because even though I love Damen with all of my being, and definitely want to take the next step—I can't stop thinking about those last six hundred years.

And how he chose to live them. (Outlandishly, according to him.)

And *whom* he chose to live them with. (Besides his ex-wife Drina, many others have been alluded to.)

And, well, as much as I hate to admit it, knowing all of that makes me feel a little insecure.

Okay, maybe *a lot* insecure. I mean, it's not like my pathetically meager list of guys I've kissed could ever compare to his six centuries' worth of conquests.

And even though I know it's ridiculous, even though I know Damen has loved me for centuries, the fact is, the heart and mind aren't always friendly.

And in my case, they're barely speaking.

Yet still, every time Damen comes over for my lesson, I always manage to turn it into a prolonged make-out session, each time starting out thinking: *This is it! It's really going to happen this time!*

Only to push him away like the worst kind of tease.

And the truth is, it's exactly like he said. He can't change his past, *it just is.* Once something is done it can't be undone. There's no rewind. No going back.

The only thing a person can ever really do is keep moving forward.

And that's exactly what I need to do.

Take that big leap forward without hesitation, without once looking back.

Simply forget the past and forge toward the future.

I just wish it were really that easy.

"Ever?" Sabine makes her way up the stairs as I run frantically around my room, trying to straighten it up before plopping in front of my desk and scrambling to look like I'm busy. "You still up?" she asks, poking her head inside. And even though her suit is wrinkled, her hair limp, and her eyes a little red and tired, her aura's hanging in there, beaming a nice shade of green.

"I was just finishing up some homework," I say, pushing my laptop away as though I'd been using it.

"Did you eat?" She leans against the doorjamb, her eyes narrowed and suspicious, as her aura reaches right toward me—the portable lie detector she unknowingly carries wherever she goes.

"Of course," I tell her. Nodding and smiling and doing my best to appear sincere, but the truth is, it feels false on my face.

I hate having to lie. Especially to her. After all that she's done for me, taking me in after the accident when my whole family died. I mean, it's not like she had to do that. Just because she's my only living relative didn't mean she couldn't say no. And believe me, half the time she probably wishes she had. Her life was way less complicated before I arrived.

"I meant something besides that red drink." She nods, motioning toward the bottle on my desk, the opalescent red liquid with the strange bitter taste I don't hate nearly as much as I used to. Which is good since, according to Damen, I'll be sipping it for the rest of eternity. Though it's not like I *can't* eat real food, it's just that I no longer want to. My immortal juice provides all of the nutrients I could ever need. And no matter how much or how little I drink, I always feel sated.

But still, I know what she's thinking. And not only because I can read all of her thoughts, but because I used to think the same things about Damen. I used to get really annoyed watching him push his food around and only *pretend* to eat. Until I found out his secret, that is.

"I, um, I grabbed something earlier," I finally say, trying not to press my lips together, avert my gaze, or cringe—all of my usual dead giveaways. "With Miles and Haven," I add, hoping it will explain the lack of dirty dishes, even though I know that providing too many details is bad, like a flashing red light signaling LIAR STRAIGHT AHEAD! Not to mention that Sabine being a lawyer, one of her firm's top litigators, makes her incredibly good at spotting a phony. Though she pretty much saves that particular gift for her professional life. In her private life, she chooses to believe.

Except for today. Today she's not buying a word of it. Instead, she just looks at me and says, "I'm worried about you."

I swivel around so I'm facing her, hoping to appear as though I'm open, ready to address her concerns, even though I'm pretty much freaked. "I'm fine," I tell her, nodding and smiling so that she'll believe it. "Really. My grades are good, I'm getting along with my friends, Damen and I are—" I pause, realizing I've never really talked to her about my relationship before, haven't really defined it, and have pretty much kept it to myself. And the truth is, now that I've started, I'm not sure how to finish.

I mean, referring to ourselves as boyfriend and girlfriend sounds so mundane and inadequate once our pasts, presents, and futures are taken into account, because clearly all of our shared history makes us so much more than that. But still, it's not like I'm going to publicly proclaim us as eternal partners or soul mates either—the *ick* factor on that is just way too high. And the truth is, I'd really rather not define it at all. At the moment, I'm confused enough as it is. Besides, what would I even tell her? That we've loved each other for centuries but still haven't made it past second base?

"Well, Damen and I are—doing really good," I finally say, gulping when I realize I said *good* instead of *great*, which may be the first real truth I've spoken all day.

"So he *was* here." She sets her brown leather briefcase onto the floor and looks at me, both of us fully aware of how easily I fell into her professional litigator's trap.

I nod, mentally kicking myself for insisting we hang out here, as opposed to his place like he originally wanted.

"I thought I saw his car whiz past." She shifts her gaze to my rumpled bed with the haphazard pillows and disheveled duvet, and when she turns back to face me, I can't help but cringe, especially when I sense what's about to be said.

"Ever." She sighs. "I'm sorry I'm not around all that much and that we're unable to spend more time together. And even though it feels like we're still sort of finding our way with each other, I want you to know that I'm here for you. If you ever need to talk to someone—I'll listen."

I press my lips together and nod, knowing she's not finished, but hoping that by staying quiet and complacent, it'll be over with soon.

"Because even though you probably think I'm too old to understand what you're going through, I do remember what it was like at your age. How overwhelming it can be with the constant pressure to measure up to models and actresses and other impossible images you see on TV."

I swallow hard and avoid her gaze, cautioning myself to not overreact, to not go all overboard with defending myself since it's much better for her to believe this than to suspect the real truth.

Ever since I got expelled, Sabine's been watching me closer than ever, and when she recently loaded up on a stack of self-help books, everything from: *How to Raise a Sane Teen in Insane Times Like These,* to: *Your Teen and the Media (And What You Can Do About it!),* it's gotten a gazillion times worse. With her underlining and highlighting all of the most disturbing adolescent behaviors, and then scrutinizing me, checking for symptoms.

"But I want you to know that you're a beautiful girl, far more beautiful than I ever was at your age, and that starving yourself to compete with all of those skinny celebrities who spend half their lives checking in and out of rehab is not only a completely unrea sonable and unattainable goal, but will only end up making you sick." She gives me a pointed look, desperately wanting to get through to me, hoping her words will penetrate. "I want you to know that you're perfect just as you are, and it pains me to see you going through this. And if this is about Damen, well then, all I have to say about that is—"

"I'm not anorexic."

She looks at me.

"I'm not bulimic, I'm not on some crazy fad diet, I'm not starving myself, I'm not striving to be a size zero, and I'm not trying to look like an Olsen twin. Seriously, Sabine, do I *look* like I'm wasting away?" I stand, allowing for an unobstructed view of me in all of my tight-jeaned glory, because if anything, I feel like the opposite of wasting away. I seem to be bulking up at a pretty good pace.

She looks me over. And I mean *really* looks me over. Starting from the top of my head and going all the way down to my toes, her eyes coming to rest on my pale exposed ankles I had no choice but to display when I discovered that my favorite jeans are too short and rolled them up to compensate.

"I just thought . . ." She shrugs, unsure of what to say now that the evidence presented before her so clearly points to a *not guilty* verdict. "Because I never see you eating anymore—and you're always sipping that red—"

"So you just assumed I'd gone from adolescent binge drinker to anorexic food avoider?" I laugh so she'll know I'm not mad—a little annoyed maybe, though more with myself than with her. I should've faked it better. I should've at least *pretended* to eat. "You have nothing to worry about." I smile. "Really. And just so we're clear, I have no intention of taking and/or dealing drugs, experimenting with body modification, cutting, branding, scarification, extreme piercing, or whatever else makes this week's *Top Ten Maladjusted Behaviors to Look for in Your Teen* list. And for the record, my sipping that red drink has nothing to do with trying to be celebrity skinny or trying to please Damen. I just happen to like it, that's all. Besides, I happen to know for a fact that Damen loves me and accepts me exactly as I—" I stop, knowing I've just started a whole other topic I'm unwilling to explore. And before she can even get to the words now formulating in her head, I just hold up my hand and say, "And *no*, that's *not* what I meant. Damen and I are—" *Hooking up, dating, boyfriend and girlfriend, friends with benefits, eternally bound.* "Well, we're together. You know, committed, like a couple. But we *aren't* sleeping together."

Yet.

She looks at me, her face as pinched and uncomfortable as I feel inside. Neither of us wanting to explore this topic, but, unlike me, she feels it's her duty.

"Ever, I wasn't insinuating—" she starts. But then she looks at me, and I look at her, and she shrugs, deciding to just let it go since we both know she most certainly was.

And I'm so relieved that it's over and that I got off relatively easy, that I'm completely taken by surprise when she says, "Well, since you really seem to care about this young man, I think I should get to know him. So let's schedule a time when we can all go to dinner. How does this weekend sound?"

This weekend?

I swallow hard and look at her, knowing exactly what she's after, hoping to kill two birds with one meal. Having found the perfect opportunity to watch me scarf down a full plate of food, while putting Damen on the stand so she can totally grill him.

"Well, that sounds great and all except that Miles's play is on Friday." I fight to keep my voice steady and sure. "And then there's supposed to be an after party—and that'll probably run pretty late—so . . ."

She nods, her eyes right on mine, her gaze so uncanny and knowing it's making me sweat.

"So it's probably not going to work," I finish, knowing I'll have to go through with it eventually, but hoping for later rather than sooner. I mean, I love Sabine, and I love Damen, I'm just not sure I'm going to love them together, especially once the interrogation begins.

She looks at me for a moment, then nods and turns away. And just when I'm able to exhale, she glances over her shoulder to say, "Well, Friday's clearly out, but that still leaves Saturday. Why don't you tell Damen to be here at eight?"

three

Even though I oversleep, I still manage to get out the door and over to Miles's on time. I guess because it doesn't take me nearly as long to get ready now that Riley's no longer around to distract me. And even though it used to bug me the way she'd perch on my dresser wearing one of her crazy Halloween costumes while grilling me about boyfriends and making fun of my clothes, ever since I convinced her to move on, to cross the bridge to where our parents and our dog Buttercup were waiting, I haven't been able to see her.

Which pretty much means she was right. I can only see the souls who've stayed behind, not the ones who've crossed over.

And like always when I think about Riley, my throat constricts and my eyes start to sting, and I wonder if I'll ever get used to the fact that she's gone. I mean, permanently and irreversibly gone. But I guess by now I should know enough about loss to realize that you never really stop missing someone—you just learn to live around the huge gaping hole of their absence.

I wipe my eyes and pull into Miles's drive, remembering Riley's promise, that she'd send me a sign, something to show she's okay. But even though I've been holding tight to her pledge, staying alert, and searching vigilantly for some indication of her presence—so far I've got nothing.

Miles opens the door and just as I start to say *hi,* he holds up his hand and says, "Don't speak. Just look at my face and tell me what you see. What's the very first thing you notice? And *don't* lie."

"Your beautiful brown eyes," I say, hearing the thoughts in his head and wishing, not for the first time, that I could show my friends how to shield their thoughts and keep all their private stuff private. But that would mean divulging my mind-reading, aura-seeing, psychic-sensing secrets, and that I can't do.

Miles shakes his head and climbs inside, yanking down on the mirrored visor and inspecting his chin. "You're such a liar. Look, it's right there! Like a shining red beacon you can't possibly miss, so don't even try to pretend you don't see it."

I glance at him as I back out of the drive, seeing the zit that dared sprout on his face, though it's his bright pink nail polish that steals my attention. "Nice nails." I laugh.

"It's for the play." He smirks, still zit gazing. "I can't even believe this! It's like I'm totally falling apart just when everything was going so perfect. Rehearsals have been great, I know all of my lines as well as everyone else's . . . I thought I was totally and completely ready, and now *this!*" He jabs at his face.

"It's just nerves," I say, glancing at him as the light turns green.

"Exactly!" He nods. "Which just proves what an amateur I am. Because professionals, *real* professionals, they don't get nervous. They just go into their creative zone and . . . *create.* Maybe I'm not cut out for this?" He looks at me, his face tense with worry. "Maybe it's just a fluke that I got the lead."

I glance at him, remembering how Drina claimed to climb inside the director's head and sway him toward Miles. But even if that's true, that doesn't mean he can't handle it, doesn't mean he wasn't the best.

"That's ridiculous." I shake my head. "Tons of actors get nervous, suffer from stage fright or whatever. Seriously. You wouldn't believe some of the stories Riley used to—" I stop, eyes wide, mouth open, knowing I can never finish that sentence. Can never divulge the stories gleaned from my dead little sister who used to enjoy spying on the Hollywood elite. "Anyway, don't you wear, like, a ton of heavy pancake makeup?"

He glances at me. "Yeah. So. What's your point? The play's Friday, which, for your information, happens to be *tomorrow*. This will *never* be gone by then."

"Maybe." I shrug. "But what I meant was, can't you use the makeup to cover it?"

Miles rolls his eyes and scowls. "Oh, so I can sport a huge flesh-colored beacon instead? Would you look at this thing? There's no disguising it. It's got its own DNA! It's casting shadows!"

I pull into the school parking lot, claiming my usual space, the one right next to Damen's shiny black BMW. And when I look at Miles again, for some reason I feel compelled to touch his face. As though my index finger is inexplicably drawn to the zit on his chin.

"What're you doing?" he asks, cringing and pulling away.

"Just—just be still," I whisper, having no idea what I'm doing, or why I'm even doing it. All I know is my finger has a definite destination in mind.

"Well don't—*touch it!*" he shouts, the exact moment I make contact. "Great, that's just great. Now it'll probably double in size." He shakes his head and climbs out of the car, and I can't help but feel disappointed to see the pimple still there.

I guess I was hoping I'd developed some kind of enhanced healing ability. Ever since Damen told me, right after I'd decided to accept my fate and start drinking the immortal juice, that I could expect to go through some changes, anything from super-enhanced psychic abilities (which I was not looking forward to), to super-enhanced physical abilities (which could certainly have its benefits in P.E.), or something else altogether (like the ability to heal others, which has my vote since it would be totally cool), I've been on the lookout for something extraordinary. But so far, all I got is an extra inch of leg, which really doesn't do much for me besides requiring a new pair of jeans. And that probably would've happened eventually anyway.

I grab my bag and climb out of my car, my lips meeting Damen's the instant he comes around to my side.

"Okay, seriously. How much longer can this possibly last?"

We both pull away and look at Miles.

"Yeah, I'm talking to you." He wags his finger. "All of the kissing, and hugging, and let us not forget the constant whispering of sweet little nothings." He shakes his head and narrows his eyes. "Seriously. I was hoping you guys would be over it by now. I mean, don't get me wrong, we're all very happy that Damen's back in school, that you've found each other again, and will most likely live happily ever after. But really, don't you think it's time to maybe try and tone it down a little? Because *some* of us aren't quite as happy as you. *Some* of us are a little bit love deprived."

"*You're* love deprived?" I laugh, not at all offended by anything he just said, knowing it has far more to do with his anxiety about the play than anything to do with Damen and me. "What happened to Holt?"

"Holt?" He balks. "Don't even talk about Holt! Do not even go there, Ever!" He shakes his head and turns on his heel, heading toward Haven who's waiting by the gate.

"What's his problem?" Damen asks, reaching for my hand and entwining my fingers with his, gazing at me with eyes that still love me, despite yesterday.

"Tomorrow's opening night." I shrug. "So he's freaking out, has a zit on his chin, and naturally he's decided to hold us responsible," I say, watching as Miles links arms with Haven as he leads her toward class.

"We're not talking to them," he says, glancing over his shoulder and frowning at us. "We're on strike until they stop acting so love struck or this zit goes away, whichever comes first." He nods, only half joking.

Haven laughs and skips alongside him, as Damen and I head into English. Going right past Stacia Miller who smiles sweetly at him and then tries to trip me.

But just as she drops her small bag in my path, hoping to incite a nice, humiliating face plant, I *see* it lifting, and I *feel* it smacking— right into her knee. And even though I feel the pain too, I'm still glad I did it.

"*Owww!*" she wails, rubbing her knee and glaring at me, even though she has no tangible proof that I'm in any way responsible.

But I just ignore her and take my seat. I've gotten better at ignoring her. Ever since she got me suspended for drinking on campus, I've done my best to stay out of her way. But sometimes—sometimes I just can't help myself.

"You shouldn't have done that," Damen whispers, attempting a stern look as he leans toward me.

"Please. You're the one who wants me to practice manifesting." I shrug. "Looks like those lessons are finally starting to pay off."

He looks at me, shaking his head as he says, "You see, it's even worse than I thought, because for your information that was psychokinesis you just did, *not* manifesting. See how much there is to learn?"

"*Psycho-what?*" I squint, unfamiliar with the term, though the act itself was sure fun.

He takes my hand, a smile playing at the corner of his lips as he says, "I've been thinking . . ."

I glance at the clock, seeing it's already five minutes past nine and knowing Mr. Robins is just now leaving the teachers' lounge.

"Friday night. What do you say we go somewhere . . . special?" He smiles.

"Like Summerland?" I look at Damen, my eyes growing wide as my pulse quickens. I've been dying to get back to that magical, mystical place. The dimension between the dimensions, where I can manifest oceans and elephants, and move things far greater than projectile Prada bags—only I need Damen to get there.

But he just laughs and shakes his head. "No, not Summerland. Though we will return there, I promise. But I was thinking more like, I don't know, maybe the Montage, or the Ritz, perhaps?" He raises his brows.

"But Miles's play is Friday and I promised we'd be there!" I say, realizing just after I've said it that I'd conveniently forgotten all about Miles's *Hairspray* debut when I thought I was going to Summerland. But now that Damen wants to check into one of the area's most swanky hotels—my memory is somehow restored.

"Okay, then, how about after the play?" he offers. But when he looks at me, when he sees how I hesitate, how I press my lips together and search for a polite way to decline, he adds, "Or not. It was just a thought."

I gaze at him, knowing I need to accept, that I *want* to accept. Hearing the voice in my head shouting: *Say yes! Say yes! You promised yourself you'd leap forward, without once looking back, and now's your chance—so just go ahead and do it! JUST! SAY! YES!*

But even though I'm convinced that it's time to move on, even though I love Damen with all of my heart and am determined to get over his past and take the next step, what comes out of my mouth is entirely different.

"We'll see," I say, averting my gaze and focusing on the door, just as Mr. Robins walks in.

four

When the fourth-period bell finally rings, I get up from my desk and approach Mr. Munoz.

"Are you sure you're finished?" he asks, looking up from a pile of papers. "If you need another minute, that's perfectly okay."

I glance over my test sheet, then shake my head. Wondering what he'd do if he ever found out that I'd finished approximately forty five seconds after he first handed it to me, then spent the next fifty minutes only pretending to struggle.

"I'm good," I tell him, knowing it's true. One of the perks of being psychic is that I no longer have to study, instead I just sort of *know* all the answers. And even though it's sometimes tempting to show off and ace all of my tests in a long steady stream of perfect scores, I usually try to hold back and get a few wrong since it's important to not overdo it.

Or at least that's what Damen says. Always reminding me how imperative it is to keep a low profile, to at least give the *appearance* of being normal—even though we're anything but. Though the first time he said it, I couldn't help but remind him of how there seemed to be an awful lot of tulip manifesting going on back when we first met. But he just said that certain allowances had to be made in his efforts to woo me, and that it took longer than necessary since

I didn't bother to look up their true meaning of *undying love,* until it was almost too late.

I hand the paper to Mr. Munoz, cringing when the tips of our fingers make contact. And even though our skin just barely brushed, it was still enough to *show* me far more than I ever needed to know, allowing for a pretty clear visual of his entire morning so far. Everything from his incredibly messy apartment with the kitchen table that's littered with takeout containers and multiple versions of the manuscript he's been working on for the past seven years, to him singing "Born to Run" at the top of his lungs as he tried to find a clean shirt before heading over to Starbucks where he bumped into a petite blonde who spilled her iced venti chai latte all down the front of it—resulting in a cold, wet, annoying stain that one flash of her beautiful smile seemed to erase. A glorious smile he can't seem to forget—a glorious smile that—*belongs to my aunt!*

"Want to wait while I grade it?"

I nod, practically hyperventilating as I focus on his red pen. Replaying the scene I just saw in my head, each time coming to the same horrific conclusion—*my history teacher is hot for Sabine!*

I can't let this happen. Can't allow her to *ever* go back there. I mean, just because they're smart, cute, and single, doesn't mean they need to date.

I stand there, frozen, unable to breathe, struggling to block out the thoughts in his head by focusing on the tip of his pen. Watching as he leaves a trail of tiny red dots that turn into checkmarks at numbers seventeen and twenty-five—just as I'd planned.

"Only two wrong. Very good!" He smiles, brushing his fingers against the stain on his shirt, wondering if he'll ever see *her* again. "Would you like to see the correct answers?"

Uh, not really, I think, eager to be out of there as soon as I can, and not just so I can get to the lunch table and see Damen, but in case his fantasy decides to pick up where I forced it to leave off.

But knowing that the normal thing would be to appear at least somewhat interested, I take a deep breath and smile and nod as though I'd like nothing more. And when he hands me the answer key, I just go through the motions, saying, "Oh, look at that, I got the wrong date." And, "Of course! How could I not know that? *Duh!*"

But he just nods, mostly because his thoughts are already back on the blonde—aka: *The only woman in the entire universe who he is absolutely forbidden to date!* Wondering if she'll be there tomorrow—same time and place.

And even though the idea of teachers in lust pretty much grosses me out in a general sense, this particular teacher's being in lust over someone who's practically *like a parent to me*—just will not do.

But then I remember how just a few months ago I had a vision of Sabine dating some cute guy in her building. And since Munoz works *here,* and Sabine works *there,* I figure there's really no threat of my two worlds colliding. But just in case I'm wrong, I still manage to say, "Um, it was a fluke."

He looks at me, brows merged, trying to make sense of my words.

And even though I know I've gone too far, even though I know I'm about to say something as far from normal as you can get, I really don't feel I have much of a choice. I cannot have my history teacher dating my aunt. I can't tolerate it. I just can't.

So I motion toward the stain on his shirt when I add, "You know, *her,* Miss Iced Venti Chai Latte?" I nod, seeing the alarmed look on his face. "I doubt she'll be back. She doesn't really go all that often."

Then before I can say anything else that will not only dash his dreams but confirm the full extent of my freakdom, I sling my bag over my shoulder and run for the door, shrugging off the last of Mr. Munoz's lingering energy as I make my way toward the lunch table where Damen is waiting—eager to be with him again after three very long hours apart.

But when I get there, it's not quite the homecoming I expected. There's a new guy sitting beside him, right in my usual place, and he's soaking up so much attention, Damen barely notices me.

I lean against the edge of the table, watching as they all break into laughter at something the new guy said. And not wanting to interrupt or come off as rude, I take the seat across from Damen rather than right beside him in my usual place.

"Omigod, you are *so* funny!" Haven says, leaning forward and briefly touching the new guy's hand. Smiling in a way that makes it clear her new boyfriend, Josh, her self-proclaimed soul mate, has been temporarily forgotten. "Too bad you missed it, Ever, he's *so* hysterical Miles even forgot to obsess on his zit!"

"Thanks for the reminder." Miles scowls, his finger seeking the spot on his chin—only it's no longer there.

His eyes go wide, looking to each of us for confirmation that his mammoth-sized zit, the bane of this morning's existence, really is gone. And I can't help but wonder if its sudden disappearance is because of me, because of when I touched it this morning, back in the parking lot. Which would mean I really do have magical healing abilities.

But just after I think it, the new guy says, "Told you it'd work. Stuff's brilliant. Keep the rest in case it returns."

And I narrow my gaze, wondering how he could've had enough time to intervene on Miles's complexion issues when it's the first I've yet to see of him.

"I gave him some salve," he says, turning toward me. "Miles and I are in homeroom together. I'm Roman, by the way."

I look at him, taking in the bright yellow aura that swirls all around him, its edges extended, beckoning, like a friendly group hug. But when I take in his deep navy blue eyes, tanned skin, blond tousled hair, and casual clothes with just the right amount of hipster chic—despite his good looks, my first reaction is to run away. Even when he flashes me one of those languid, easy, make-your-heart-swoon kind of smiles, I'm so on edge, I can't seem to return it.

"And you must be Ever," he says, retracting his hand, the one I hadn't even noticed was extended and waiting to be shaken until he pulled it away.

I glance at Haven who's clearly horrified by my rudeness, then over at Miles who is too busy mirror gazing to notice my faux pas. But when Damen reaches under the table and squeezes my knee, I clear my throat, look at Roman, and say, "Um, yeah, I'm Ever." And even though he shoots me that smile again, it still doesn't work. It just makes my stomach go all jumpy and queasy.

"Seems we have a lot in common," he says, though I can't imagine what that could possibly be. "I sat two rows behind you in history. And the way you were struggling, I couldn't help but think, well there's a girl who hates history almost as much as I do."

"I don't hate history," I say, only it comes out too quickly, too defensively, my voice containing a sharp abrasive edge that makes everyone stare. So I glance at Damen, looking for confirmation, sure I can't be the only one who feels the unsettled stream of energy that starts with Roman and flows right to me.

But he just shrugs and sips his red drink as though everything's perfectly normal and he hasn't noticed a thing. So I turn back to Roman and delve into his mind, eavesdropping on a steady stream of harmless thoughts that while slightly juvenile for sure, are basically benign. Which pretty much means the problem is mine.

"Really?" Roman raises his brows and leans toward me. "All that delving into the past, exploring all those long ago places and dates, examining the lives of people who lived centuries before and bear absolutely no relevance now—that doesn't bother you? Or bore you to death?"

Only when those people, places, and dates involve my boyfriend and his six hundred years of carousing!

But I only think it. I don't say it. Instead, I just shrug and say, "I did fine. In fact, it was easy. I aced it."

He nods, his eyes grazing over me, not missing an inch. "Good to know." He smiles. "Munoz is giving me the weekend to catch up, perhaps you can tutor me?"

I glance at Haven, watching as her eyes grow dark and her aura turns a jealous puke green, then at Miles who's moved on from his zit and is now texting Holt, and then I look at Damen who's oblivious to us both, his gaze far away, focused on something I can't see. And even though I know I'm being ridiculous, that everyone else seems to like him and I should do what I can to help, I just shrug when I say, "Oh, I'm sure that's not necessary. You don't need me."

Unable to ignore the prick of my skin and the ping in my stomach when his eyes meet mine—revealing a set of flawless white teeth when he says, "Nice of you to give me the benefit of the doubt, Ever. Though I'm not sure you should."

five

"What's up with you and the new kid?" Haven asks, lagging behind as everyone else heads for class.

"Nothing." I shake off her hand and forge straight ahead, her energy streaming right through me as I watch Roman, Miles, and Damen laugh and carry on as though they're old friends.

"Please." She rolls her eyes. "It's so obvious you don't like him."

"That's ridiculous," I say, my eyes focused on Damen, my gorgeous and glorious boyfriend/soul mate/eternal partner/cohort (I really need to find the right word) who's barely spoken to me since this morning in English. And I'm hoping it's not because of the reason I think—because of my behavior yesterday and my refusal to commit to this weekend.

"I'm totally serious." She looks at me. "It's like—it's like you hate new people or something." Which happened to come out much kinder than the actual words in her head.

I press my lips together and stare straight ahead, resisting the urge to roll my eyes.

But she just peers at me, hand on one hip, heavily made-up eyes squinting from under the flaming red stripe in her bangs. "Because if I remember right, and we both know I do, you hated Damen when he first came to this school."

"I didn't *hate* Damen," I say, rolling my eyes despite my recent vow not to. Thinking: *Correction, I only gave the* appearance *of hating Damen. When the truth is, I loved him that whole entire time. Well, except for that short period of time when I truly did hate him. But still, even then, I loved him. I just didn't want to admit it.* . . .

"Um, excuse me, but I beg to differ," she says, artfully messy black hair falling into her face. "Remember how you didn't even invite him to your Halloween party?"

I sigh, completely annoyed by all this. All I want to do is get to class so I can pretend to pay attention while I telepathically IM Damen.

"Yes, and if you'll remember that's also the night we hooked up," I finally say, though the second it's out, I regret it. Haven's the one who found us making out by the pool, and it pretty much broke her heart.

But she just ignores it, more determined to make her case than revisit that particular past. "Or maybe you're jealous because Damen has a new friend. You know, someone other than you."

"That's ridiculous," I say, though it comes out too quickly to ever be believed. "Damen has plenty of friends," I add, even though we both know it's not true.

She looks at me, lips pursed, completely unmoved.

But now that I'm this far in, I've no choice but to continue, so I say, "He has you, and Miles, and—" *And me,* I think, but I don't want to say it because it's a sad little list, which is exactly her point. And the truth is, Damen never hangs with Haven and Miles unless I'm there too. He spends every free moment with me. And the times we're not together he sends a steady stream of thoughts and images to make up for the distance. It's like we're always connected. And I have to admit that I like it that way. Because only with Damen can I be my true self—my thought-hearing, energy-sensing, spirit-seeing self. Only with Damen can I let my guard down and be the real me.

But when I look at Haven, I can't help but wonder if maybe she's right. Maybe I am jealous. Maybe Roman really is just some nice normal guy who moved to a new school and wants to make some new friends—as opposed to the creepy threat I assume him to be. Maybe I really have become so paranoid, jealous, and possessive I automatically assume that just because Damen wasn't as focused on me as he usually is, I'm about to be replaced. And if that's the case, well, it's way too pathetic to admit. So I just shake my head and fake a laugh when I say, "Again, ridiculous. All of this is seriously ridiculous." Then I try to look as though I really do mean it.

"Yeah? Well, what about Drina, then? How do you explain *that*?" She smirks and says, "You hated her from the moment you saw her, and don't even try to deny it. And then, once you found out she knew Damen, you hated her even more."

I cringe when she says it. And not only because it's true, but because hearing the name of Damen's ex-wife always makes me cringe. I can't help it, it just does. But I have no idea how to explain it to Haven. All she knows is that Drina pretended to be her friend, ditched her at a party, and then disappeared forever. She has no memory of Drina trying to kill her with the poisonous salve she used for that creepy tattoo she recently had removed from her wrist, no memory of—

Oh my God! The salve! Roman gave Miles a salve for his zit! I knew there was something strange about him. I knew I wasn't making it up!

"Haven, what class does Miles have now?" I ask, my eyes scanning the campus, unable to find him and in too big of a hurry to use remote sensing, which I still haven't mastered.

"I think English, why?" She gives me a strange look.

"Nothing, I just—I gotta run."

"Fine. Whatever. But just so you know, I still think you hate new people!" she shouts.

But it lingers behind me. I'm already gone.

I sprint across campus, focusing on Miles's energy and trying to sense which classroom he's in. And as I round a corner and see a door on my right, without even thinking, I burst in.

"Can I help you?" the teacher asks, turning away from the board, holding a broken piece of white chalk in his hand.

I stand before the class, cringing as a few of Stacia's minions mock me as I fight to catch my breath.

"Miles," I pant, pointing at him. "I need to speak to Miles. It'll only take a sec," I promise, as his teacher crosses his arms and gives me a dubious look. "It's important," I add, glancing at Miles who's now closed his eyes and is shaking his head.

"I assume you have a hall pass?" his teacher asks, a stickler for the rules.

And even though I know it might very well alienate him and end up working against me, I don't have time to get bogged down in all this red tape, the high school bureaucracy designed to keep us all safe—but that is actually, at this very moment, keeping me from handling a matter that is clearly life and death!

Or at least it might be.

I'm not sure. Though I'd like a chance to find out.

And I'm so frustrated, I just shake my head and say, "Listen, you and I both know I don't have a hall pass, but if you'll just do me the favor of letting me speak with Miles outside for a sec, I promise to send him right back."

He looks at me, his mind sifting through all the alternatives, all the different ways this could play out: kicking me out, escorting me to class, escorting me to Principal Buckley's office—before glancing at Miles and sighing when he says, "Fine. Make it quick."

The second we head into the hall and the door closes behind us, I look at Miles and say, "Give me the salve."

"What?" He gapes.

"The salve. The one Roman gave you. Give it to me. I need to see it," I tell him, extending my hand and wiggling my fingers.

"Are you crazy?" he whispers, looking around even though it's just wall-to-wall carpet, taupe colored walls, and us.

"You have no idea how serious this is," I say, my eyes on his, not wanting to scare him, though I will if I have to. "Now come on, we don't have all day."

"It's in my backpack." He shrugs.

"Then go get it."

"Ever, seriously. What the—?"

I just fold my arms and nod. "Go on. I'll wait."

Miles shakes his head and disappears inside the room. Emerging a moment later with a sour expression and a small white tube in the palm of his hand. "Here. Happy now?" He tosses it to me.

I take the tube and examine it, twirling it between my thumb and index finger. It's a brand that I recognize, from a store that I frequent. And I don't understand how that could be.

"You know, in case you've forgotten, my play is tomorrow, and I really don't need all of this extra drama and stress right now, so if you don't mind . . ." He extends his hand, waiting for me to return the salve so he can get back to class.

Only I'm not willing to hand it over just yet. I'm looking for some kind of needle hole or puncture mark, something to prove it's been tampered with, that it's not what it seems.

"I mean, today at lunch when I saw how you and Damen toned down the whole smoochy business, I was ready to high-five you, but now it's like you've replaced it with something way worse. I mean, seriously, Ever. Either unscrew the cap and use it, or give it back already."

But I don't give it back. Instead, I close my fingers around it and try to read its energy. But it's just some stupid zit cream. The kind that actually works.

"Are we done here?" He frowns at me.

I shrug and give the tube back. To say I'm embarrassed would be putting it mildly. But when Miles shoves it into his pocket and heads for the door, I can't help but say, "So you noticed?" The words feel hot and sticky in my throat.

"Noticed what?" He stops, clearly annoyed.

"The, um, the absence of the whole *smoochy business?*"

Miles turns, performing an exaggerated eye roll before leveling his gaze right on mine. "Yeah, I noticed. I figured you guys were just taking my threat seriously."

I look at him.

"This morning—when I said Haven and I were on strike until you guys stopped with all of your—" He shakes his head. "Whatever. Can I please get to class?"

"Sorry." I nod. "Sorry about all the—"

But before I can finish, he's already gone, the door closed firmly between us.

six

When I get to sixth period art, I'm relieved to see Damen's already there. Since Mr. Robins kept us so busy in English and we barely spoke at lunch, I'm looking forward to a little alone time with him. Or at least as alone as you can be in a classroom with thirty other students.

But after slipping on my smock and gathering my supplies from the closet, my heart sinks when I see that, once again, Roman has taken my place.

"Oh, hey, Ever." He nods, placing his brand-new blank canvas on *my* easel while I stand there, cradling my stuff in my arms and staring at Damen who's so immersed in his painting he's completely oblivious to me.

And I'm just about to tell Roman to scram when I remember Haven's words, how she said I hate new people. And fearing she might be right, I force a smile onto my face and place my canvas on the easel on Damen's other side, promising myself to get here much earlier tomorrow so I can reclaim my space.

"So tell me. Wot are we doin' 'ere, mate?" Roman asks, lodging a paintbrush between his front teeth and glancing between Damen and me.

And that's another thing. Normally, I find British accents really appealing, but with this guy, it just grates. But that's probably because it's totally bogus. I mean, it's so obvious with the way he only slips it in when he wants to seem cool.

But as soon as I think it, I feel guilty again. Everyone knows that trying too hard to look cool is just another sign of insecurity. And who wouldn't feel a little insecure on their first day at this school?

"We're studying the *isms*," I say, determined to play nice despite the nagging ping in my gut. "Last month we got to pick our own, but this month, we're all doing photorealism since nobody picked that last time."

Roman looks at me, starting with my growing-out bangs and working his way all the way down to my gold Haviana flip-flops—a slow leisurely cruise along my body that makes my stomach go all jumpy and twisted—and not in a good way.

"Right. So you make it look real then, like a photograph," he says, his eyes on mine.

I meet his gaze, a gaze he insists on holding for several seconds too long. But I refuse to squirm or look away first. I'm determined to stay in the game for as long as it takes. And even though it may seem totally benign on the surface, something about it feels dark, threatening, like some kind of dare.

Or maybe not.

Because right after I think that, he says, "These American schools are amazing! Back home, in soggy old London—" he winks, "it was always theory over practice."

And I'm instantly ashamed for all of my judgmental thoughts. Because apparently, not only is he from London, which means his accent is real, but Damen, whose psychic powers are *way* more refined than mine, doesn't seem the least bit alarmed.

If anything, he seems to like him. Which is even worse for me, because it pretty much proves that Haven is right.

I really am jealous.

And possessive.

And paranoid.

And apparently I hate new people too.

I take a deep breath and try again, talking past the lump in my throat and the knot in my stomach, determined to come off as friendly, even if it means I have to fake it at first. "You can paint anything you want," I say, using my upbeat friendly voice, which in my old life, before my whole family died in the accident and Damen saved me by making me immortal, was pretty much the only voice I ever used. "You just have to make it look real, like a photograph. Actually, we're supposed to use an actual photograph to show our inspiration, and, of course, for grading purposes too. You know, so we can prove that we accomplished what we set out to."

I glance at Damen, wondering if he's heard any of this and feeling annoyed that he's chosen his painting over communicating with me.

"And what's he painting?" Roman asks, nodding at Damen's canvas, a perfect depiction of the blooming fields of Summerland. Every blade of grass, every drop of water, every flower petal, so luminous, so textured, so tangible—it's like being there. "Looks like paradise." He nods.

"It is," I whisper, so awed by the painting I answered too quickly, without time to think about what I just said. Summerland is not just a sacred place—it's our secret place. One of the many secrets I've promised to keep.

Roman looks at me, brows raised. "So it's a real place then?"

But before I can answer, Damen shakes his head and says, "She wishes. But I made it up, it only exists in my head." Then he shoots me a look, tacking on a telepathic message of—*careful*.

"So how do you ace the assignment, then? If you don't have a photo to prove it exists?" Roman asks, but Damen just shrugs and gets back to painting.

But with Roman still glancing between us, his eyes all squinty and questioning, I know I can't leave it like that. So I look at him and say, "Damen's not so big on following the rules. He prefers to make his own." Remembering all the times he convinced me to ditch school, bet at the track, and worse.

And when Roman nods and turns toward his canvas, and Damen sends me a telepathic bouquet of red tulips, I know that it worked—our secret is safe and all is okay. So I dip my brush in some paint and get back to work. Eager for the bell to ring so we can head back to my house, and let the real lesson begin.

After class, we pack up our stuff and head for the parking lot. And despite my bid to be nice to the new guy, I can't help but smile when I see he's parked clear on the other side.

"See you tomorrow," I call, relieved to put some distance between us, because despite everyone's instant infatuation with him, I'm just not feeling it, no matter how hard I try.

I unlock my car and toss my bag on the floor, starting to slide onto my seat as I say to Damen, "Miles has rehearsal and I'm heading straight home. Want to follow?"

I turn, surprised to find him standing before me, swaying ever so slightly from side to side with a strained look on his face. "You okay?" I lift my palm to his cheek, feeling for heat or clamminess, some sign of unease, even though I really don't expect to find any. And when Damen shakes his head and looks at me, for a split second all the color drains right away. But then it's over as soon as I blink.

"Sorry, I just—my head feels a bit strange," he says, pinching the bridge of his nose and closing his eyes.

"But I thought you never get sick, that *we* don't get sick?" I say, unable to hide my alarm as I reach for my backpack. Thinking a sip of immortal juice might make him feel better since he requires so much more than I. And even though we're not exactly sure why, Damen figures that six centuries of chugging it have resulted in some kind of dependency, requiring him to consume more and more with each passing year. Which probably means I'll eventually require more too. And even though it seems like a long way off, I just hope he shows me how to make it by then so I won't have to bug him for refills all the time.

But before I can get to it, he retrieves his own bottle and takes a long hearty swig, pulling me to him and pressing his lips to my cheek when he says, "I'm okay. Really. Race you home?"

seven

Damen drives fast. Insanely fast. I mean, just because we both have advanced psychic radar, which comes in handy for zoning in on cops, opposing traffic, pedestrians, stray animals, and anything else that might get in our way, that doesn't mean we should abuse it.

But Damen thinks otherwise. Which is why he's already waiting on my front porch before I can even pull in and park.

"I thought you'd never make it." He laughs, following me up to my room, where he plops onto my bed, pulls me down with him, and leans in for a nice lingering kiss—a kiss that, if it were up to me, would never end. I'd happily spend the rest of eternity wrapped in his arms. Just knowing we have an infinite number of days to spend side by side provides more happiness than I can bear.

Though I didn't always feel that way. I was pretty upset when I first learned the truth. So upset that I spent some time away from him until I could get it all straight in my head. I mean, it's not everyday you hear someone say: *Oh, by the way, I'm an immortal, and I made you one too.*

And while I was pretty reluctant to believe him at first, after he walked me through it, reminding me of how I died in the accident, how I looked right into his eyes the moment he returned me to life, and how I recognized those eyes the first time I met him at school—well, there was no denying it was true.

Though that doesn't mean I was willing to accept it. It was bad enough dealing with the barrage of psychic abilities brought on by my NDE (near death experience—they insist on calling it *near,* even though I really did *die*), and how I started hearing other people's thoughts, getting their life stories by touch, talking to the dead, and more. Not to mention that being immortal, as cool as it may sound, also means I'll never get to cross the bridge. I'll never make it to the *other side* to see my family again. And when you think about it, that's a pretty big trade.

I pull away, my lips reluctantly leaving his as I gaze into his eyes—the same eyes I've gazed into for four hundred years. Though no matter how hard I try, I can't summon our past. Only Damen, who's stayed the same for the last six hundred years—neither dying nor reincarnating—holds the key.

"What're you thinking?" he asks, his fingers smoothing the curve of my cheek, leaving a trail of warmth in their path.

I take a deep breath, knowing how committed he is to staying in the present, but determined to know more of my history—*our* history. "I was thinking about when we first met," I say, watching his brow lift as he shakes his head.

"Were you? And what exactly do you remember from that time?"

"Nothing." I shrug. "Absolutely nothing. Which is why I'm hoping you'll fill me in. You don't have to tell me everything—I mean, I know how you hate looking back. I'm just really curious about how it all started—how we first met."

He pulls away and rolls onto his back, his body still, his lips unmoving, and I fear this is the only response that I'll get.

"Please?" I murmur, inching toward him and curling my body around his. "It's not fair that you get all the details while I'm left out here in the dark. Just give me something to go on. Where did we live? What did I look like? How did we meet? Was it love at first sight?"

He shifts ever so slightly, then rolls onto his side, burying his hand in my hair as he says, "It was France, 1608."

I gulp, taking a quick intake of breath as I wait to hear more.

"Paris, actually."

Paris! I immediately picture elaborate gowns, stolen kisses on the Pont Neuf, gossiping with Marie Antoinette . . .

"I attended a dinner at a friend's house—" He pauses, his gaze moving past mine, centuries away now. "And you were working as a servant."

A servant?

"One of their servants. They were very wealthy. They had many."

I lie there, stunned. This is *not* what I expected.

"You weren't like the others," he says, his voice lowered to almost a whisper. "You were beautiful. Extraordinarily beautiful. You looked a lot like you do now." He smiles, gathering a chunk of my hair and rubbing it between his two fingers. "And also like now, you were orphaned, having lost your family in a fire. And so, left penniless, with no one to support you, you were employed by my friends."

I swallow hard, not sure how I feel about this. I mean, what's the point of reincarnating if you're forced to relive the same kind of painful moments all over again?

"And yes, just so you know, it *was* love at first sight. I fell completely and irreversibly in love with you. The very moment I saw you I knew that my life would never be the same."

He looks at me, his fingers on my temples, his gaze luring me in, presenting the moment in all its intensity, unfolding the scene as though I'm right there.

My blond hair is hidden under a cap, my blue eyes are shy and afraid to make contact, and with clothes so drab and fingers so calloused, my beauty is wasted, easily missed.

But Damen sees it. The moment I enter the room his eyes find mine. Looking past my scruffy exterior to the soul that refuses to hide. And he's so dark, so striking, so refined, so handsome—I turn away. Knowing the buttons on his coat alone are worth more than I'll make in a year. Knowing without looking twice that he's out of my league . . .

"Still, I had to move cautiously because—"

"Because you were already married to Drina!" I whisper, watching the scene in my head and overhearing one of the dinner guests inquire about her, our eyes meeting briefly as Damen says:

"Drina is in Hungary. We have gone our separate ways." Knowing he'll be the source of scandal, but wanting me to hear it more than caring what they'll think . . .

"She and I were already living apart, so it wasn't an issue. The reason I had to tread cautiously is because fraternizing outside of one's class was severely frowned upon back then. And because you were so innocent, so vulnerable in so many ways, I didn't want to cause you any trouble, especially if you didn't feel the same way."

"But I did feel the same way!" I say, watching as we move past that night, and how every time I went into town, I'd manage to run into him.

"I'm afraid I resorted to following you." He looks at me, his face chagrined. "Until we finally bumped into each other so often, you began to trust me. And then . . ."

And then we met in secret—stolen kisses just outside the servant's entrance, a passionate embrace in a dark alleyway or inside his carriage . . .

"Only now I know that it wasn't nearly as *secret* as I'd thought . . ." He sighs. "Drina was never in Hungary, she was there all along. Watching, planning, determined to win me back—no matter the cost." He takes a deep breath, the regret of four centuries displayed on his face. "I wanted to take care of you, Ever. I wanted to give you anything and everything your heart desired. I wanted to treat you like the princess you were born to be. And when I finally convinced you to come away with me, I'd never felt so happy and alive. We were to meet at midnight—"

"But I never showed," I say, *seeing* him pacing, worried, distressed, convinced I'd changed my mind . . .

"It wasn't until the next day that I learned you'd been killed in an accident, run over by a coach on your way to meet me." And when he looks at me, he shows me his grief—his unbearable, all-consuming, soul-crushing grief. "At the time, it never occurred to me that Drina was responsible, I had no idea until she confessed it to you. It seemed like an accident, a horrible, unfortunate accident. And I guess I was too numb with grief to suspect anything else—"

"How old was I?" I ask, barely able to breathe, knowing I was young, but wanting the details.

He pulls me closer, his fingers tracing the planes of my face when he says, "You were sixteen, and your name was Evaline." His lips play at my ear.

"Evaline," I whisper, feeling an instant connection to my tragic former self who, orphaned young, loved by Damen, and dead at sixteen—is not so different from my current self.

"It wasn't until many years later when I saw you again in New England, having incarnated as a Puritan's daughter—that I began to believe in happiness again."

"*A Puritan's daughter?*" I gaze into his eyes, watching as he shows me a dark-haired, pale-skinned girl in a severe blue dress. "Were all of my lives so boring?" I shake my head. "And what kind of horrible accident took me that time?"

"Drowning." He sighs, and the moment he says it, I'm overcome by his grief all over again. "I was so devastated I sailed right back to London, where I lived off and on for many years. And I was just about to head off to Tunisia when you resurfaced as a beautiful, wealthy, and rather spoiled I might say—landowner's daughter in London."

"Show me!" I nuzzle against him, eager to view a more glamorous life—his finger tracing my brow as a pretty brunette in a gorgeous green dress with a complicated updo and a smattering of jewels appears in my mind.

A rich, spoiled, conniving flirt—her life a series of parties and shopping trips—whose sights are set firmly on someone else—until she meets Damen . . .

"And that time?" I ask, sad to see her go, but needing to know how she went.

"A terrible fall." He closes his eyes. "By that point, I was sure I was being punished—granted eternal life, but one without love."

He cradles my face in his hands, his fingers emitting such tenderness, such reverence, such delicious warm tingle—I close my eyes and snuggle closer. Focusing on the feel of his skin as our bodies press tightly together, everything around us slipping away until there's nothing but us—no past, no future, nothing but this moment in time.

I mean, I'm with him, and he's with me, and that's the way it's meant to eternally be. And while all those prior lives may be interesting, their only real purpose was to get us to this one. And now that Drina is gone, there's nothing that can stand in our way, nothing that can keep us from moving forward—except me. And even though I want to know *everything* that happened before, for now it can wait. It's time for me to move past my petty jealousies and insecurities, to stop finding excuses and finally commit to taking that big leap forward after all of these years.

But just as I'm about to tell him, he moves away so abruptly, it's a moment before I can get to his side.

"What is it?" I cry, seeing his thumbs pressed to his temples as he struggles to breathe. And when he turns to me, there's no recognition. His gaze goes right through me.

But just as soon as I perceive it, it's already passed. Replaced with the loving warmth I've grown used to, as he rubs his eyes and shakes his head, looking at me when he says, "I haven't felt like this since before—" He stops and stares into space. "Well, maybe never." But when he sees the concern on my face, he adds, "But I'm fine, really." And when I refuse to loosen my grip, he smiles and says, "Hey, how about a trip to Summerland?"

"Seriously?" I say, my eyes lighting up.

The first time I visited that wonderful place, that magical dimension between the dimensions—I was dead. And I was so entranced by its beauty I was reluctant to leave. The second time I visited was with Damen. And after he showed me all of its glorious possibilities, I've longed to return. But as Summerland can only be accessed by the spiritually advanced (or those already dead), I can't get there alone.

"Why not?" He shrugs.

"Well, what about my lessons," I say, trying to appear interested in studying and learning new tricks, when the truth is, I'd much rather go to Summerland where everything is effortless and instant. "Not to mention how you're not feeling so well." I squeeze his arm again, noticing how the usual warmth and tingle still hasn't fully returned.

"There are lessons to be learned in Summerland too." He smiles. "And if you'll hand me my juice, I'll feel well enough to make us the portal."

But even after I hand it over and he takes several long hearty gulps, he can't make it appear.

"Maybe I can help?" I say, staring at the sweat on his brow.

"No—I just—I almost had it. Just give me another second," he mumbles, clenching his jaw, determined to get there.

So I do. In fact, I let the seconds turn into minutes, and still nothing.

"I don't understand." He squints. "This hasn't happened since—since I first learned how to do it."

"Maybe it's because you're not feeling well." I watch as he takes another drink, followed by another, and then another. And when he closes his eyes and tries again, he gets the exact same results as before. "Can I try?"

"Forget it. You don't know how," he says, his voice containing an edge I try not to take personally, knowing it's due more to his frustration with himself than with me.

"I *know* I don't know how, but I thought maybe you could teach me and then I—"

But before I can finish, he's up from the bed, pacing before me. "It's a *process,* Ever. It took me years to learn how to get there. You can't just skip to the end of the book without reading the middle." He shakes his head and leans against my desk, his body rigid and tense, his gaze refusing mine.

"And when was the last time you *read* a book without already knowing the beginning, middle, and end?" I smile.

He looks at me, his face a series of hard edges and angles, but only for a moment before he sighs and moves toward me, taking my hand as he says, "You want to try?"

I nod.

He looks me over, clearly doubting it'll work, but wanting to please me more than anything else. "Okay then, make yourself comfortable, but don't cross your legs like that. It cuts off the chi."

"Chi?"

"A fancy word for energy." He smiles. "Unless you want to sit in the lotus position, then that's perfectly fine."

I kick off my flip-flops and press my soles against the carpeted floor, getting as comfortable and relaxed as my excitement will allow.

"Usually it requires a long series of meditations, but in the interest of time, and since you're already pretty advanced, we're just going to cut to the chase, okay?"

I nod, eager to get started.

"I want you to close your eyes and imagine a shimmering veil of soft golden light hovering before you," he says, entwining his fingers with mine.

So I do, picturing an exact replica of the one that got me there before, the one Damen placed in my path to save me from Drina. And it's so beautiful, so brilliant, and so luminous, my heart swells with joy as I raise my hand toward it, eager to immerse it in that radiant shower of glistening light, longing to return to that mystical place. And just as my fingers make contact and are about to submerge, it shrinks from my sight and I'm back in my room.

"I can't believe it! I was *so* close!" I turn toward Damen. "It was right there before me! Did you see it?"

"You came remarkably close," he says. And even though his gaze is tender, his smile is forced.

"What if I try it again? What if we do it together this time?" I say, my hope plummeting the instant he shakes his head and turns away.

"Ever, we *were* doing it together," he mutters, wiping his brow and averting his gaze. "I'm afraid I'm not turning out to be a very good teacher."

"That's ridiculous! You're a great teacher, you're just having an off day, that's all." But when I look at him, it's clear he's not swayed. So I switch tactics, placing the blame back on me when I say, "It's my fault. I'm a bad student. I'm lazy, sloppy, and spend most of my time trying to distract you from my lessons so we can make out." I squeeze his hand. "But I'm past all that now. And I'm about to get very serious. So just give me another chance, you'll see."

He looks at me, doubting it'll work, but not wanting to disappoint me, he takes my hand and we both try again, the two of us closing our eyes, envisioning that glorious portal of light. And just as it starts to take shape, Sabine walks through the front door and starts up the stairs, catching us so off guard, we scramble to opposite sides of the room.

"Damen, I thought that was your car in the drive." She slips off her jacket and covers the space from the door to my desk in a handful of steps. The amped-up energy of her office still clinging to her as she shakes his hand and focuses on the bottle balanced on his knee. "So *you're* the one who got Ever hooked." She glances between us, her eyes narrowed, her lips pursed, like she's got all the evidence she needs.

I peek at Damen, panic rising in my throat, wondering how he'll explain. But he just laughs it off when he says, "Guilty! Most people don't have the taste for it, but for whatever reason, Ever seems to like it." Then he smiles in a way that's meant to be persuasive, if not charming, and if you ask me, it nails both.

But Sabine just continues to gaze at him, completely unmoved. "That's all she seems to be interested in anymore. I buy bags and bags of groceries, but she refuses to eat."

"That's not true!" I say, annoyed that she's starting this all over again, especially in front of Damen. But when I see the chai latte stain on her blouse, my annoyance turns to outrage. "How'd you get that?" I motion toward the spot like it's a scarlet letter, a mark of disgrace, knowing I have to do whatever it takes to dissuade her from returning anytime soon.

She gazes down at her blouse, her fingers rubbing against it as she pauses to think, then she shakes her head and shrugs when she says, "I bumped into someone." And the way she says it, so casual, so offhand, so blasé, it's obvious she's not nearly as impressed with the encounter as Munoz seemed to be.

"So, are we still on for dinner Saturday night?" she asks.

I swallow hard, telepathically urging Damen to just nod and smile and answer in the affirmative even though he has no idea what she's talking about, since I failed to mention it before.

"I made reservations for eight."

I hold my breath, watching as he nods and smiles just like I asked him to. Even choosing to take it a step further by adding, "Wouldn't miss it."

He shakes Sabine's hand and heads out the door, his fingers entwined around mine, sending a warm wonderful thrum through my body. "Sorry about the whole dinner thing," I say, gazing up at him. "I guess I was hoping she'd get really busy and forget all about it."

He presses his lips to my cheek, then slides into his car. "She cares about you. Wants to make sure I'm good enough, sincere, and not out to hurt you. Believe me, we've been through this before. And though I may have come close once or twice, I don't remember ever failing inspection." He smiles.

"Aw yes, the strict Puritan father," I say, figuring he's the perfect description of an overbearing parental type.

"You'd be surprised." Damen laughs. "The wealthy landowner was much more of a gatekeeper. And yet still, I managed to sneak by."

"Maybe someday you'll show me *your* past," I say. "You know, how your life was before we met. Your home, your parents, how you became this way . . ." My voice trails off, seeing the flash of pain in his eyes and knowing he's still unwilling to discuss it. He always shuts down, refuses to share, which only makes me even more curious.

"None of that matters," he says, releasing my hand and fiddling with his mirrors, anything to avoid looking at me. "All that matters is *now*."

"Yeah, but Damen—" I start, wanting to explain that it's not just curiosity I'm after, but a closeness, a bond, wishing he'd trust me with those long-ago secrets. But when I look at him again, I know better than to press. Besides, maybe it's time I extend a little trust too.

"I was thinking . . ." I say, my fingers fiddling with the hem on my shirt.

He looks at me, his hand on the clutch, ready to shift into reverse.

"Why don't you go ahead and make that reservation." I nod, my lips pressed together, my gaze focused on his. "You know, for the Montage or the Ritz?" I add, holding my breath as his beautiful dark eyes graze over my face.

"You sure?"

I nod. Knowing I am. We've been waiting for this moment for hundreds of years, so why delay any longer? "More than sure," I say, my eyes meeting his.

He smiles, his face lighting up for the first time all day. And I'm so relieved to see him looking normal again after that strange behavior from before—his remoteness at school, his inability to make the portal appear, his not feeling well—all of it so unlike the Damen I know. He's always so strong, sexy, beautiful, and invincible—immune to weak moments and bad days. And seeing him vulnerable like that has left me far more shaken than I care to admit.

"Consider it done," he says, filling my arms with dozens of manifested red tulips before speeding away.

eight

The next morning when I meet Damen in the parking lot, all my worries disappear. Because the moment he opens my door and helps me out of my car, I notice how healthy he looks, how devastatingly handsome he is, and when I look in his eyes, it's clear that all of yesterday's weirdness is over. We are more in love than ever.

Seriously. All through English he can barely keep his hands off of me. Constantly leaning toward my desk and whispering into my ear, much to Mr. Robins's annoyance, and Stacia and Honor's disgust. And now that we're at lunch, he hasn't let up a bit, stroking my cheek and gazing into my eyes, pausing only to take the occasional sip of his drink before picking up right where he left off, murmuring sweet nothings into my ear.

Usually when he acts like that, it's partly out of love, and partly to tone down all of the noise and energy—all of the random sights, sounds, and colors that constantly bombard me. Ever since I broke the psychic shield I'd made a few months back, a shield that shut everything out and made me as clueless as I was before I died and came back psychic, I've yet to find a way to replace it that will allow me to channel the energies I want while blocking the energies I don't want. And since Damen's never struggled with this, he's not sure how to teach me.

But now that he's back in my life, it no longer seems all that urgent, because the mere sound of his voice can silence the world, while the touch of his skin makes my whole body tingle. And when I look in his eyes, well, let's just say that I'm instantly overcome by this warm, wonderful, magnetic *pull*—like it's just him and I and everything else has ceased to exist. Damen's like my perfect psychic shield. My ultimate other half. And even when we can't be together, the telepathic thoughts and images he sends provide that same calming effect.

But today, all of those sweet murmurings aren't just to shield me—they're mostly about our upcoming plans. The suite he booked at the Montage Resort. And how he's yearned so long for this night.

"Do you have any idea what it's like to wait for something for four hundred years?" he whispers, his lips nipping at the curve of my ear.

"Four hundred? I thought you've been around for six hundred?" I say, pulling away to get a better view of his face.

"Unfortunately a couple of centuries had to pass before I found you," he whispers, his mouth making its way from my neck to my ear. "Two very lonely centuries, I might add."

I swallow hard. Knowing the *loneliness* he refers to does *not* necessarily mean he was *alone*. In fact, quite the contrary. But still, I don't call him on it. In fact, I don't say a word. I'm committed to moving past all of that, getting over my insecurities and moving forward. Just like I promised I would.

I refuse to think about how he spent those first two hundred years without me.

Or how he spent the next four hundred getting over the fact that he'd lost me.

Nor will I even begin to consider the six-hundred-year head start he has on studying and *practicing* the—um—sensual arts.

And I will absolutely, positively, *not* dwell on all of the beautiful, worldly, experienced women he *knew* over the span of those years.

Nope.

Not me.

I refuse to even go there.

"Shall I pick you up at six?" he asks, gathering my hair at my nape and twisting it into a long blond rope. "We can go to dinner first."

"Except we don't really eat," I remind him.

"Ah, yes. Good point." He smiles, releasing my hair so that it flows back around my shoulders and drops down to my waist. "Though I'm sure we can find something else to occupy our time?"

I smile, having already told Sabine that I'm staying at Haven's and hoping she doesn't try to follow up. She used to be so good about taking me at my word, but ever since I was caught drinking, got suspended, and basically stopped eating, she's been prone to following through.

"Are you sure you're okay with all this?" Damen asks, misreading the look on my face as indecision, when it's really just nerves.

I smile and lean in to kiss him, eager to erase any lingering doubts (mine more than his), just as Miles tosses his bag on the table and says, "Oh, Haven, look! They're back. The lovebirds have returned!"

I pull away, my face flushing with embarrassment as Haven laughs and sits down beside him, her eyes scanning the tables as she says, "Where's Roman? Anyone seen him?"

"He was in homeroom." Miles shrugs, removing the top from his yogurt and hunching over his script.

And he was in history, I think, remembering how I ignored him all through class, despite his numerous attempts to get my attention, and how after the bell rang, I hung back, pretending to look for something in my bag. Preferring the weight of Mr. Munoz's penetrating stare and his conflicted thoughts about me (my good grades versus my undeniable weirdness) to dealing with Roman.

Haven shrugs and opens her cupcake box, sighing when she says, "Well, it was nice while it lasted."

"What're you talking about?" Miles looks up as she points straight ahead, her lips twisted to the side, her eyes completely dejected, as we all follow her finger, all the way to where Roman is talking and laughing with Stacia, Honor, Craig, and the rest of the A-list crew. "Big deal." He shrugs. "You just wait, he'll be back."

"You don't know that," Haven says, shedding the skirt from her red velvet cupcake, her gaze still focused on Roman.

"Please. We've seen it a million times before. Every new kid with the slightest potential for cool has ended up at that table at some point. Only the truly cool never last long—because the truly cool end up here." He laughs, tapping the yellow fiberglass table with the tips of his bright pink nails.

"Not me," I say, eager to steer the conversation away from Roman, knowing I'm the only one who's happy to see he's abandoned us for a much cooler crowd. "I started out here from the very first day," I remind them.

"Yeah, go figure." Miles laughs. "Though I was referring to Damen. Remember how he got sucked over to the other side for a while? But eventually he came to his senses and found his way back, just like Roman will."

I gaze down at my drink, twisting the bottle around in my hand. Because even though I know Damen was never sincere about his brief flirtation with Stacia, that he only did it to get to me, to see if I cared, the images of the two of them standing so close together are forever burned into my brain.

"Yes, I did," Damen says, squeezing my hand and kissing my cheek, sensing my thoughts even if he can't always read them. "I certainly came to my senses."

"You see? So, we can only have faith that Roman will too." Miles nods. "And if he doesn't, then he was never truly cool to begin with, *right?*"

Haven shrugs and rolls her eyes, licking a glob of frosting from her thumb and mumbling, "Whatever."

"Why do you care so much anyway?" Miles peers at her. "I thought you were all about Josh?"

"I *am* all about Josh," she says, avoiding his gaze as she wipes some nonexistent crumbs from her lap.

But when I look at her and *see* the way her aura wavers and flares a deceitful shade of green, I can tell it's not true. She's smitten and that's all there is to it. And if Roman becomes smitten too, then it's *adios Josh, hello creepy new guy.*

I unzip my lunch pack, going through the motions of pretending I'm still interested in food when I hear: "Ay, mate, what time's the premiere?"

"Curtain's at eight. Why? You coming?" Miles asks, his eyes lighting up, his aura glowing in a way that makes it pretty obvious he hopes that he will.

"Wouldn't miss it," Roman says, sliding onto the space beside Haven and bumping her shoulder in the smarmiest, most insincere way. Clearly aware of the effect it elicits and not afraid to exploit it.

"So how was life among the A-list? Everything you dreamed it would be?" she asks in a voice that, if you couldn't see her aura, you'd think she was flirting. But I know she's serious, because auras don't lie.

Roman reaches toward her, gently pushing her bangs away from her face. A gesture so intimate her cheeks flush bright pink. "*Wot's* that now?" he says, his gaze fixed on hers.

"You know, table A? Where you were sitting?" She mumbles, struggling to keep her composure while under his spell.

"The lunchtime caste system," Miles says, breaking their enchantment and pushing his half-eaten yogurt aside. "It's the same at every school. Everyone divides into cliques designed to keep others out. They can't help themselves, they just do. And those people you were just with? They're the top clique, which, in the high school caste system, makes them The Rulers. As opposed to the people you're sitting with now—" He points at himself. "Who are otherwise known as The Untouchables."

"Bullocks!" Roman says, pulling away from Haven and popping the top on his soda. "Complete rubbish. I don't buy it."

"Doesn't matter if you do. It's still a fact." Miles shrugs, gazing longingly at table A. Because despite how he goes on and on about our table being the truly cool table, the truth is, he's painfully aware that in the eyes of the Bay View student body, there's nothing cool about it.

"It may be your fact, but it's not mine. I don't do with segregation, mate. I like a free and open society, room to roam around and explore all my options." Then, looking at Damen, he says, "What about you? You believe in all this?"

But Damen just shrugs and continues gazing at me. He couldn't care less about A-lists and B-lists, who's cool and who's not. I'm the only reason he enrolled in this school, and I'm the only reason he stays.

"Well, it's nice to have a dream." Haven sighs, inspecting her short black nails. "But it's even nicer when there's a remote possibility of it coming true."

"Aw, but that's where you're wrong, luv. It's not a dream at all." Roman smiles in a way that makes her aura beam a bright shimmery pink. "I'll make it happen. You'll see."

"So what? You fancy yourself the Che Guevara of Bay View High?" My voice contains a sting I don't bother to hide. Though to be honest, I'm more surprised by my use of the word *fancy* than the tone of my voice. I mean, since when do I talk like that? But when I glance at Roman and see his expansive, overwhelming, yellow-orange aura, I know he's affecting me too.

"I rather *fancy* that, yes." He smiles his languid grin, his eyes gazing into mine so deeply, I feel like I'm naked—like he sees everything, *knows* everything, and there's nowhere to hide. "Just think of me as a revolutionary, because by the end of next week, this lunchtime caste system will come to an end. We're going to break these self-imposed barriers, push all the tables together, and have ourselves a party!"

"Is that your prediction?" I narrow my gaze, trying to deflect all of his intrusive energy away.

But he just laughs, not the least bit offended. A laugh that, on the surface, is so warm, engaging, and all-encompassing—no one would guess at the subtext beneath—the creepy edge, the hint of malice, the barely concealed threat meant solely for me.

"I'll believe it when I see it," Haven says, wiping red crumbs from her lips.

"Seeing *is* believing," Roman says, his eyes right on mine.

"So what's your take on all that?" I ask, just after the bell rings and Roman, Haven, and Miles head off to class as Damen and I lag behind.

"Of all what?" he asks, pulling me to a stop.

"Of Roman. And all of his lunch-table revolution nonsense?" I say, desperate for some validation that I'm not jealous, possessive, or crazy—that Roman really is a creep—and that it has nothing to do with me.

But Damen just shrugs. "If you don't mind, I'd rather not focus on Roman right now. I'm far more interested in *you*."

He pulls me toward him, bestowing me with a long, deep, breath-stealing kiss. And even though we're standing right in the middle of the quad, it's as though everything around us no longer exists. Like the entire world has shrunk down to this one single point. And by the time I break away, I'm so charged, so heated, and so breathless, I can barely speak.

"We're going to be late," I finally manage, taking his hand and pulling him toward class.

But he's stronger than I am, so he simply stays put. "I was thinking—what do you say we skip it?" he whispers, his lips on my temple, my cheek, then my ear. "You know, just blow off the rest of the day—since there are so many other, *better* places we could be."

I gaze at him, nearly swayed by his magnetism, but I shake my head and pull away. I mean, I get that he finished school hundreds of years ago and now finds it all rather tedious. And even though I mostly find it tedious too, since having instant knowledge of all the stuff they're trying to teach really does make it seem pretty pointless, it's still one of the few things in my life that feels somewhat normal. And ever since the accident, when I realized I'd never be normal again, well, it made me prize it that much more.

"I thought you said we were supposed to maintain a normal façade at all costs," I say, pulling him along as he grudgingly lags behind. "Isn't attending class and feigning interest part of that façade?"

"But what could be more normal than two hormonal teens, ditching school and getting an early start on the weekend?" He smiles, the warmth of his beautiful dark eyes nearly luring me in.

But I shake my head again and hold firm, gripping his arm even tighter as I drag him toward class.

nine

Since we're spending the night together, Damen doesn't follow me home after school. Instead, we share a brief kiss in the parking lot before I climb into my car and head for the mall.

I want to buy something special for tonight—something pretty for Miles's play and my big date—both of us starring in our own kind of debut. But after checking my watch and seeing I don't have as much time as I thought, I wonder if I should've taken Damen up on his offer to ditch school.

I cruise through the parking lot, wondering if I should try to find Haven. We haven't really hung out that much since that whole weird thing with Drina, and then when she met Josh, well, even though he doesn't go to our school, they've been pretty much joined at the hip ever since. He even managed to wean her from her support group addiction. Her after-school ritual of scoping out random church basements and loading up on punch and cookies, while making up some sob story about that particular day's addiction.

And up until now, I haven't really minded seeing less of her since she seems so happy. Like she's finally found someone who not only likes her but who's good for her too. But lately I'm starting to miss her, and I'm thinking a little time together might do me some good.

I spot her and Roman leaning against his vintage red sports car, watching as Haven grabs hold of his arm and laughs at something he said. The severity of her black skinny jeans, black shrunken cardigan, Fall Out Boy tank, and purposely messy dyed black hair with shocking red stripe, all softened by her rosy pink aura, its edges expanding, reaching, until it swallows them both. Leaving no room for doubt that if Roman feels the same way, Josh will soon be replaced. And even though I'm determined to stop it before it's too late, I've just started to cruise by when Roman glances over his shoulder and peers at me with a gaze so insistent, so intimate, so loaded with unknown intent—I punch the pedal and zoom past.

Because despite the fact that my friends all think he's so cool, despite the fact that the A-list agrees, despite the fact that Damen isn't the least bit alarmed—I don't like him.

Even though my feelings are based on nothing more substantial than a constant ping in my gut whenever he's near—the fact is: That new guy really gives me the creeps.

Since it's hot, I head over to the indoor mall of South Coast Plaza as opposed to the outdoor mall of Fashion Island, even though the locals would probably do the opposite.

But I'm not a local. I'm an Oregonian. Which means I'm used to my pre-spring weather being much more, well, pre-springlike. You know, gobs of rain, overcast skies, and plenty of mud. Like a *real* spring. Not this hot, weird, unnatural, summer hybrid that tries to pass as spring. And from what I hear, it's only going to get worse. Which makes me miss home even more.

Normally, I go out of my way to avoid places like this—a place so overrun with light and noise and all of that crowd-generated energy that always overwhelms me and sets me on edge. And without Damen by my side, standing in as my psychic shield, I'm back to relying on my iPod again.

Though I refuse to wear my hoodie and sunglasses to block out the noise like I used to. I'm done with looking like a freak. Instead, I narrow my focus to what's right before me, and block out all the peripherals like Damen taught me to do.

I insert my earbuds and crank up the volume, allowing the noise to bar everything but the swirling rainbow of auras and the few disembodied spirits floating about (which, despite my narrowed focus, really are right in front of me). And when I head into Victoria's Secret, aiming straight for the naughty nighties section, I'm so focused, so intent on my mission, I fail to see Stacia and Honor just off to the side.

"O. Migawd!" Stacia sings, approaching me with such purpose you'd think I was a bin labeled: GUCCI—HALF OFF! "You *cannot* be serious." She points at the negligee I hold in my hand, her perfectly manicured nail motioning toward the slit that starts from both the top and bottom and meets at a crystal-encrusted circle somewhere in the middle.

And even though I was merely curious, and not even thinking about buying it, seeing her face all scrunched up like that and hearing the mocking thoughts in her head makes me feel totally foolish.

I drop it back on the rack and fidget with my earbud, pretending as though I didn't hear a thing as I move toward the matching cotton sets, which are way more my style and speed.

But just as I begin browsing through several hot-pink-and-orange-striped camis, I realize they're probably nowhere near Damen's speed. He'd probably prefer something a little more racy. Something with a lot more lace and a lot less cotton. Something that could actually be considered *sexy*. And without even looking, I know Stacia and her faithful lapdog have followed.

"Aw, look, Honor. Freak can't decide between skanky or sweet." Stacia shakes her head and smirks at me. "Trust me, when in doubt, always go with skanky. It's pretty much a sure thing. Besides, from what I recall about Damen, he's not so big on sweet."

I freeze, my stomach clenching with unreasonable jealousy as my throat squeezes tight. But only for a moment before I force myself to resume breathing and browsing, refusing to let her think, even for a second, that her words might've gotten to me.

Besides, I know all about what happened between them, and I'm happy to report that it was neither skanky nor sweet. Mostly because it wasn't anything at all. Damen merely *pretended* to like her so he could get to me. And yet, just the thought of him even pretending still makes me queasy.

"Come on, let's go. She can't hear you," Honor says, scratching her arm and glancing between Stacia and me, then checking her phone for the hundredth time to see if Craig answered her text.

But Stacia remains rooted, enjoying herself far too much to give up so easily. "Oh, she can hear me just fine," she says, a smile playing at the corner of her lips. "Don't let the iPod and earbuds fool you. She can hear everything we say and everything we think. Because Ever's not just a freak, she's also a witch."

I turn away and head for the other side of the store, browsing a rack of push-up bras and corsets, telling myself: *Ignore her, ignore her, just focus on shopping and she'll go away.*

But Stacia's not going anywhere. Instead, she grabs hold of my arm and pulls me right to her, saying, "Come on, don't be shy. *Show* her. Show Honor what a freak you are!"

Her eyes stare into mine, sending a flood of disturbing dark energy coursing right through me as she squeezes my arm so tight her thumb and index finger practically meet. And I know she's trying to bait me, incite me, aware of exactly what I'm capable of after that time when I lost control in the hallway at school. Only that time she didn't do it on purpose—she had no idea what I could do.

Honor starts to fidget, standing beside her and whining, "Come on, Stacia. Let's go. This is *bor*-ing."

But Stacia ignores her and grips my arm harder, her nails pressing into my flesh as she whispers, "Go on, tell her. Tell her what you see!"

I close my eyes, my stomach swirling as my head fills with images similar to the ones I saw before: Stacia scratching and clawing her way to the top of the popularity pyramid, stomping much harder than necessary on all those beneath her. Including Honor, *especially* Honor, who's so afraid of being unpopular she does nothing to stop it . . .

I could tell her what a horrible friend Stacia really is, expose her for the awful person I know her to be. . . . I could pry Stacia's hand from my arm and fling her across the room so hard she'd fly straight through the plate glass window before crashing into the mall directory. . . .

Only I can't. The last time I let loose at school, when I told Stacia all the awful things I know about her, it was a colossal mistake— one I don't have the luxury of making again. There's so much more to hide now, much bigger secrets at stake—secrets that belong not only to me but to Damen as well.

Stacia laughs as I fight to stay calm and not overreact. Reminding myself that while appearing weak is okay, giving in to weakness is definitely *not*. It's absolutely imperative to appear normal, clueless, and allow her the illusion that she's so much stronger than me.

Honor checks her watch, rolling her eyes, wanting to leave. And just as I'm about to pull away, and maybe even *accidentally* backhand Stacia while I'm at it, I *see* something so awful, so repulsive, I knock an entire rack of lingerie to the floor in an attempt to break free.

Bras, thongs, hangers, and fixtures—all of it crashing to the ground in one big heap.

With me as the cherry on top.

"O. Migawd!" Stacia shrieks, grabbing hold of Honor as they fall all over themselves laughing at me. "You are such a freakin' *spaz!*" she says, going straight for her cell so she can capture it all on video. Zooming in to get close-up footage of me attempting to break free of a red lace garter belt that's wrapped around my neck. "Better get crackin' and get this cleaned up!" She squints, adjusting her angle as I struggle to stand. "You know what they say, you break it, you buy it!"

I get to my feet, watching as Stacia and Honor bolt for the door the moment a salesperson arrives. Stacia pausing long enough to glance over her shoulder and say, "I'm watching you, Ever. Believe me, I'm not through with you yet." Before running away.

ten

The moment I sense Damen turning onto my street, I run to the mirror (again) and fidget with my clothes, making sure everything is right where it should be—the dress, the bra, the new lingerie—and hoping it all stays in place (well, at least until it's time to come off).

After the Victoria's Secret salesgirl and I cleaned up the mess, she helped me choose this really pretty matching bra and panty set that isn't made of cotton, isn't embarrassingly sexy, and doesn't actually support or cover much of anything, but then I guess that's the point. Then I moved on to Nordstrom where I bought this pretty green dress and some cute strappy wedges to go with it. And on the way home I stopped for a quick manicure/pedicure, which is something I haven't done since, well, since before the accident that robbed me of my old life forever—when I used to be popular and girly like Stacia.

Only I was never *really* like Stacia.

I mean, I may have been popular and a cheerleader, but I was never a bitch.

"What are you thinking?" Damen asks, having let himself in and coming straight up to my room since Sabine's not at home.

I gaze at him, watching as he leans against the doorjamb and smiles. Taking in his dark jeans, dark shirt, dark jacket, and the black motorcycle boots he always wears and feeling my heart skip two beats.

"I was thinking about the last four hundred years," I say, cringing when his eyes grow dark and worried. "But not in the way that you think," I add, eager to assure him I wasn't obsessing over his past yet again. "I was thinking about all of our lifetimes together, and how we never . . . um . . ."

He lifts his brow as a smile plays at his lips.

"I guess I'm just glad those four hundred years are over," I mumble, watching as he moves toward me, slips his arms around my waist, and pulls me tight to his chest. My eyes grazing over the planes of his face, his dark eyes, smooth skin, his irresistible lips, drinking all of him in.

"I'm glad too," he says, his eyes teasing mine. "Nope, on second thought, scratch that, because the truth is, I'm more than glad. In fact—I'm ecstatic." He smiles, but a moment later he's merging his brows, saying, "No, that still doesn't explain it. I think we need a new word." He laughs, lowering his mouth to my ear as he whispers, "You are more beautiful tonight than you've *ever* been. And I want everything to be perfect. I want it to be everything you dreamed it would be. I just hope I don't disappoint you."

I balk, pulling away to gaze at his face, wondering how he could even think such a thing, when all of this time it's been *me* who's been worried about disappointing *him*.

He places his finger under my chin, lifting my face until my lips meet his. And I kiss him back with such fervor, he pulls away and says, "Maybe we should head straight for the Montage instead?"

"Okay," I murmur, my lips seeking his. Regretting the joke when he pulls away and I see how hopeful he is. "Except that we can't. Miles will *kill* me if I miss his debut." I smile, waiting for him to smile too.

Only he doesn't. And when he looks at me with his face so drawn and serious, I know I strayed too close to the truth. All of my lives have always ended on this night—the night we'd planned to be together. And even though I don't remember the details, he clearly does.

But then just as quickly his color's returned and he takes my hand when he says, "Well, lucky for us you're quite *unkillable* now, so there's nothing that can keep us apart."

The first thing I notice as we head for our seats is that Haven's sitting beside Roman. Taking full advantage of Josh's absence by pressing her shoulder against his and cocking her head in a way that allows her to gaze up at him adoringly and smile at everything he says. The second thing I notice is that my seat is also beside Roman's. Only unlike Haven, I'm not at all thrilled. But since Damen's already claimed the outside seat, and I don't want to make a big show of moving, I reluctantly sink down onto mine. Feeling the invasive push of Roman's energy as his eyes peer into mine—his attention so focused on me, I can't help but squirm.

I gaze around the mostly full theater, trying to get my mind off of Roman and am relieved when I see Josh heading down the aisle, clad in his usual tight black jeans, studded belt, crisp white shirt, and skinny checkered tie, his arms loaded down with candy and bottles of water as his black swoop of hair flops into his eyes. And I can't help but breathe a sigh of relief, seeing how perfect he and Haven are for each other, and I'm thrilled that he's not been replaced.

"Water?" he asks, plopping onto the seat on Haven's other side and passing two bottles my way.

I take one for myself and try to pass the other to Damen, but he just shakes his head and sips his red drink.

"*Wot* is that?" Roman asks, leaning across me and motioning toward the bottle, his unwelcome touch sending a chill through my skin. "You suck that stuff down like it's spiked. In which case, share the wealth, mate. Don't leave us out here in the cold." He laughs, extending his hand and wiggling his fingers, glancing between us with a dare in his eye.

And just as I'm about to butt in, fearing that Damen's so nice he might agree to give Roman a taste, the curtain unfolds and the music begins. And even though Roman gives up and leans back in his seat, his gaze never once wavers from me.

Miles was amazing. So amazing that every now and then I find myself actually focusing on the lines that he speaks and the lyrics he sings, while the rest of the time my mind is preoccupied with the fact that I'm about to lose my virginity—for the very first time—in four hundred years.

I mean, it's so amazing to think that out of all of those incarnations, out of all the times we met and fell in love, we never once managed to seal the deal.

But tonight, all of that changes.

Everything changes.

Tonight we bury the past and move toward the future of our eternal love.

When the curtain finally closes, we all get up and head for backstage. But just as we reach the back door, I turn to Damen and say, "Damn! We forgot to stop by the store and pick up some flowers for Miles."

But Damen just smiles. Shaking his head as he says, "What're you talking about? We've got all the flowers we need right here."

I squint, wondering what he's up to, because according to my eyes, he's as empty-handed as I. "What're *you* taking about?" I whisper, feeling that warm wonderful charge course through me as he places his hand on my arm.

"Ever," he says, an amused look on his face. "Those flowers already exist on the quantum level. If you want to access them on a physical level, all you have to do is manifest them like I taught you to do."

I glance all around, making sure no one's eavesdropping on our strange conversation and feeling embarrassed when I admit that I can't. "I don't know how," I say, wishing he'd just make the flowers and get it over with already. This is really no time for a lesson.

But Damen's not buying it. "Of course you can. Have I taught you nothing?"

I press my lips together and stare at the floor, because the truth is, he's tried to teach me plenty. But I'm a horrible student and I've slacked off so much it'll be better for both of us if I leave the manifesting of flowers to him.

"You do it," I say, wincing at the disappointment that transforms his face. "You're so much quicker than I am. If I try to do it, it'll turn into a big scene, people will notice, and then we'll be forced to explain. . . ."

He shakes his head, refusing to be swayed by my words. "How will you ever learn if you always rely on me?"

I sigh, knowing he's right but still not wanting to waste precious time trying to manifest a bouquet of roses that may or may not ever appear. All I want is to get the flowers in hand, tell Miles *Bravo,* and move on to the Montage and the rest of our plans. And a moment ago it seemed like he only wanted that too. But now he's gone all serious and professorlike on me, and to be honest, it's kind of wrecking the mood.

I take a deep breath and smile sweetly, my fingers crawling along the edge of his lapel when I say, "You're absolutely right. And I will get better, I promise. But I was thinking that maybe just this once, you could do it since you're so much quicker than I am—" I stroke the spot just under his ear, knowing he's *this* close to caving. "I mean, the sooner we get the bouquet, the sooner we can leave, and then . . ."

And I'm not even finished before he's closing his eyes, his hand held before him as though gripping a spray of spring blooms, as I glance all around, making sure no one is watching, hoping to get this over with soon.

But when I look at Damen again, I start to panic. Because not only is his hand still empty, but a trail of sweat is coursing its way down his cheek for the second time in two days.

Which wouldn't seem all that strange except for the fact that Damen doesn't sweat.

Just like he never gets sick and never has *off* days, he also never sweats. No matter what the temperature outside, no matter what the task at hand, he always remains cool, calm, and perfectly able to handle whatever's before him.

Until yesterday, when he failed to access the portal.

And now, as he fails to manifest a simple bouquet for Miles.

And when I touch his arm and ask if he's okay, I get only the slightest trickle of the usual tingle and heat.

"Of course I'm okay." He squints, raising his lids just enough to peer at me, before closing them tightly again. And even though our gaze was brief, what I glimpsed in his eyes made me grow cold and weak.

Those were not the warm loving eyes I've grown used to. Those eyes were cold, distant, remote—just like I glimpsed earlier this week. And I watch as he focuses, his brow furrowed, his upper lip beaded with sweat, determined to get this over and done with so we can both move on to our perfect night. And not wanting this to drag on any further or repeat the other day when he failed to make the portal appear, I stand right beside him and close my eyes too. *Seeing* a beautiful bouquet of two dozen red roses clutched in his hand, *inhaling* their heady sweet scent while *feeling* the soft plush of petals that just happen to be mounted above long thorny stems—

"Ouch!" Damen shakes his head and brings his finger to his

mouth, even though the wound is already healed long before it can get there. "I forgot to make a vase," he says, clearly convinced he made the flowers himself, and I have every intention of keeping it that way.

"Let me do it," I say, in an effort to please him. "You're absolutely right, I need the practice," I add, closing my eyes and envisioning the one in the dining room at home, the one with the complicated pattern of swirls and etches and luminous facets.

"Waterford crystal?" He laughs. "How much do you want him to think we spent on this thing?"

I laugh too, relieved that all the weirdness is over and he's back to joking again. Taking the vase he thrusts into my hands as he says, "Here. You give these to Miles while I get the car and pull it around."

"You sure?" I ask, noting how the skin around his eyes appears tense and pale, and his forehead is the slightest bit clammy. "Because we can just run in, say *congrats,* and run out. It doesn't have to be a big deal."

"This way we can avoid the long line of cars and make an even quicker getaway." He smiles. "I thought you were anxious to get there."

I am. I'm as anxious as he. But I'm also concerned. Concerned about his inability to manifest, concerned about the fleeting cold look in his eyes—holding my breath as he takes a swig from his bottle, reminding myself of how quickly his wound healed, convincing myself it's a good sign.

And knowing my concern will only make him feel worse, I clear my throat and say, "Fine. You go get the car. And I'll meet you inside."

Unable to ignore the startling coolness of his cheek when I lean in to kiss it.

eleven

By the time I get backstage, Miles is surrounded by family and friends and still dressed in the white go-go boots and minidress of his very last scene as *Hairspray*'s Tracy Turnblad.

"Bravo! You were amazing!" I say, handing over the flowers in place of a hug since I can't risk taking on any additional energy when I'm so nervous inside I can barely handle my own. "Seriously, I had no idea you could sing like that."

"Yes you did." He sweeps his long wig to the side and buries his nose in the petals. "You've heard me perform car karaoke plenty of times."

"Not like that." I smile, and I'm serious. In fact, he was so good I plan to catch a repeat performance on another, less nervous-making night. "So where's Holt?" I ask, already knowing the answer but just trying to make conversation until Damen arrives. "Surely you've made up by now?"

Miles frowns and motions toward his dad, while I cringe and mouth *sorry*. Having forgotten he's out of the closet with his friends, but not yet his parents.

"Don't you worry, all is well," he whispers, batting his false eyelashes and running his hands through his blond-streaked locks. "I had a temporary meltdown, but it's over with now, and all is for-given. And speaking of Prince Charming . . ."

I turn toward the door, eager to see Damen walk through it. My heart going into overdrive at just the mere thought of him—the whole, wonderful, glorious thought of him—and not doing much to mask my disappointment when I realize he's referring to Haven and Josh.

"What do you think?" he asks, nodding at them. "They gonna make it?"

I watch as Josh slides his arm around Haven's waist, cupping his fingers and pulling her closer. But no matter how hard he tries, it's no use. Despite the fact that they're perfect together, she's focused on Roman—mirroring the way he stands, the way he tilts his head back when he laughs, the way he holds his hands—all of her energy flowing straight toward him as though Josh doesn't exist. But even though it seems mostly one-sided, unfortunately Roman's the type who'd be more than willing to take her out for a test drive.

I turn back to Miles and force a casual shrug.

"There's a cast party at Heather's," Miles says. "We're all headed there soon. You guys coming?"

I give him a blank look. I don't even know who that is.

"She played Penny Pingleton?"

I don't know who that is either, but I know better than to admit it, so I nod like I do.

"Don't tell me you guys were macking so much you missed the whole show!" He shakes his head in a way that makes it clear he's only partly joking.

"Don't be ridiculous, I saw the whole thing!" I say, my face flush-ing a thousand shades of red and knowing he'll never believe me even though it's more or less true. Because even though we were behaving ourselves and not at all *macking,* it was almost like our hands we're *macking*—with the way Damen entwined his fingers with mine—and like our thoughts were *macking*—with the telepathic messages we sent back and forth. Because even though my eyes were watching the whole entire time—my mind was elsewhere, already occupying our room at the Montage.

"So you coming or not?" Miles asks, his mind correctly guessing *not,* and not nearly as upset as I thought he might be. "So, where you two headed, anyway? What could be more exciting than partying with the cast and crew?"

And when I look at him, I'm so tempted to tell him, to share my big secret with someone I know I can trust. But just as I've convinced myself to spill it, Roman walks up with Josh and Haven in tow.

"We're heading over, anybody need a ride? It's only a two-seater, but there's room for one more." Roman nods at me, his gaze pushing, probing, even after I turn away.

Miles shakes his head. "I'm grabbing a ride with Holt, and Ever better-dealed me. Some top-secret plan she refuses to spill."

Roman smiles, his lips lifting at the corners as his eyes graze over my body. And even though, technically speaking, his thoughts could probably be considered more flattering than crude, the fact that they're coming from him is enough to give me the creeps.

I avert my gaze, glancing toward the door, knowing Damen should've been here by now. And I'm just about to send him a telepathic message, telling him to step it up and meet me inside, when I'm interrupted by the sound of Roman's voice saying, "Must've kept it secret from Damen too, then. He already left."

I turn, my eyes meeting his, feeling that undeniable ping in my gut as a chill blankets my skin. "He didn't *leave,*" I say, not even trying to clear the edge from my voice. "He just went to pull the car around back."

But Roman just shrugs, his gaze filled with pity when he says, "Whatever you say. I just thought you should know that just now, when I stepped out for a smoke, I saw Damen pulling out of the parking lot and speeding away."

twelve

I burst through the door and into the alley, gazing around the narrow empty space as my eyes adjust to the darkness, making out a row of overflowing Dumpsters, a trail of broken glass, a hungry stray cat—but no Damen.

I stumble forward, my eyes searching relentlessly as my heart beats so fast I fear it might break free from my chest. Refusing to believe he's not here. Refusing to believe that he ditched me. Roman's awful! He's lying! Damen would never just up and leave me like this.

Trailing my fingers along the brick wall for guidance, I close my eyes and try to tune in to his energy, calling him to me in a telepathic message of love, need, and worry, but getting only a solid black void in response. Then I slalom through cars all heading for the exit, cell phone pressed to my ear while I peer into windows, leaving a series of messages on his voice mail.

Even when my right heel breaks off my sandal, I just toss them aside and keep going. I don't care about my shoes. I can make a hundred more pairs.

But I can't make another Damen.

And as the lot slowly empties, with still no sign of him, I crumble to the curb, feeling sweaty, exhausted, deflated. Watching the cuts and blisters on my feet simultaneously mend, and wishing I could close my eyes and access his mind—get a read on his thoughts, if not his whereabouts.

But the truth is, I've never been able to get inside his head. It's one of the things I liked best about him. His being so psychically off limits made me feel normal. And wouldn't you know, the one thing that once seemed so appealing is now the very thing that's working against me.

"Need a lift?"

I look up to find Roman standing over me, jangling a set of keys in one hand, my broken sandals in the other.

I shake my head and look away, knowing I'm in no position to refuse a ride, though I'd rather crawl through a trail of hot coals and broken glass than climb inside a two-seater with him.

"C'mon," he says. "I promise not to bite."

I gather my things, tossing my cell into my bag and smoothing my dress as I stand up and say, "I'm good."

"Really?" He smiles, moving so close our toes nearly touch. "'Cause, to be honest, you're not looking so good."

I turn, making my way toward the exit, not bothering to stop when he says, "What I meant was the *situation* isn't looking so good. I mean, look at you, Ever. You're disheveled, shoeless, and though I can't be too sure, it appears that your boyfriend has ditched you."

I take a deep breath and keep going, hoping he'll soon tire of this game, tire of *me*, and move on.

"And yet, even in that frenetic, slightly desperate state, I have to admit, you're still smokin'—if you don't mind my saying."

I stop, suddenly turning to face him despite my vow to keep moving. Cringing as his eyes slowly rake over my body, lingering on my legs, my waist, and my chest—with an unmistakable gleam.

"Makes one wonder what Damen's thinking, 'cause if you ask me—"

"No one asked you," I say, feeling my hands starting to shake and reminding myself that I'm completely in charge here, that I've no reason to feel threatened. That even though I may look like your average defenseless girl on the outside, I'm anything but. I'm stronger than I used to be, so strong that if I really wanted, I could take him down with one swing. I could pick him up off his feet and toss him clear across the parking lot to the other side of the street. And don't think I'm not tempted to prove it.

He smiles, that lazy grin that works on just about everyone but me, his steely blue eyes peering straight into mine with a gaze so knowing, so personal, so amused—my first instinct is to flee.

But I don't.

Because everything about him feels like a challenge, and no way am I letting him win.

"I don't need a ride," I finally say. Turning to pick up the pace and feeling his chill as he trails right behind me. His icy cold breath on the back of my neck when he says, "Ever, please, slow down a minute, would ya? I didn't mean to upset you."

But I don't slow down. I keep going. Determined to put as much distance between us as I possibly can.

"Come on now." He laughs. "I'm only trying to help. Your friends have all left, Damen's buggered off, the cleaning crew went home, which makes me your only hope left."

"I've plenty of options," I mumble, wishing he'd just go away so I can try to manifest a car, some shoes, and be on my way.

"None that I can see."

I shake my head and keep walking. This conversation is over.

"So what you're saying is, you'd rather foot it all the way home than get in a car with me?"

I reach the end of the street and punch the signal again and again, willing the light to turn green so I can get to the other side and be rid of him.

"I don't know how we got off to such a bad start, but it's pretty clear that you hate me and I've no idea why." His voice is smooth, inviting, as though he really wants to start over, let bygones be bygones, make amends, and all that.

But I don't want to start over. Nor do I want to make amends. I just want him to turn around, go somewhere else, and leave me alone so I can find Damen.

And yet, I can't let it go, can't let him get the last word. So I glance over my shoulder and say, "Don't flatter yourself, Roman. Hating requires caring. In which case, I couldn't possibly hate you."

Then I storm across the street even though the light has yet to turn green. Dancing around a couple of speeders intent on beating the yellow, and feeling the insistent chill of his gaze.

"What about your shoes?" he shouts. "Shame to just leave 'em like this. I'm sure the heel can be fixed."

But I just keep moving. *Seeing* him bow deeply behind me, his arm sweeping upward in an exaggerated arc, my sandals dangling from the tips of his fingers. His all-encompassing laugh chasing behind me, following me across the boulevard and onto the street.

thirteen

The moment I cross the street I duck behind a building, peer around the corner, and wait until Roman's cherry red Aston Martin Roadster pulls onto the road and drives away. Then I wait a few minutes more until I'm fully convinced he really is gone and won't be returning anytime soon.

I need to find Damen. I need to find out what happened to him, why he disappeared without saying a word. I mean, he's (we've) been looking forward to this night for four hundred years, so the fact that he's not here beside me proves something's gone terribly wrong.

But first I need a car. You can't get anywhere in Orange County without one. So I close my eyes and picture the first thing that comes to mind—a sky blue VW Bug—just like the one Shayla Sparks, the coolest senior to ever walk the halls of Hillcrest High, used to drive. Remembering its cartoonish round shape and the black cloth top that seemed so glamorous and yet took such a beating in the relentless Oregon rain. Picturing it so clearly it's as though it's right there before me—all shiny and curvy and adorably cute. *Feeling* my fingers bend around the door handle, and the soft stroke of leather as I slide onto the seat, and when I place a single red tulip in the flower holder before me, I open my eyes and see that my ride is complete.

Only I don't know how to start the engine.

I forgot to manifest a key.

But since that's never stopped Damen, I just close my eyes again and *will* the engine to life, remembering the exact sound Shayla's car used to make as my ex–best friend Rachel and I stood on the curb after school, watching in envy as her super cool friends piled into the front and back seats.

And the moment the engine turns, I head toward Coast Highway. Figuring I'll start at the Montage, the place we were supposed to end up, and take it from there.

The traffic is thick this time of night, but it doesn't slow me. I just focus on all of the surrounding cars, *seeing* what everyone's next move is going to be, then adjusting my journey around it. Moving quickly and smoothly into each open space, until I arrive at the entrance, jump out of the Bug, and sprint for the lobby.

Stopping only when the valet calls out from behind me, "Hey, wait up! What about the key?"

I pause, my breath coming in short shallow gasps, not realizing until I catch him staring at my feet that I'm not only keyless but shoeless as well. Yet knowing I can't afford to waste any more time than I already have, and reluctant to go through the whole manifesting process in front of him, I run through the door, yelling, "Just leave it running, I'll only be a sec!"

I make a beeline for the front desk, bypassing a long line of disgruntled people, all of them weighed down with golf bags and monogrammed luggage, all of them complaining about checking in late due to a four-hour delay. And when I cut in front of the middle-aged couple that was supposed to be next, the griping and grumbling hits the next level.

"Has Damen Auguste checked in?" I ask, ignoring the protests behind me, as my fingers curl around the edge of the counter and I fight to steady my nerves.

"I'm sorry, *who?*" The clerk's gaze darts to the couple behind me, shooting them a look meant to say—*don't worry, I'll be done with this psycho chick soon!*

"Damen. Auguste." I enunciate slowly, succinctly, with far more patience than I have.

She squints at me, her thin lips barely moving as she says, "I'm sorry, that information is confidential." Flicking her long dark ponytail over her shoulder in a move so final, so dismissive, it's like a period at the end of a sentence.

I narrow my eyes, focusing on her deep orange aura and knowing it means strict organization and self-control are the virtues she prizes the most—something I showed a glaring lack of when I jumped the turnstile a moment ago. And knowing I need to get on her good side if I've any hope of obtaining the info I need, I resist the urge to act all huffy and indignant, and calmly explain how I'm the *other* guest who's sharing the room.

She looks at me, looks at the couple behind me, then says, "I'm sorry, but you'll have to wait your turn. Just. Like. Everyone. Else."

And I know I have less than ten seconds between now and when she calls for security.

"I *know.*" I lower my voice and lean toward her. "And I really am sorry. It's just that—"

She looks at me, her fingers inching toward the phone as I take in her long straight nose, thin unadorned lips, and the hint of puffiness just under her eyes, and just like *that*, I *see* my way in.

She's been dumped. She's been dumped so recently she still cries herself to sleep every night. Reliving the horrible event every day, *all day*—the scene following her wherever she goes, from her waking state to her dreams.

"It's just that, well—" I pause, trying to make it seem as though it hurts too much to say the actual words, when the truth is I'm not sure which words I'll actually use. Then I shake my head and start over, knowing it's always better to stick with some semblance of the truth when you need the lie to seem real. "He didn't show up when he was supposed to, and because of that . . . well . . . I'm not sure if he's even still coming." I swallow hard, cringing when I realize the tears in my eyes are for real.

But when I look at her again, seeing her face soften—the grim judging mouth, the squinty narrowed eyes, the superior tilt of her chin—all of it suddenly transformed by compassion, solidarity, and unity—I know that it worked. We're like sisters now, loyal members of an all-female tribe, recently jilted by men.

I watch as she taps some commands on her keyboard, tuning in to her energy so I can see what she sees—the letters on the screen flashing before me, showing that our room, suite 309, is still empty.

"I'm sure he's just running late," she says, though she doesn't believe it. In her mind, all men are scum, of this she's convinced. "But if you can show me some ID and prove that you're you, I can—"

But before she can finish, I'm already gone, turning away from the desk and running outside. I don't need a key. I could never check into that sad empty room, waiting for a boyfriend who clearly won't show. I need to keep moving, keep searching. I need to hit the only other two places where he might be. And as I jump in my car and head for the beach—I pray that I'll find him.

fourteen

I park near the Shake Shack and head toward the ocean, feeling my way down the dark winding path, determined to locate Damen's secret cave even though I've only been there one other time, which happens to be the one *other* time we came really close to doing the deed. And we would have too—if it weren't for me. I guess I have a long history of slamming the brakes at the most crucial moment. Either that, or I end up dying. So obviously, I was hoping tonight would be different.

But the moment my feet hit the sand and I make my way down to his hideout, I'm sorry to see that it's pretty much the same as we left it: blankets and towels folded and stacked in the corner, surfboards lined up against the walls, a wet suit draped over a chair—but no Damen.

And with only one place left on my list, I cross my fingers and run for my car. Amazed by the way my limbs move with such speed and grace, the way my feet merely glance over the sand, covering the distance so quickly, I've barely started and I'm already back in my car pulling out of my space. Wondering just how long I've been able to do this, and what other immortal gifts I might have.

• • •

When I arrive at the gate, Sheila, the gate guard who's used to seeing me by now and knows I'm on Damen's permanent list of welcome guests, just smiles and waves me right in. And as I head up the hill toward his house and pull into his drive, the first thing I notice is that the lights are all off.

And I mean *all* of them. Including the one over the door that he always leaves on.

I sit in the Bug, its engine idling as I gaze up at those cold dark windows. Part of me wanting to break down the door, tear up the stairs, and burst into his "special" room—the one where he stores his most precious mementos—the portraits of himself as painted by Picasso, Van Gogh, and Velázquez, along with the piles of rare, first-editions tomes—the priceless relics of his long and storied past, all hoarded into one overstuffed, gilt-laden room. While the other part prefers to stay put, knowing I don't need to enter to prove he's not there. The cold, foreboding exterior, with its stone-covered walls, tiled roof, and vacant windows, is completely devoid of his warm loving presence.

I close my eyes, struggling to recall the last words he said—something about getting the car so that *we* could make an even quicker getaway. Sure that he really meant *we*—that *we* were supposed to make the quick getaway so that *we* could finally be together—our four-hundred-year quest culminating on this one perfect night.

I mean, he couldn't have been looking for a quicker getaway from *me*—

Could he?

I take a deep breath and climb out of my car, knowing the only way to get answers is to keep moving. The soles of my cold wet feet slipping along the dew-covered walkway as I fumble for the key, remembering too late that I left it at home, never dreaming I'd need it tonight of all nights.

I stand before the front door, memorizing its curving arch, mahogany finish, and bold, detailed carvings, before I close my eyes and picture another just like it. *Seeing* my imaginary door unlock and swing open, never having tried this before, but knowing it's possible after seeing Damen unlock a gate at our school—a gate that'd been decidedly locked just a few moments before.

But when I open my eyes again, all I've managed to manifest is another giant wood door. And having no idea how to dispose of it (since up until now I've only manifested things I wanted to keep), I lean it against the wall and head toward the back.

There's a window in his kitchen, the one just behind the sink that he always leaves cracked. And after sliding my fingers under the rim and pushing the window all the way up, I crawl over a sink overflowing with empty glass bottles before jumping to the ground, my feet landing with a muffled *thud* as I wonder if breaking and entering applies to concerned girlfriends too.

I gaze around the room, taking in the wooden table and chairs, the rack of stainless steel pots, the high-tech coffeemaker, blender, and juicer—all part of the collection of the most modern kitchen gadgets money can buy (or Damen can manifest). Carefully selected to give the appearance of a normal, well-to-do life, like accessories in a beautifully decorated model home, perfectly staged and completely unused.

I peer into his fridge, expecting to see the usual abundant supply of red juice, only to find just a few bottles instead. And when I peek inside his pantry, the place where he allows the newer batches to ferment or marinate or whatever they do in the dark for three days—I'm shocked to find that it's barely stocked too.

I stand there, staring at the handful of bottles, my stomach thrumming, my heart racing, knowing something's terribly wrong with this picture. Damen's always so obsessive about keeping plenty of juice on hand—even more so now that he's responsible for supplying me—that he would never allow things to get to this point.

But then again, he's also been going through an awful lot of it lately, chugging it to the point where his consumption has nearly doubled. So it's entirely possible he hasn't had time to make a new batch.

Which sounds good in theory, sure, but it's not at all plausible.

I mean, who am I fooling? Damen's extremely organized with these things, even bordering on obsessive. He would never let his brewing duties slide—not for one day.

Not unless something was terribly wrong.

And even though I don't have any proof, I just know in my gut that the way he's been acting so *off* lately—with the sudden blank looks that are impossible to miss no matter how quickly they fade, not to mention the sweating, the headaches, the inability to manifest everyday objects, or access the Summerland portal—well, when I add it all up, it's clear that he's sick.

Only Damen doesn't get sick.

And when he pricked his finger on that thorny rose just a little while ago, I watched as it healed right before me.

But still, maybe I should start calling the hospitals—just to be sure.

Except Damen would *never* go to the hospital. He'd see it as a sign of weakness, defeat. He's far more likely to crawl off like a wounded animal, hiding out somewhere where he could be alone.

Only he doesn't have any wounds because they instantly heal. Besides, he'd never crawl off without telling me first.

Then again, I was also convinced he'd never drive off without me, and look how that turned out.

I riffle through his drawers, searching for the Yellow Pages—yet another accessory in his quest to seem normal. Because while it's true that Damen would never take himself to the hospital, if there were an accident, or some other event beyond his control, then it's possible that someone else might've taken him without his consent.

And while that completely contradicts Roman's (most likely bogus) story of watching Damen speed away, that doesn't stop me from calling every hospital in Orange County, asking if a Damen Auguste has been admitted, and coming up empty each time.

When the last hospital is called, I consider calling the police but quickly decide against it. I mean, what would I say? That my six-hundred-year-old immortal boyfriend went missing?

I'd have just as much luck cruising Coast Highway, searching for a black BMW with dark tinted windows and a good-looking driver inside—the proverbial needle in the haystack of Laguna Beach.

Or—I can always just settle in here, knowing he's got to turn up eventually.

And as I climb the stairs to his room, I comfort myself with the thought that if I can't be with him, then at least I can be with his things. And as I settle myself upon his velvet settee, I gaze among the things he prizes the most, hoping I'm still one of them too.

fifteen

My neck hurts. And my back feels weird. And when I open my eyes and glimpse my surroundings—I know why. I spent the night in this room. Right here on this ancient velvet settee, which was originally intended for light banter, coquettish flirting, but definitely not sleeping.

I struggle to stand, my muscles tightening in protest as I stretch toward the sky then down toward my toes. And after bending my torso from side to side and swiveling my neck to and fro, I head over to his thick velvet drapes and yank them aside. Flooding the room with a light so bright my eyes water and sting, barely having enough time to adjust before I've closed them again. Ensuring the edges overlap and no amount of sunlight is allowed to creep in, returning the space to its usual state of permanent midnight, having been warned by Damen that those harsh Southern California rays can wreak havoc on the contents of this room.

Damen.

Just thinking about him makes my heart swell with such longing, such all-consuming ache—my head grows dizzy and my whole body sways. And as I grab hold of an elaborate wood cabinet, grasping its fine detailed edge, my eyes search the room, reminding me that I'm not nearly as alone as I think.

Everywhere I look his image surrounds me. His likeness perfectly captured by the world's greatest masters, matted in museum-quality frames, and mounted on these walls. The Picasso in the dark somber suit, the Velázquez on the rearing white stallion—each of them depicting the face I thought I knew so well—only now the eyes seem distant and mocking, the chin raised and defiant, and those lips, those warm wonderful lips that I crave so bad I can taste them, appear so remote, so aloof, so maddeningly distant, as though warning me not to come near.

I close my eyes, determined to block it all out, sure that my panicked state of mind is influencing me for the worst. Forcing myself to take several deep breaths, before trying his cell phone again. His voice mail prompting yet another round of: *Call me . . . where are you . . . what happened . . . are you okay . . . call me*—messages I've left countless times already.

I slip my phone back into my bag and gaze around the room one last time, my eyes carefully avoiding his portraits while assuring myself there's nothing I missed. No blatant clue to his disappearance that I might've overlooked, no small, seemingly insignificant hint that might make the *how* and *why* a little easier to grasp.

And when I'm satisfied I've done all I can, I grab my purse and head to the kitchen, stopping just long enough to leave a short note, repeating all the same words I said on the phone. Knowing the moment I walk out the door my connection to Damen will feel even more tenuous than it already does.

I take a deep breath and close my eyes, picturing the future that just yesterday seemed so sure—the one of Damen and me, both of us happy, together, complete. Wishing it was possible to manifest such a thing, yet knowing deep down it's no use.

You can't manifest another person. Or at least not for very long.

So I shift my attention to something I *can* create. Picturing the most perfect red tulip—its soft waxy petals and long fluid stem the ideal symbol for our undying love. And when I feel it take shape in my hand, I head back to the kitchen, tear up the note, and leave the tulip on the counter instead.

sixteen

I miss Riley.

I miss her so much it's like a physical ache.

Because the second I realized I had no choice but to inform Sabine that Damen wouldn't be making it to dinner (which I waited to do until ten minutes past eight when it was clear he wouldn't show), the questions began. And they pretty much kept coming for the remainder of the weekend, with her asking stuff like: *What's wrong? I know something's wrong. I wish you would talk to me. Why won't you tell me? Is it something with Damen? Are you two in a fight?*

And even though I did talk to her (over dinner when I somehow managed to eat enough to convince her that I really and truly do *not* have an eating disorder), trying to assure her that everything was A-OK, that Damen was just busy, and that I was overtired after spending such a long, fun-filled night at Haven's—it was clear she didn't believe me. Or at least not the part about me being fine. She totally believed the part about me staying at Haven's.

Instead, she kept insisting that there had to be a better explanation for my constant sighing and mood swings, the way I went from morose to manic to mopey and back again. But even though I felt bad for lying to her—I stuck with my story. I guess it seemed easier since lying to Sabine made it easier to lie to myself. Fearing that *retelling* the story, explaining how even though my heart refuses to believe it, my head can't help but wonder if he might've purposely ditched me—might somehow *make* it come true.

If Riley were here, things would be different. I could talk to her. I could tell her the whole sordid tale from beginning to end. Knowing she'd not only understand, but that she'd get answers too.

Her being dead is like an all-access pass. Allowing her to go anywhere she wants merely by thinking about it. Making no place off-limits—the entire planet is fair game. And I've no doubt she'd be far more effective than all of my frantic phone calls and drive-bys combined.

Because in the end, all my disjointed, clumsy, ineffective investigating really amounts to is: _____ (nothing).

Leaving me just as clueless this Monday morning as I was on Friday night when it occurred. And no matter how many times I call Miles or Haven, their answer is always the same—*nothing to report, but we'll call you if anything changes.*

But if Riley were here, she'd close this case in no time. Getting quick results and in-depth answers—she'd be able to tell me just exactly what I'm dealing with, and how to proceed.

But the fact is, Riley's not here. And despite her promising me a sign, seconds before she left, I'm starting to doubt it'll happen. And maybe, just maybe, it's time I stop looking and get on with my life.

I slip on some jeans, slide my feet into some flip-flops, pull on a tank top, and chase it with a long-sleeved T—and just as I'm about to walk out the door and head for school, I turn right around and grab my iPod, hoodie, and sunglasses, knowing I'd better prepare for the worst since I've no idea what I'll find.

•   •   •

"Did you find him?"

I shake my head, watching as Miles climbs into my car, throws his bag on the floor, and shoots me a look filled with pity.

"I tried calling," he says, brushing his hair off his face, his nails still sporting a bright flashy pink. "Even tried to swing by his house but didn't get past the front gate. And trust me, you do *not* want to mess with Big Sheila. She takes her job *very* seriously." He laughs, hoping to lighten the mood.

But I just shrug, wishing I could laugh along with him, but knowing I can't. I've been a wreck since Friday and the only cure is to see Damen again.

"You shouldn't worry so much," Miles says, turning toward me. "I'm sure he's fine. I mean, it's not like it's the first time he's disappeared."

I glance at him, sensing his thoughts before the words leave his lips. Knowing he's referring to the last time Damen disappeared, the time I sent him away. "But that was different," I tell him. "Trust me, that was nothing like this."

"How can you be so sure?" His voice is careful, measured, his eyes still on me.

I take a deep breath and stare at the road, wondering whether or not I should tell him. I mean, I haven't *really* talked to anyone in so long, haven't confided in a friend since well before the accident—before everything changed. And sometimes, having to hoard all of these secrets can really feel lonely. I long to get out from under their weight and gossip like a normal girl again.

I look at Miles, sure that I can trust him, but not all that sure if I can trust me. I'm like a soda can that's been dropped and shaken, and now all of my secrets are rushing to the top.

"You okay?" he asks, eyeing me carefully.

I swallow hard. "Friday night? After your play?" I pause, knowing

I've got his full attention. "Well . . . we, um . . . we sort of made plans."

"Plans?" He leans toward me.

"*Big* plans." I nod, a smile hinting at the corner of my lips, then instantly fading when I remember how it all went so tragically wrong.

"How big?" he asks, eyes on mine.

I shake my head, gazing at the road ahead when I say, "Oh, just your usual Friday night. You know, room at the Montage, new lingerie, chocolate dipped strawberries, and two flutes of champagne . . ."

"Omigod, you *didn't*!" he squeals.

I glance at him, watching as his face falls when he realizes the truth.

"Oh God, I mean, you *really* didn't. You didn't get a chance to, since he . . ." He looks at me. "Oh Ever, I'm *so* sorry."

I shrug, seeing the devastation I feel so clearly displayed on his face.

"Listen," he says, reaching for my arm as I stop at a light, then pulling away when he remembers how I don't like to be touched by anyone other than Damen, not knowing that it's only because I go out of my way to avoid any and all unsolicited energy exchange. "Ever, you're gorgeous, seriously. I mean, especially now that you stopped wearing those dumpy hoodies and baggy—" He shakes his head. "Anyway, I think it's safe to say that there's no way Damen would have *willingly* walked out on you. I mean, let's face it, the guy's totally in love, anyone can see it. And believe me, with the way you two are constantly going at it, everyone *has* seen it. There's just no possible way he could've bailed!"

I glance at him, wanting to remind him of what Roman said about Damen speeding away, and how I have this terrible feeling he's somehow connected, maybe even responsible—but just as I'm about to, I realize I can't. I've no evidence to go on, nothing to prove it.

"You call the police?" he asks, his expression suddenly serious.

I press my lips together and squint at the light straight ahead, hating the fact that I did indeed call the cops. Knowing that if everything turns out to be fine, and Damen shows up unscathed, he's going to be pretty unhappy about my drawing that kind of attention his way.

But what was I supposed to do? I mean, if there *was* an accident or something, I figured they'd be the first to know. So Sunday morning, I went down to the station and filed a report, answering all of the usual questions like: *male, Caucasian, brown eyes, brown hair* . . . Until we got to his age and I nearly choked when I almost said: *um . . . he's approximately six hundred and seventeen years old . . .*

"Yeah, I filed a report," I finally say, pressing hard on the gas the second the light turns green and watching the speedometer rise. "They took down the info and said they'd look into it."

"That's it? Are you kidding? He's underage, he's not even an adult!"

"Yeah, but he's also emancipated. Which is like a whole other set of circumstances, making him legally responsible for himself, and other things I don't quite understand. Anyway, it's not like I'm privy to their investigation techniques, it's not like they filled me in on the big plan," I say, slowing to a more normal speed, now that we've entered the school zone.

"Do you think we should pass out flyers? Or hold a candlelight vigil like you see on the news?"

My stomach curls when he says it, even though I know he's just being his usual overly dramatic, though well-meaning self. But up until now, I hadn't imagined it ever coming to that. I mean, surely Damen will show up soon. He's *got* to. He's *immortal*! What could possibly happen to him?

But no sooner do I think it than I pull into the parking lot and see him climbing out of his car. Looking so sleek, so sexy, so gorgeous—you'd think everything was perfectly normal. That the last few days had never occurred.

I slam on the brakes, my car lurching forward then back, causing the driver behind me to slam on their brakes too. My heart racing, my hands shaking, as I watch my completely gorgeous, up until now MIA boyfriend, run a hand through his hair so deliberately, so insistently, and with such focused concentration you'd think it was his most pressing concern.

This is not what I expected.

"What the *hell*?" Miles shrieks, gaping at Damen as a whole slew of cars honk behind us. "And what's he doing parked all the way over *there*? Why isn't he in the second-best spot, saving the *best* one for us?"

And since I don't know the answers to any of those questions, I pull up beside Damen, thinking he might.

I lower my window, feeling inexplicably shy and awkward when he merely glances at me before looking away. "Um, is everything okay?" I ask, wincing when he just barely nods, which is pretty much the most imperceptible acknowledgment of my presence he could possibly give.

He reaches into his car and grabs his bag, taking the opportunity to admire himself in the driver's side window as I swallow hard and say, "Because you sort of took off Friday night . . . and I couldn't find you or reach you all weekend . . . and I got kinda worried . . . I even left you some messages . . . did you get them?" I press my lips together and cringe at my pathetic, ineffective, wuss-laden inquiry.

You *sort* of took off? I got *kinda* worried?

When what I really want to scream is:

HEY YOU—IN THE SUPER-SLICK ALL-BLACK ENSEMBLE— WHAT THE HELL HAPPENED?

Watching as he slips his bag onto his shoulder and gazes at me, his quick powerful stride closing the distance between us in a handful of seconds. But only the physical distance, not the emotional one, because when I look into his eyes they seem miles away.

And just when I realize I've been holding my breath, he leans into the window, his face close to mine when he says, "Yeah. I got your messages. All fifty-nine of them."

I can feel his warm breath on my cheek as my mouth drops open and my eyes search his, seeking the heat his gaze always provides, and shivering when I come away cold, dark, and empty. Though it's nothing like the lack of recognition I glimpsed the other day. No, this is far worse.

Because now when I look in his eyes—it's clear that he knows me—he just wishes he didn't.

"Damen, I—" My voice cracks as a car honks behind me and Miles mutters something unintelligible under his breath.

And before I've had a chance to clear my throat and start over, Damen's shaking his head and walking away.

seventeen

"Are you *all right*?" Miles asks, his face displaying all of the heart-break and pain I'm too numb to feel.

I shrug, knowing I'm not. I mean, how can I be all *right* when I'm not even sure what's all *wrong*?

"Damen's an asshole," he says, a hard edge to his voice.

But I just sigh. Even though I can't explain it, and even though I don't understand it, I just know in my gut that things are far more complicated than they might seem.

"No he's not," I mumble, climbing out of the car and closing the door much harder than necessary.

"Ever, please . . . I mean, I'm sorry to be the one to point it out, but you *did* just see what I saw, right?"

I head toward Haven who's waiting by the gate. "Trust me, I saw *everything*," I say. Replaying the scene in my mind, each time pausing on his distant eyes, his tepid energy, his complete lack of interest in me—

"So you agree? That he's an asshole?" Miles watches me carefully, assuring himself I'm not the kind of girl who would ever allow a guy to treat her like that.

"Who's an asshole?" Haven asks, glancing between us.

Miles looks at me, his eyes asking permission, and after seeing me shrug, he looks at Haven and says, "Damen."

Haven squints, her mind swimming with questions. But I've got my own set of questions, questions with no probable answer. Such as:

What the hell just happened back there?

And:

Since when does Damen have an aura?

"Miles can fill you in," I say, glancing between them before walking away. Wishing more than ever that I could be normal, that I could lean on them and cry on their shoulders like a regular girl. But there just happens to be more to this situation than meets their mortal eyes. And even though I can't yet prove it—if I want answers, I'll have to go straight to the source.

When I get to class, instead of hesitating at the door, like I thought I would, I surprise myself by bursting right in. And when I see Damen leaning against the edge of Stacia's desk, smiling and joking and flirting with her—I feel like I've stepped into a major case of déjà vu.

You can handle this, I think. *You've been here before.*

Remembering the time, not so long ago, when Damen pretended to be interested in Stacia, but only to get to me.

But the closer I get, the more I realize that this is nothing at all like the last time. Back then all I had to do was look into his eyes to find the smallest glimmer of compassion, a sliver of regret he just couldn't hide.

But now, watching as Stacia outdoes herself with her hair-tossing, cleavage-flaunting, eyelash-batting routine—it's like I'm invisible.

"Um, excuse me," I say, causing them to look up, clearly annoyed by the interruption. "Damen, could I, um, could I talk to you for a sec?" I shove my hands in my pockets so he can't see them shake, forcing myself to breathe like a normal, relaxed person would—in and out, slow and steady, with no gasping or wheezing.

Watching as he and Stacia glance at each other, then burst out laughing at the exact same time. And just as Damen's about to speak, Mr. Robins walks in and says, "Seats, everyone! I want to see you all in your seats!"

So I motion to our desks, and say, "Please, after you."

I follow behind, resisting the urge to grab him by the shoulder, spin him around, and force him to look me in the eye as I scream:

Why did you leave me? What on earth happened to you? How could you do that—on that night—of all nights?

Knowing that sort of direct, confrontational approach will only work against me. That if I want to get anywhere at all, then I'll have to act cool, calm, and easy.

I toss my bag to the floor, stacking my book, notebook, and pen on my desk. Smiling as though I'm no more than a casual friend interested in a little Monday morning chat when I say, "So, what'd you do this weekend?"

He shrugs, his eyes grazing over me before resting on mine. And it's a moment before I realize the horrible thoughts that I hear are coming straight from his head.

Well, if I'm gonna have a stalker, at least she's hot, he thinks, his brows merging together as I instinctively reach for my iPod, wanting to tune him out, yet knowing I can't risk missing something important, no matter how much it might hurt. Besides, I've never had access to Damen's mind before, never been able to hear what he's thinking. But now that I can, I'm not sure that I want to.

And when he twists his lips to the side and narrows his eyes, thinking: *Too bad she's totally psycho—definitely not worth risking a tap.*

The bite of his words is like a stake in my chest. And I'm so taken aback by his casual cruelty, I forget they weren't spoken out loud when I shriek, "Excuse me? What did you just say?"

Causing all of my classmates to turn and stare, their sympathies lying with Damen for having to sit next to me.

"Is something wrong?" Mr. Robins asks, glancing between us.

I sit there, totally speechless. My heart caving when Damen looks at Mr. Robins and says, "I'm fine. She's the freak."

eighteen

I followed him. I'm not ashamed to admit it. I had to. He left me no choice. I mean, if Damen's going to insist on avoiding me, then surveillance is my only option.

So I followed him out of English, waited for him after second period—third and fourth too. Staying in the background and observing from afar, wishing I'd agreed to let him transfer to all of my classes like he originally wanted, but thinking it was too creepy, too codependent, I wouldn't let him. So now I'm forced to linger outside his door, eavesdropping on his conversations along with the thoughts in his head—thoughts that, I'm horrified to report, are depressingly vain, narcissistic, and shallow.

But that's not the real Damen. Of this I'm convinced. Not that I think he's a manifest Damen because those never last more than a few minutes. What I mean is, something's happened to him. Something serious that's making him act and think like—well, like most of the guys in this school. Because even though I never had access to his mind until now, I *know* he didn't think like that before. He didn't act like that either. No, this new Damen is like an entirely new creature, where only the outside is familiar—while the inside is something else altogether.

I head toward the lunch table, steeling myself for what I might find, though it's not until I've unzipped my lunch pack and shined my apple on my sleeve, that I realize that the real reason I'm alone isn't because I'm early.

It's because everyone else has abandoned me too.

I look up, hearing Damen's familiar laugh, only to find him surrounded by Stacia, Honor, and Craig, along with the rest of the A-list crew. Which wouldn't be all that surprising with the way things are going, except for the fact that Miles and Haven are there too. And as my eyes sweep the length of the table, I drop my apple and my mouth runs dry when I see that *all* of the tables are now pushed together.

The lions are now lunching with lambs.

Which means Roman's prediction came true.

Bay View High School's lunchtime caste system has come to an end.

"So, what do you think?" Roman says, sliding onto the bench opposite me, hooking his thumb over his shoulder as a smile widens his cheeks. "Sorry for just dropping in on you like this, but I saw you admiring my work, so I thought I'd stop by for a chat. Are you *all right?*" He leans toward me, his face appearing genuinely concerned, though luckily I'm not stupid enough to fall for it.

I meet his gaze, determined to hold it for as long as I can. Sensing he's responsible for Damen's behavior, Miles's and Haven's defection, and the entire school living in harmony and peace—but lacking the evidence needed to prove it.

I mean, to everyone else he's a hero, a true Che Guevara, a lunchtime revolutionary.

But to me he's a threat.

"So I assume you made it home safely?" he asks, chugging his soda though his eyes are on me.

I glance at Miles, watching as he says something to Craig that makes them both laugh, then I move on to Haven, seeing her lean toward Honor, whispering into her ear.

But I don't look at Damen.

I refuse to watch him gaze into Stacia's eyes, place his hand on her knee, and tease her with his very best smile as his fingers creep along her thigh . . .

I saw plenty of that already in English. Besides, I'm pretty sure that whatever they're up to is just foreplay—the first tentative step toward the kind of horrible things I saw in Stacia's head. The vision that freaked me so bad I took down a whole rack of bras in my panic. And yet, by the time I got myself upright and settled again, I was sure she'd done it on purpose, never considered it to be some kind of prophecy. And even though I still think she created it just out of spite, and that their being together now is merely a coincidence, I have to admit it's pretty disturbing to see it played out.

But even though I refuse to watch it, I still try to listen—hoping to hear something pertinent, some vital information exchange. But just as I focus my attention and try to tune in, I'm met by a big wall of sound—all of those voices and thoughts merging together, making it impossible to distinguish any particular one.

"You know, Friday night?" Roman continues, his long fingers tapping the sides of his soda can, refusing to budge from this line of questioning, even though I refuse to participate. "When I found you alone? I have to tell you, Ever, I felt awful leaving you like that, but then again, you insisted."

I glance at him, uninterested in playing this game but thinking that if I just answer his question, then maybe he'll leave. "I made it home just fine. Thanks for your concern."

He smiles, the grin that probably makes a million hearts swoon—but only chills mine. Then he leans in and says, "Aw, now look at that, you're being sarcastic, aren't you?"

I shrug and gaze down at my apple, rolling it back and forth across the table.

"I just wish you'd tell me what I've done to make you hate me so much. I'm sure there's got to be some kind of peaceful solution, some way to remedy this."

I press my lips together and stare at my apple, rolling it along on its side as I push it hard against the table, feeling its flesh soften and give as the skin starts to break.

"Let me take you to dinner," he says, his blue eyes focused on mine. "What do you say? A right and proper date. Just the two of us. I'll get the car detailed, buy some new clothes, make a reservation somewhere swank—a good time guaranteed!"

I shake my head and roll my eyes, the only response I plan to give.

But Roman's undaunted, refusing to fold. "Aw, come on, Ever. Give a bloke a chance to change your mind. You can opt out at anytime, scout's honor. Hell, we'll even make up a safe word. You know, if at any time you decide things have strayed too far from your comfort level, you just shout out the safe word, all activity will cease, and neither of us will ever speak of it again." He pushes his soda aside and slides his hands toward mine, the tips of his fingers creeping so close, I yank mine away. "Come on, give a little, will ya? How can you say no to an offer like that?"

His voice is deep and persuasive, his gaze right on mine, but I just continue rolling my apple, watching the flesh burst free of the skin.

"I promise it'll be nothing like those rubbish dates that wanker Damen probably takes you on. For one thing, I'd never leave a girl as gorgeous as you to fend for herself in a parking lot." He looks at me, a smile playing at his lips when he says, "Well, I suppose I did leave a gorgeous girl like you to fend for herself, but only because I was honoring your request. See? I've already proven I'm at your service, willing to jump at your every command."

"What's with you?" I finally say, peering into those blue eyes without flinching or looking away. Wishing he'd just give it a rest and rejoin the only other lunch table in this school, the one where everybody's welcome but me. "I mean, does *everyone* have to like you? Is that it? And if so, don't you think that's just a *tad* insecure?"

He laughs. And I mean, a genuine, thigh-slapping laugh. And when he finally calms down, he shakes his head and says, "Well no, not *everyone*. Though I do have to admit, it *is* usually the case." He leans toward me, his face mere inches from mine. "What can I say? I'm a likable guy. Most people find me quite charming."

I shake my head and look away, tired of being toyed with and eager to put an end to this game. "Well, I'm sorry to break it to you, but I'm afraid you're going to have to count me among the rare few who aren't the least bit charmed by you. But please, do us both a favor and try not to view it as a challenge and set out to change my mind. Why don't you just go rejoin your table and leave me alone. I mean, why bring everyone together if you don't plan to enjoy all the fun?"

He looks at me, smiling and shaking his head as he slides off the bench, his eyes right on mine when he says, "Ever, you are mad hot. Seriously. And if I didn't know better, I'd think you were purposely trying to drive me insane."

I roll my eyes and look away.

"But, not wanting to wear out my welcome and recognizing the signs of a bloke being told to *sod off,* I think I'll just—" He jabs his thumb toward the table where the whole school is sitting. "Though, of course, if you change your mind and want to come join me, I'm sure I can convince them to make room."

I shake my head and motion for him to go, my throat hot and tight, unable to speak, knowing that despite all appearances, I haven't won this one—in fact, I'm not even close.

"Oh, and I thought you might want these," he says, placing my shoes on the table, as though my strappy, faux snakeskin wedges are some kind of peace offering. "But don't worry, no need to thank me." He laughs, glancing over his shoulder to say, "You might want to take it easy on that apple though, you're giving it quite the beating."

I squeeze tighter, watching as he heads straight for Haven, trails a finger down the length of her neck and presses his lips to her ear. Causing me to grip the apple so hard it explodes in my hand—its sticky wet juice slipping down the length of my fingers and onto my wrist—as Roman looks over and laughs.

nineteen

When I get to art, I head straight for the supply closet, slip into my smock, gather my supplies, and am just heading back into the room when I see Damen standing in the doorway, wearing a strange look on his face. A look that, while it may be strange, also fills me with hope, as his eyes are sort of vacant, his jaw slack, and he seems lost and unsure, like he might need my help.

Knowing I need to seize the moment while it's standing there slack jawed before me, I lean toward him, gently touching his arm as I say, "Damen?" My voice shaky, scratchy, as though it's the first time I've used it all day. "Damen, honey, are you okay?" My eyes graze over him, fighting the urge to press my lips hard against his.

He looks at me with a flash of recognition that's soon joined by kindness, longing, and love. And as my fingers strain toward his cheek, my eyes fill with tears, seeing his reddish brown aura fade and knowing he's mine once again—

And then:

"Ay mate, move along, move along, you're holdin' up the flow of traffic 'ere."

And just like *that,* the old Damen's gone, and the new Damen's back.

He pushes past me, his aura flaring, his thoughts repulsed by my touch. Then I press against the wall, cringing as Roman follows behind, *accidentally* brushing his body against mine.

"Sorry 'bout that, luv." He smiles, his face leering.

I close my eyes and grasp the wall for support. My head swaying as the euphoric swirl of his bright sunshiny aura—his intense, expansive, optimistic energy—washes right through me. Infusing my mind with images so hopeful, so friendly, so innocuous, they fill me with shame—shame for all my suspicions—shame for being so unkind—

And yet—there's something not quite right about it. Something off in the rhythm. Most minds are a jumble of beats, a rush of words, a swirl of pictures, a cacophony of sounds all tumbling together like the most disjointed jazz. But Roman's mind is orderly, organized, with one thought flowing cleanly into the next. Making it sound forced, unnatural, like a prerecorded script—

"By the looks of you, darlin', it seems that was almost as good for you as it was for me. You sure you won't change your mind about that date?"

His chilled breath presses my cheek, his lips so close I fear he might try to kiss me. And just as I'm about to push him away, Damen walks past us and says, "Dude, seriously, what're you doing? That spaz is not worth your time."

That spaz is not worth your time that spaz is not worth your time that spaz is not worth your time that spaz is not worth your time that spaz is not worth your time that spaz is not—

"Ever? Have you grown?"

I look up to find Sabine standing next to me, handing me a freshly rinsed bowl that's meant for the dishwasher. And it's only after I blink a few times that I remember it's my job to put it there.

"Sorry, what?" I ask, my fingers gripping the soapy wet porcelain as I ease it onto the rack. Unable to think about anything but Damen, and the hurtful words I use to torture myself with, by replaying them again and again.

"You look like you've grown. In fact, I'm sure of it. Aren't those the jeans I just bought you?"

I gaze down at my feet, startled to find several inches of ankle exposed. Which is even more bizarre when I remember how just this morning the hems dragged on the floor. "Um—maybe," I lie, knowing that we both know they are.

She squints, shaking her head when she says, "I thought for sure they'd be the right size. Looks like you're going through a growth spurt." She shrugs. "But then, you're only sixteen, so I suppose it's not too late."

Only sixteen, but damn close to seventeen, I think, longing for the day when I turn eighteen, graduate, and head off on my own so I can be alone with my weird creepy secrets and Sabine can get back to her regularly scheduled life. Having no idea how I'll ever repay her for her kindness, and now adding a pair of overpriced jeans to the tab.

"I was done growing by fifteen, but it looks like you're going to end up a lot taller than me." She smiles, handing me a fistful of spoons.

I smile weakly, wondering just how tall I'll get and hoping I don't turn into some kind of giantess freak, some Ripley's *Believe it or Not!* cover girl. Knowing that growing three inches in the course of one day is no ordinary growth spurt—not by a long shot.

But now that she mentions it, I've also noticed that my nails are starting to grow so fast I have to clip them nearly every day, and that my bangs are now past my chin even though I've only been growing them for the past few weeks. Not to mention how the blue of my eyes seems to be deepening, while my slightly crooked front teeth have righted themselves. And no matter how much I abuse it, how irregularly I cleanse it, my complexion remains clear, poreless, and completely blemish-free.

And now I've grown three inches since breakfast?

Obviously, it can only be due to one thing—the immortal juice I've been drinking. I mean, even though I've been immortal for the better half of a year, nothing really changed (well, other than my instantaneous healing abilities) until I started drinking it. But now that I have, it's like all my better physical traits are suddenly magnified and enhanced, while the more mediocre ones are fully improved.

And while part of me feels excited by the prospect and curious to see what else is in store, the other part can't help but notice how I'm developing toward full immortal capacity just in time to spend the rest of eternity alone.

"Must be that juice you're always guzzling." Sabine laughs. "Maybe I should try it. I wouldn't mind breaking the five-foot-four barrier without the aid of high heels!"

"No!" I say, the words spilling from my lips before I can stop them, knowing that answering like that will only pique her interest.

She looks at me, brows merged, damp sponge in hand.

"I mean, I'm sure you won't like it. In fact, you'll most likely hate it. Seriously, it's got kind of a weird taste." I nod, attempting a light breezy expression, not wanting her to know how her statement has left me totally freaked.

"Well, I won't know until I try, right?" she says, her eyes still on mine. "Where do you get it anyway? I don't remember ever seeing it in stores. And I've never seen a label on it either. What's it even called?"

"I get it from Damen," I say, enjoying the feel of his name on my lips, even though it does nothing to fill up the void his absence has left.

"Well, ask him to get me some too, will you?"

And the moment she says it, I know this is no longer just about the juice. She's trying to get me to open up, to explain his absence at our Saturday night dinner, and every day since.

I close the dishwasher and turn away. Pretending to wipe down a counter that's already clean and avoiding her eyes when I say, "Well, I can't actually do that. Mostly because . . . we're um . . . we're sort of taking a break," I say, my voice cracking in the most embarrassing way.

She reaches for me, wanting to hug me, comfort me, tell me it will all be okay. And even though my back is turned so that I can't see her in the physical sense, I can still *see* it in my head, so I step to the side and move out of her way.

"Oh Ever—I'm so sorry—I didn't know—" she says, her hands hanging awkwardly at her sides, unsure what to do with them now that I've moved.

I nod, feeling guilty for being my usual cold distant self. Wishing I could somehow explain that I can't risk the physical contact because I can't risk knowing her secrets. That it will only distract me and provide images I don't need to see. I mean, I'm barely handling my own secrets, so it's not like I'm eager to add hers to the mix.

"It—it was kind of sudden," I say, knowing she's not willing to let the case rest until she's gotten a little more out of me. "I mean, it just sort of happened—and—well, I don't really know what to say . . ."

"I'm here if you need to talk."

"I'm not ready to talk about it yet. It's—it's too new still and I'm trying to sort it all out. Maybe later . . ." I shrug, hoping that by the time *later* arrives, Damen and I will be back together again, and the whole issue resolved.

twenty

When I get to Miles's, I'm a little nervous, having no idea what to expect. But when I see him outside, waiting on his front stoop, I heave a small sigh of relief, knowing things aren't nearly as bad as I thought.

I pull up to his drive, lower my window, and call, "Hey Miles, hop in!"

Then I watch as he glances up from his phone, shaking his head as he says, "Sorry, I thought I told you, I'm getting a ride from Craig."

I gape, my smile frozen in place as I replay his words in my head.

Craig? As in Honor's boyfriend Craig? The sexually confused Cro-Magnon jock whose true preferences I learned by eavesdropping on his thoughts? The one who practically lives to make fun of Miles because it makes him feel "safe"—like he's not one of "them."

That Craig?

"Since when are you friends with Craig?" I ask, shaking my head and squinting at him.

Miles reluctantly rises and comes around to my side. Pausing from his texting pursuits long enough to say, "Since I decided to get a life, branch out, and expand my horizons. Maybe you should try it too. He's pretty cool once you get to know him."

I watch as his thumbs get back to work, as I struggle to get a grip on his words. Feeling like I've landed in some crazy, implausible, alternate universe where cheerleaders gossip with goths, and jocks hang with drama freaks. A place so unnatural it could never truly exist.

Except that it does exist. In a place called Bay View High.

"This is the same Craig that called you a fag and gave you a swirly on your first day of school?"

Miles shrugs. "People change."

I'll say.

Except that they don't.

Or at least not that much in one day unless they have a very good reason for doing so—unless someone else, someone behind the scenes, is *prompting* them, *engineering* it so to speak. Manipulating them against their will and causing them to say and do things that are totally against their true nature—all without their permission, without their even realizing it.

"Sorry, I thought I told you, but I guess I got busy. But you don't need to come by anymore, I've got it all covered," he says, dismissing our friendship with a shrug, as though it bore no more importance than a ride to school.

I swallow hard, resisting the urge to grab him by the shoulders and demand to know what happened—why he's acting like this—why *everyone* is acting like this—and why they've all unanimously decided against me.

But I don't. Somehow, I manage to restrain myself. Mostly because I have a terrible suspicion I might already know. And if it turns out that I'm right, then it's not like Miles is responsible anyway.

"Okay, well, good to know." I nod, forcing a smile I definitely don't feel. "I guess I'll just see you around then," I say, my fingers drumming against the gearshift, waiting for a response that's not coming anytime soon, and backing out of his drive only when Craig pulls up behind me, honks his horn twice, and motions for me to move.

In English, it's even worse than I anticipated. And I'm not even half-way down the aisle before I notice that Damen is now sitting by Stacia.

And I'm talking hand-holding, note-passing, whispering distance from Stacia.

While I remain alone in the back like a complete and total reject.

I press my lips together as I make my way toward my desk, listening to *all* of my classmates hiss:

"*Spaz! Watch out, Spaz! Don't fall, Spaz!*"

The same words I've been hearing since the moment I got out of my car.

And even though I've no idea what it means, I can't say I'm all that bothered by it—until Damen joins in. Because the moment he starts laughing and sneering along with the rest, all I want to do is go back. Back to my car, back home where it's safe—

But I don't. I can't. I need to stay put. Assuring myself that it's temporary—that I'll soon get to the bottom of it—that there's no possible way I've lost Damen for good.

And somehow, this helps me get through it. Well, that, and Mr. Robins telling everyone to *shush*. So when the bell finally rings, and everyone's filed out, I'm almost out the door when I hear:

"Ever? Can I speak to you for a moment?"

I grip the door handle, my fingers closed and ready to twist.

"I won't keep you long."

And I take a deep breath and surrender, my fingers cranking the sound on my iPod the second I see his face.

Mr. Robins never keeps me after class. He's just not the stop and chat type. And all of this time I was sure that completing my homework and acing my tests insured me against this exact kind of thing.

"I'm not sure how to say this, and I don't want to overstep my bounds here—but I really feel I must say something. It's about—"

Damen.

It's about my one true soul mate. My eternal love. My biggest fan for the last four hundred years, who is now completely repulsed by me.

And how just this morning he asked to change seats.

Because he thinks I'm a stalker.

And now, Mr. Robins, my recently separated, well-meaning English teacher who hasn't a clue, about me, about Damen, about much of anything outside of musty old novels written by long-dead authors, wants to explain how relationships work.

How young love is intense. How it all feels so urgent, like it's the most important thing in the world while it's happening—only it's not. There will be plenty of other loves, if I just allow myself to move on. And I have to move on. It's imperative. Mostly because:

"Because stalking is not the answer," he says. "It's a crime. A very serious crime, with serious consequences." He frowns, hoping to relay the seriousness of all this.

"I'm not stalking him," I say, realizing too late that defending myself against the *S* word before going through all the usual steps of: *He said what? Why would he do that? What could he mean?* like a normal, more clueless person would, makes me appear suspiciously guilty. So I swallow hard when I add, "Listen, Mr. Robins, with all due respect, I know you mean well, and I don't know what Damen told you, but—"

I look in his eyes, *seeing* exactly what Damen told him: *that I'm obsessed with him, that I'm crazy, that I drive by his house day and night, that I call him over and over again, leaving creepy, obsessive, pathetic messages*—which may be partially true, *but still.*

But Mr. Robins isn't about to let me finish, he just shakes his head and says, "Ever, the last thing I want to do is choose sides or get between you and Damen, because frankly, it's just none of my business and it's something you're ultimately going to have to work out on your own. And despite your recent expulsion, despite the fact that you rarely pay attention in class, and leave your iPod on long after I've asked you to turn it off—you're still one of my best and brightest students. And I'd hate to see you jeopardize what could turn out to be a very bright future—*over a boy.*"

I close my eyes and swallow hard. Feeling so humiliated I wish I could just vanish into thin air—disappear.

No, actually it's much worse than that—I feel mortified, disgraced, horrified, dishonored, and everything else that defines wanting to slink off in shame.

"It's not what you think," I say, meeting his gaze and silently urging him to believe it. "Despite whatever stories Damen might've told you, it's not at all what it appears to be," I add, hearing Mr. Robins sigh along with the thoughts in his head. How he wishes he could share how lost he felt when his wife and daughter walked out, how he never thought he'd make it through another day—but fearing it's inappropriate, which it *is.*

"If you just give yourself some time, focus your attention on something else," he says, sincerely wanting to help me, and yet afraid of overstepping his bounds. "You'll soon find that—"

The bell rings.

I shift my backpack onto my shoulder, press my lips together, and look at him.

Watching as he shakes his head and says, "Fine. I'll write you a tardy pass. You're free to go."

twenty-one

I'm a YouTube star. Apparently the footage of me untangling my-self from a seemingly never-ending string of Victoria's Secret bras, thongs, and garter belts has not only earned me the oh so clever nickname of *Spaz* but has also been viewed 2323 times. Which just happens to be the number of students enrolled here at Bay View. Well, with a few of the faculty members tossed in.

It's Haven who tells me. Finding her at her locker after barely making it through a gauntlet of people shouting, "Hey, Spaz! Don't fall, Spaz!" she's kind enough not only to fill me in on the origin of my newfound celebrity but to lead me to the video so I can watch the spectacle of myself *spazzing* out right there on my iPhone.

"Oh, that's just great," I say, shaking my head, knowing it's the least of my problems, but still.

"It's pretty fuggin' bad," she agrees, closing her locker and look-ing at me with an expression that could only be read as pity—well, pity on a time crunch with only a few seconds to spare for a spaz like me. "So—anything else? 'Cause I need to get going, I promised Honor I'd—"

I look at her, I mean, really look at her. Seeing how the flame-red stripe in her hair is now pink, and how her usual pale-skinned, darkly clad, Emo look has been swapped for the spray-tanned, sparkle-dress, fluffy-haired ensemble of those same cliquey clones she always made fun of. But despite her new dress code, despite her new A-list membership, despite all the evidence presented before me, I still don't believe she's responsible for anything she wears, says, or does at this point. Because even though Haven has a tendency to latch on to others and mimic their ways—she still has her standards. And I know for a fact that the Stacia and Honor brigade is one group she never aspired to join.

But still, knowing all that doesn't make it any easier to accept. And even though I know it's useless, even though it clearly won't change a thing, I still look at her and say, "I can't believe you're friends with them. I mean, after everything they've done to me." I shake my head, wanting her to know just how much that hurts.

And even though I hear her response a few seconds earlier, it does little to soften the blow when she says, "Did they push you? Did they shove you or trip you or make you fall on top of that rack? Or did you do that all on your own?" She looks at me, brows raised, lips pursed, narrowed eyes focused on mine. As I stand there stunned, mute, my throat searing so hot I couldn't speak if I tried.

"It's like—lighten up already, would you?" She rolls her eyes and shakes her head. "They meant for it to be funny. And you'd be a helluva lot happier if you could just unclench, stop taking yourself and everything around you so damn seriously, and fuggin' learn to live a little! I mean, seriously, Ever. Think about it, okay?"

She turns, merging seamlessly into the crowd of students, all of them heading for the extra long table in their new lunchtime exodus, while I make a run for the gate.

I mean, why torture myself? Why hang around just so I can watch Damen flirt with Stacia, and get called *spaz* by my friends? Why have all of these advanced psychic abilities if I'm not going to exploit them and put them to good use—like ditching school?

"Leaving so soon?"

I ignore the voice behind me and keep going. Roman's pretty much the last person I'm willing to talk to at this point.

"Ever, hey, hold up! Seriously." He laughs, picking up his pace until he's right alongside me. "Where's the fire?"

I unlock my car and slide in, yanking the door and almost getting it closed, until he stops it with the palm of his hand. And even though I know I'm stronger, that if I really wanted I could just slam the door closed and be on my way, the fact that I'm still not used to my new immortal strength is the one thing that stops me. Because as much as I dislike him, I'm a little reluctant to slam it so hard I sever his hand.

I'd much rather save that kind of thing for when I might need it.

"If you don't mind, I really need to get going." I pull the door again, but he just grips it tighter. And when I combine the amused look on his face with the surprising strength in his fingers, I feel the strangest ping in my gut when I realize those two seemingly random things support my deepest suspicions.

But when I look at him again, watching as he lifts his hand to sip from his soda, exposing a wrist that's free of all markings, bearing no tattoos of a snake eating its own tail—the mythical Ouroboros symbol which happens to be the sign of an immortal turned rogue—it just doesn't add up.

Because the fact is, not only does he eat and drink, not only are his aura and thoughts accessible (well, to me anyway), but as much as I hate to admit it, from what I can see, he bears no outward signs of evil. And when you put that together, it's obvious my suspicions are not only paranoid but unfounded as well.

Which means he's not the malevolent immortal rogue I supposed him to be.

Which also means he's not responsible for Damen dumping me, or Miles's and Haven's defection. Nope, that would point right back to me.

And even though all the evidence supports that—I refuse to accept it.

Because when I look at him again, my pulse quickens, my stomach pings, and I'm overcome by a feeling of unease and dread. Making it impossible for me to believe he's just some jolly young chap from England who wound up at our school and found himself all smitten with me.

Because the one thing I know for sure is: Everything was fine until he arrived.

And nothing's been the same since.

"Skipping out on lunch, are you?"

I roll my eyes. I mean, it's pretty obvious what I'm up to, so I won't waste my time with an answer.

"And I see you have room for one more. Mind if I join you?"

"As a matter of fact, I do. So if you'd kindly remove your—" I motion toward his hand, flicking my fingers in the international sign for *scram*.

He holds up his hands in surrender, shaking his head when he says, "I don't know if you've noticed, Ever, but the more you evade me, the faster I chase. It'll be a lot easier for both of us if you just stop running."

I narrow my gaze, trying to *see* past the sunshiny aura and well-ordered thoughts, but I'm blocked by a barrier so impenetrable it's either the end of the road, or he's way worse than I thought.

"If you insist on the chase," I say, my voice much surer than I feel. "Then you better start training. 'Cause, dude, you're in for a marathon."

He winces, body flinching, eyes widening as though he's been stung. And if I didn't know better, I'd think it was real. But the fact is, I do know better. He's just hamming it up, practicing a few facial expressions for dramatic effect. And I don't have time to be the butt of his joke.

I shift into reverse and back out of my space, hoping to leave it at that.

But he just smiles, slapping the hood of my car when he says, "As you wish, Ever. Game on."

twenty-two

I don't go home.

I started to. In fact, I had every intention of driving home, hauling upstairs, and flinging myself on my bed, burying my face in a fat pile of pillows and crying my eyes out like a big pathetic baby.

But then, just as I was turning onto my street, I thought better. I mean, I can't allow myself that kind of luxury. I can't waste the time. So instead, I make a U-turn and head toward downtown Laguna. Making my way through those steep narrow streets, driving past well-tended cottages with beautiful gardens and the double-lot McMansions that sit right beside them. Heading for the address of the only person I know who can help me.

"Ever." She smiles, pushing her wavy auburn hair off her face as her large brown eyes settle on mine. And even though I arrived unannounced, she doesn't seem the least bit surprised. But then her being psychic makes her pretty hard to startle.

"I'm sorry for just showing up and not calling first, I guess I—"

But she doesn't let me finish. She just opens the door and waves me right in, ushering me toward the kitchen table where I sat once before—the last time I was in trouble and had nowhere to turn.

I used to loathe her, *really* loathed her. And when she started convincing Riley to move on—to cross the bridge to where our parents and Buttercup were waiting—it got even worse. But even though I used to count her as my worst enemy besides Stacia, all of that seems like so long ago now. And as she fusses around the kitchen, setting out cookies and brewing green tea, I watch, feeling guilty for not keeping in touch, for only coming around when I'm desperately in need.

We exchange the usual pleasantries, then she takes the seat across from me and cradles her teacup as she says, "You've grown! I know I'm short, but you positively tower over me now!"

I shrug, unsure how to deal with this but knowing I better get used to it. When you grow several inches in a matter of days, people tend to notice. "I guess I'm a late bloomer. You know, going through a growth spurt—or—something," I say, my smile feeling clumsy on my lips, realizing I need to come up with a much more convincing reply, or at least learn how to reply with conviction.

She looks me over and nods. Not buying a word of it but deciding to just let it go. "So, how's the shield holding up?"

I swallow hard, blinking once, twice. I was so focused on my mission I'd forgotten about the shield she helped me create. The one that blocked out all the noise and sound the last time Damen went away. The one I dismantled the moment he returned.

"Oh, um, I kind of got rid of it," I say, cringing as the words spill from my lips, remembering how it took the better part of an afternoon just to put it in place.

She smiles, gazing at me from over the top of her cup. "I'm not surprised. Being normal's not all it's cracked up to be, once you've experienced something *more*."

I break off a piece of oatmeal cookie and shrug. Knowing that if it were up to me, I'd choose *normal* over *this* any day.

"So, if this isn't about the shield—then what is it?"

"You mean you don't know? What kind of psychic are you?" I laugh, far too loud for such a dumb, feeble joke.

But Ava just shrugs, tracing a heavily ringed finger along the rim of her cup as she says, "Well, I'm no advanced mind reader like you. Though I do sense something rather serious in the works."

"It's about Damen," I start, pausing to press down on my lips. "He's—he's changed. He's become cold, distant, cruel even, and I—" I drop my gaze, the truth behind the words making them so much harder to say. "He won't return my calls, won't talk to me at school, he even moved his seat in English, and now he—he's dating this girl who—well, she's just *awful*. I mean, really, truly awful. And now he's awful too—"

"Ever—" she starts, her voice warm and gentle, her eyes kind.

"It's not what you think," I tell her. "It's not that at all. Damen and I didn't break up, we weren't having problems, it was nothing like that. It's like, one day everything was great—and the next— *not*."

"And did something happen to precipitate this change?" Her face is thoughtful, her eyes on mine.

Yeah, Roman happened. But since I can't explain my suspicions, that he's an immortal rogue (despite all evidence to the contrary), employing some sort of mass mind control or hypnosis or spell casting (which I'm not even sure is possible) over the entire Bay View student body, I just tell her about Damen's recent bout of odd behavior—the headaches, the sweating, and a few other safe-to-talk-about nonsecret things.

Then I sit there, holding my breath as she sips her tea and looks out the window at the beautiful garden beyond, her gaze returning to me when she says, "Tell me everything you know about Summerland."

I stare at the two halves of my uneaten cookie and clamp my lips shut, never having heard the word mentioned so openly and casually like that. I'd always thought of it as Damen's and my sacred space, never realizing that mere mortals might know of it too.

"Certainly you've visited?" She sets down her cup and raises her brow. "During your near-death experience perhaps?"

I nod, remembering both of my visits, the first time when I was dead, the second with Damen. And I was so taken with that magical, mystical dimension with its vast fragrant fields and pulsating trees—I was reluctant to leave.

"And did you visit its temples while you were there?"

Temples? I didn't see any temples. Elephants, beaches, and horses— things we both manifested, but certainly no buildings or dwellings of any kind.

"Summerland is legendary for its temples, or Great Halls of Learning as they're called. I'm thinking your answer lies there."

"But—but I'm not even sure how to get there without Damen. I mean, short of dying and all . . ." I look at her. "How do you even know about it? Have you been there?"

She shakes her head. "I've been trying to access it for years. And though I've come close a few times, I've never been able to get through the portal. But maybe if we merge our energy together, pool our resources so to speak, we just might get through."

"It's impossible," I say, remembering the last time I tried to access it that way. And even though Damen was already showing signs of distress, he's still way more advanced than Ava on her very best day. "It's not that easy. Even if we do pool our energy, it's still a lot more difficult than you think."

But she just shakes her head and smiles, rising from her seat as she says, "But we'll never know until we try, right?"

twenty-three

I follow her down a short hallway. My flip-flops snapping against a red woven rug as I think: *This'll never work.*

I mean, if I couldn't access the portal with Damen, how can I possibly access it with Ava? Because even though she seems to be a pretty gifted psychic, her skills are mostly saved for the party circuit, telling fortunes over a fold-up card table, embellishing them in hopes of a generous tip.

"It'll never work if you don't believe," she says, pausing before an indigo door. "You need to have faith in the process. And so, before we enter, I need you to clear your mind of all negativity. I need you to rid yourself of any sad or unhappy thoughts, or anything else that's dragging you down and serves the word *can't.*"

I take a deep breath and stare at the door, fighting the urge to roll my eyes as I think: *Great. I should've known.* This is just the sort of hokey stuff you're forced to tolerate when you're dealing with Ava.

But all I say is, "Don't worry about me, I'm good." Nodding in a way I hope is convincing, wanting to avoid her usual twenty-step meditation, or whatever woo-woo practice she might have in mind.

But Ava just stands there, hands on hips, eyes on mine. Refusing to let me in until I agree to lighten my emotional load.

So when she says, "Close your eyes," I do. But only to speed things along.

"Now I want you to imagine long spindly roots sprouting from the soles of your feet and delving deep into the earth, carving into the soil and stretching their limits. Digging deeper and deeper into the ground until they've reached the earth's core and can't go any farther. Got it?"

I nod, picturing what she asks, but only so we can get this show on the road and not because I believe in it.

"Now take a deep breath, take several deep breaths, and let your whole body relax. Feel your muscles loosening, while your tension fades away. Allowing any lingering negative thoughts or emotions to disappear. Just banish them from your energy field and tell them good riddance. Can you do that?"

Um, whatever, I think. Just going through the motions and feeling pretty surprised when my muscles really do start to relax. And I mean, *really* relax. Like I'm at peace after a long hard battle.

I guess I wasn't aware of just how tense I've been or how much negativity I was lugging around until Ava made me release it. And even though I'm willing to do just about anything to get into that room and closer to Summerland, I have to admit that some of this mumbo-jumbo stuff might really work.

"Now draw your attention up until you're focused on the crown of your head, the area right at the top. And imagine a solid beam of the purest golden white light penetrating that very spot and easing its way all down your neck, your limbs, your torso, all the way down to your feet. Feel that warm, wonderful light healing every part of you, coating every last cell both inside and out, allowing any lingering sadness or anger to be transformed into loving energy by this powerful healing force. Feel the light surging inside you like a steady beam of lightness, love, and forgiveness with no beginning or end. And when you start to feel lighter, when you start to feel yourself purified and cleansed, open your eyes and look at me, but only when you're ready."

So I do, I go through the whole white light ritual, determined to participate and at least pretend to take these steps seriously since it's important to Ava. And just as I imagine a golden beam coursing through my body, coating my cells and all that, I also try to calculate just how long I should delay opening my eyes so it won't look too fake.

But then, something odd happens. I find myself feeling lighter, happier, stronger, and despite the desperate state I arrived in—fulfilled.

And when I do open my eyes, I see that she's smiling at me, her entire body surrounded by the most beautiful violet aura I've ever seen.

She opens the door and I follow her inside, blinking and squinting as I adjust to the deep purple walls of this small spare room that, from the looks of it, seems to double as a shrine.

"Is this where you give your readings?" I ask, taking in the large collection of crystals and candles and iconic symbols that cover the walls. Watching as she shakes her head and settles onto an elaborate embroidered floor cushion, patting the one right beside her and motioning for me to sit too.

"Most of the people who show up here are occupying a dark emotional space, and I can't risk letting them in. I've worked very hard to keep the energy in this room pure, clean, and free of all darkness, and I don't allow anyone to enter until their energy is cleared, including me. That cleansing exercise I just put you through, I do it first thing every morning, just after I wake, and then again before entering this room. And I recommend you do it too. Because even though I know you thought it was nonsense, I also know you're surprised by how much better you feel."

I press my lips together and avert my gaze. Knowing she doesn't have to read my mind to know what I'm thinking. My face always betrays me—it's incapable of lying.

"I get the whole healing light thing," I say, gazing at the bamboo blinds covering the window and the shelf lined with stone statues of deities from all over the globe. "And I have to admit that it did make me feel better. But what was that root thing all about? It seemed kind of weird."

"That's called *grounding*." She smiles. "When you came to my door, your energy felt very scattered and this helps to contain it. I suggest you perform that exercise daily as well."

"But won't it keep us from reaching Summerland? You know, by *grounding* us here?"

She laughs. "No, if anything, it'll help you stay focused on where you really want to go."

I gaze around the room, noticing how it's so crammed with stuff, it's hard to take it all in. "So is this like your sacred space?" I finally say.

She smiles, her fingers picking at a loose thread on her cushion. "It's the place where I come to worship and meditate and try to reach the dimensions beyond. And I have a very strong hunch that this time, I'll get there."

She folds her legs into the lotus position and motions for me to do so as well. And at first I can't help but think that my new long and gangly legs will never bend and entwine like hers. But a moment later I'm shocked by the way they just slip right into place, folding around each other in a way that's so natural and comfortable without the least bit of resistance.

"Ready?" she asks, her brown eyes on mine.

I shrug, gazing at the soles of my feet, amazed to see them so visible as they rest on top of my knees, wondering what kind of ritual she'll put us through next.

"Good. Because now it's your turn to lead." She laughs. "I've never been there before. So I'm counting on you to show us the way."

twenty-four

I had no idea it would be so easy. Didn't believe we'd be able to get there. But just after I lead us through the ritual of closing our eyes and imagining a brilliant portal of shimmering light, we joined hands and toppled right through, landing side by side on that strange buoyant grass.

Ava looks at me, her eyes wide, her mouth open, but unable to form any words.

I just nod and gaze all around, knowing just how she feels. Because even though I've been here before, that doesn't make it any less surreal.

"Hey, Ava," I say, rising to my feet and brushing the seat of my jeans, eager to play tour guide and show her just how magical this place can be. "Imagine something. Anything. Like an object, an animal, or even a person. Just close your eyes and see it as clear as you can and then . . ."

I watch as she closes her eyes, my excitement building as her brows merge together and she focuses on her object of choice.

And when she opens her eyes again, she clasps her hands to her chest and stares straight ahead, crying, "Oh! Oh, it can't be—but look—it looks just like him and he's *so* real!"

She kneels on the grass, clapping her hands together and laughing with glee as a beautiful golden retriever leaps into her arms and smothers her cheeks with wet sloppy licks. Hugging him tightly to her chest, murmuring his name again and again, and I know it's my duty to warn her he's not the real deal.

"Ava, um, I'm sorry but I'm afraid he won't—" but before I can finish, the dog slips from her grasp, fading like a pattern of vibrating pixels that soon vanish completely. And when I see the devastation on her face, my stomach sinks, feeling guilty for initiating this game. "I should've explained," I say, wishing I hadn't been so impulsive. "I'm so sorry."

But she just nods, blinking back tears as she brushes the grass from her knees. "It's okay. Really. I knew it was too good to be true, but just to see him like that again, just to have that moment—" She shrugs. "Well, even if it wasn't real, I don't regret it for a second. So don't you regret it either, okay?" She grasps my hand and squeezes it tight. "I've missed him so much, and just to have him for those few brief seconds was like a rare and precious gift. A gift I got to experience thanks to you."

I nod, swallowing hard, hoping she means it. And even though we could spend the next several hours manifesting everything our hearts desire, the truth is, my heart desires only one thing. Besides, after witnessing Ava's reunion with her beloved pet, the pleasure of material goods no longer seems worth it.

"So this is Summerland," she says, gazing all around.

"This is it." I nod. "But all I've ever seen of it is this field, that stream, and a few other things that didn't exist until I manifested them here. Oh, and see that bridge? Way over there, off in the distance, where the fog settles in?"

She turns, nodding when she sees it.

"Don't go near it. It leads to the *other side*. That's the bridge Riley told you about, the one I finally convinced her to cross—after a little coaxing from you."

Ava stares at it, her eyes narrowed as she says, "I wonder what happens if you try to go across? You know, without dying, without that kind of invite?"

But I just shrug, not having nearly enough curiosity to ever try and find out. "I wouldn't recommend it," I say, seeing the look in her eyes and realizing she's actually weighing her options, wondering if she should try to cross it, out of sheer curiosity if nothing else. "You might not come back," I add, trying to relay the potential serious-ness since she doesn't seem to get it. But I guess Summerland has that effect—it's so beautiful and magical it tempts you to take chances you normally wouldn't.

She looks at me, still not fully convinced but too eager to see more than to just sit around here. So she links her arm through mine, and says, "Where do we begin?"

Since neither of us has any idea just where to begin—we begin by walking. Heading through the meadow of dancing flowers, mak-ing our way through the forest of pulsating trees, crossing the rainbow-colored stream filled with all manner of fish, until finding a trail that, after curving and winding and meandering forever, leads us to a long empty road.

But not a yellow brick road or one paved with gold. This is just a regular street, made of everyday asphalt, like the kind you see at home.

Though I have to admit that it's better than the streets at home because this one is clean and pristine, with no potholes or skid marks. In fact, everything around here appears so shiny and new you'd think it'd never been used, when the truth is—or at least the truth according to Ava—Summerland is older than time.

"So what exactly do you know about these temples, or Great Halls of Learning as you call them?" I ask, gazing up at an impres-sive white marble building with all sorts of angels and mythical creatures carved into its columns and wondering if it could be the place that we seek. I mean, it looks fancy yet serious, impressive but not exactly formidable, everything I imagine a hall of higher learning to be.

But Ava just shrugs as though she's no longer interested. Which is a tad more noncommittal than I'd like.

She was so sure the answer lay here, was so insistent on binding our energy and traveling together, but now that we've made it, she's a little too enamored with the power of instant manifestation to concentrate on anything else.

"I just know they exist," she says, her hands held out before her, turning them this way and that. "I've come across their mention many times in my studies."

And yet, all you seem to be studying now are those large jewel-encrusted rings you've manifested onto your fingers! I think, not stating the actual words but knowing that if she's interested enough to look, she'll see the annoyance stamped on my face.

But she just smiles as she manifests an armful of bangles to match her new rings. And when she starts gazing down at her feet, in pursuit of new shoes, I know it's time to rein her back in.

"So what should we do when we get there?" I ask, determined to get her to focus on the true reason we're here. I mean, I did my part, so the least she could do is reciprocate and help me find the way. "And what do we research once we find it? Sudden headaches? Extreme bouts of uncontrollable sweatiness? Not to mention, will they even let us in?"

I turn, fully expecting a lecture on my persistent negativity, my rampant pessimism that vanishes for a while but never fully subsides—only to find that she's no longer there.

And I mean, she's completely, unmistakably, one hundred percent *not* present!

"Ava!" I call, turning around and around, squinting into the shimmering mist, the eternal radiance that emanates from nowhere specific but manages to permeate everything here. "Ava, where are you?" I shout, running down the middle of the long, empty road, stopping to peer into windows and doorways, and wondering why there are so many stores and restaurants and art galleries and salons when there's no one around to use them.

"You won't find her."

I turn, seeing a petite dark-haired girl standing behind me. Her stick-straight hair hanging to her shoulders, and her nearly black eyes framed by bangs so severe they seem slashed with a razor.

"People get lost here. Happens all the time."

"Who—who are you?" I say, taking in her starched white blouse, plaid skirt, blue blazer, and kneesocks, the outfit of your typical private school girl, but knowing this is no ordinary student—not if she's here.

"I'm Romy," she says. Except that her lips didn't move. And the voice that I heard came from behind me.

And when I spin around, I find the same exact girl laughing as she says, "And she's Rayne."

I turn again, seeing Rayne still behind me as Romy comes around to join her. Two identical girls standing before me, everything about them—their hair, their clothes, their faces, their eyes—exactly the same.

Except for the kneesocks. Romy's have fallen, while Rayne's are pulled tight.

"Welcome to Summerland." Romy smiles, as Rayne looks me over with suspicious narrowed eyes. "We're sorry about your friend." She nudges her twin, and when she doesn't respond, she says, "Yes, even Rayne is sorry. She just won't admit it."

"Do you know where I can find her?" I ask, gazing between them and wondering where they could've come from.

Romy shrugs. "She doesn't want to be found. So we found you instead."

"What're you talking about? And where did you even come from?" I ask, never having seen another person on my previous visits here.

"That's only because you didn't *want* to see another person," Romy says, answering the thought in my head. "You didn't *desire* it until now."

I look at her, my face blank, my mind spinning with the realization—*she can read my thoughts?*

"Thoughts are energy." She shrugs. "And Summerland consists of rapid, intense, magnified energy. So intense you can read it."

And the moment she says it, I remember my visit with Damen, and how we were able to communicate telepathically. But at the time, I thought it was just us.

"But if that's true, then why wasn't I able to read Ava's mind? And how was she able to just disappear like that?"

Rayne rolls her eyes, while Romy leans forward, her voice soft and low as though speaking to a small child even though they appear younger than I. "Because you have to *desire* it in order for it to be." Then, seeing the blank look on my face, she explains, "Within Summerland exists the possibility for everything. *For all things.* But you must first desire it to bring it into existence. Otherwise it remains only a possibility—one of many possibilities—unmanifested and incomplete."

I gaze at her, trying to make sense of her words.

"The reason you didn't see people before is because you didn't want to. But now, look around and tell me what you see."

And when I look around, I see that she's right. The shops and restaurants are now filled with people, a new art installation is being hung in the gallery, and a crowd gathers on the museum steps. And as I focus on their energy and thoughts, I realize just how diverse this place really is, every nationality and religion is present and accounted for, with everyone coexisting in peace.

Wow, I think, my eyes darting everywhere, trying to take it all in.

Romy nods. "And so the moment you desired to find your way to the temples, we showed up to help you. While Ava faded away."

"So I *made* her disappear?" I ask, beginning to grasp the truth of all this.

Romy laughs, while Rayne shakes her head and rolls her eyes, looking at me like I'm the densest person she's ever met. "Hardly."

"So all of these people—" I motion toward the crowd. "Are all of them—*dead?*" I direct my question at Romy, having given up on Rayne.

Watching as she leans in and whispers into her sister's ear, causing Romy to pull away and say, "My sister says you ask too many questions."

Rayne scowls, popping her hard on the arm with her fist, but Romy just laughs.

And as I gaze at the two of them, taking in Rayne's steady glare and Romy's insistence on speaking in riddles, I realize that as entertaining as it's been, they're starting to get on my nerves. I've got things to do, temples to find, and engaging in this kind of confusing banter is turning into a big waste of time.

Remembering too late that they both can read my thoughts when Romy nods and says, "As you wish. We'll show you the way."

twenty-five

They lead me down a series of streets, the two of them marching side by side, their stride so measured and quick I struggle to follow. We pass vendors peddling all types of wares—everything from hand-dipped candles to small wooden toys—their patrons lining up for those carefully wrapped goods and offering only a kind word or smile in exchange. We walk alongside fruit stands, candy stores, and a few trendy boutiques, before pausing on a corner as a horse-drawn carriage crosses our path followed by a chauffeur-driven Rolls-Royce.

And just as I'm about to ask how all of these things can exist in one place, how seemingly ancient buildings can sit beside the sleek-est, most modern designs, Romy looks at me and says, "I already told you. Summerland contains the possibility of *all things*. And since different people desire different things, most everything you can think of has been brought into existence."

"So all of this was *manifested*?" I say, gazing around in awe, as Romy nods and Rayne storms straight ahead. "But who's manifesting these things? Are they day-trippers like me? Are they living or dead?" I glance between Romy and Rayne, knowing my question applies to them too, because even though they *appear* to be normal on the outside, there's something very strange about them, something almost—eerie—and *timeless* as well.

And just as my gaze settles on Romy, Rayne decides to address me for the first time today, saying, "You desired to find the temples and so we are helping you. But make no mistake, we are under no obligation to answer your questions. Some things in Summerland are just none of your business."

I swallow hard, looking at Romy and wondering if she'll step in and apologize for her sister, but she just leads us down another well-populated street, into an empty alleyway, and onto a quiet boulevard where she stops before a magnificent building.

"Tell me what you see," she says, as both she and her sister peer closely at me.

I gawk at the glorious building before me, my eyes wide as my mouth drops in awe, taking in its beautiful elaborate carvings, its grand sloping roof, its imposing columns, its impressive front doors—all of its vast and varied parts rapidly changing and shifting, conjuring images of the Parthenon, the Taj Mahal, the great pyramids of Giza, the Lotus Temple, my mind reeling with imagery as the building reshapes and reforms, until all of the world's greatest temples and wonders are clearly represented in its ever-changing façade.

I see—I see everything! I think, unable to utter the words. The awesome beauty before me has rendered me speechless.

I turn to Romy, wondering if she sees what I see, and watching as she pops Rayne hard on the arm when she says, "I *told* you!"

"The temple is constructed from the energy, love, and knowledge of *all good things*." She smiles. "Those who can see that are permitted to enter."

The second I hear that, I sprint up the grand marble steps, eager to get past this glorious façade and see what's inside. But just as I reach the huge double doors, I turn back to say, "Are you coming?"

Rayne just stares, her eyes narrowed, suspicious, wishing they'd never bothered with me. While Romy shakes her head and says, "Your answers lie inside. You're no longer in need of us now."

"But where do I start?"

Romy peers at her sister, a private exchange passing between them. Then she turns to me and says, "You must seek the akashic records. They are a permanent record of everything that has ever been said, thought, or done—or ever will be said, thought, or done. But you will only find them if you are meant to. If not—" She shrugs, wishing to leave it right there, but the look of sheer panic in my eyes drives her to continue. "If you are not meant to know, then you will not know. It's as simple as that."

I stand there, thinking how that wasn't the least bit reassuring, and feeling almost relieved when they both turn to leave.

"And now we must go, Miss Ever Bloom," she says, using my full name even though I'm sure I never revealed it. "Though I'm sure we'll meet again."

I watch as they move away, remembering one last question when I call, "But how do I get back? You know, once I'm done here?"

Watching as Rayne's back stiffens and Romy turns, a patient smile spread across her face as she says, "The same way you arrived. Through the portal, of course."

twenty-six

The moment I turn toward the door it opens before me. And since it's not one of those automatic doors like the kind they have in supermarkets, I'm guessing it means I'm worthy of entering.

I step into a large spacious entry filled with the most brilliant warm light—a luminous showering radiance that, like the rest of Summerland, permeates every nook and cranny, every corner, every space, allowing no shadows or dark spots, and doesn't seem to emanate from any one place. Then I move along a hall flanked on either side by a row of white marble columns carved in the style of ancient Greece, where robe-wearing monks sit at long carved wooden tables, alongside priests, rabbis, shamans, and all manner of seekers. All of them peering at large crystal globes and levitating tablets—each of them studying the images that unfold.

I pause, wondering if it would be rude to interrupt and ask if they can point me in the direction of the akashic records. But the room is so quiet and they're all so engrossed, I'm reluctant to disturb them, so I keep going instead. Passing a series of magnificent statues carved from the purest white marble, until entering a large ornate room that reminds me of the great cathedrals of Italy (or at least the pictures I've seen). Bearing the same sort of domed ceilings, stained-glass windows, and elaborate frescoes containing the kind of glorious images that would make Michelangelo weep.

I stand in the center, my head thrown back in awe as I struggle to take it all in. Twirling around and around until I grow tired and dizzy, realizing it's impossible to glimpse it all in one sitting. And knowing I've wasted enough time already, I shut my eyes tightly and follow Romy's advice—that I must first *desire* something in order for it to be. And just after asking to be led to the answers I seek, I open my eyes and a long hallway appears.

Its light is dimmer than what I've grown used to seeing—it's sort of glowy, incandescent. And even though I've no idea where it leads, I start walking. Following the beautiful Persian runner that seems to go on forever, running my hands along a wall covered in hieroglyphs, my fingertips grazing the images as their likeness appears in my head—the entire story unfolding merely by touch, like some sort of telepathic Braille.

Then suddenly, with no sign or warning, I'm standing at the entrance to yet another elaborate room. Only this one is elaborate in a different way—not by carvings or murals—but by its pure unadulterated simplicity.

Its circular walls are shiny and slick, and even though they first appear to be merely white, on closer inspection I realize there's nothing *mere* about it. It's a *true* white, a white in the purest sense. One that can only result from the blending of *all* colors—an entire spectrum of pigments all merging together to create the ultimate color of light—just like I learned in art class. And other than the massive cluster of prisms hanging from the ceiling, containing what must amount to thousands of fine-cut crystals, all of them shimmering and reflecting and resulting in a kaleidoscope of color that now swirls around the room, the only other object in this space is a lone marble bench that's strangely warm and comfortable, especially for a substance known to be anything but.

And after taking a seat and folding my hands in my lap, I watch as the walls seamlessly seal up behind me as though the hallway that led me here never existed.

But I'm not afraid. Even though there's no visible exit and it appears that I'm trapped in this strange circular room, I feel safe, peaceful, cared for. As though the room is cocooning me, comforting me, its round walls like big strong arms in a welcoming hug.

I take a deep breath, wishing for answers to all of my questions, and watching as a large crystal sheet appears right before me, hovering in what was once empty space, waiting for me to make the next move.

But now that I'm so close to the answer, my question has suddenly changed.

So instead of concentrating on: *What's happened to Damen and how do I fix it?* I think: *Show me everything I need to know about Damen.*

Thinking this may be my only chance to learn everything I can about the elusive past he refuses to discuss. Convincing myself that I'm not at all prying, that I'm looking for solutions and that any information I can get will only help my cause. Besides, if I'm truly not worthy of knowing, then nothing will be revealed. So what harm is there in asking? And no sooner is the thought complete, than the crystal starts buzzing. Vibrating with energy as a flood of images fills up its face, the picture so clear it's like HDTV.

There's a small cluttered workshop, its windows covered by a swath of heavy dark cotton, its walls lit up by a profusion of candles. And Damen is there, no older than three, wearing a plain brown tunic that hangs well past his knees, and sitting at a table littered with small bubbling flasks, a pile of rocks, tins filled with colorful powders, mortars and pestles, mounds of herbs, and vials of dye. Watching as his father dips his quill into a small pot of ink and records the day's work in a series of complicated symbols, pausing every so often to read from a book titled: *Ficino's Corpus Hermeticism,* as Damen copies him, scribbling onto his own scrap of paper.

And he looks so adorable, so round-cheeked and cherubic, with the way his brown hair flops over those unmistakable dark eyes and curls down the nape of his soft baby neck, I can't help but reach toward him. It all looks so real, so accessible, and so *close,* I'm fully convinced that if I can only make contact, I can experience his world right beside him.

But just as my finger draws near, the crystal heats up to an unbearable degree and I yank my hand back, watching my skin briefly bubble and burn before healing again. Knowing the boundaries are now set, that I'm allowed to observe but not interfere.

The image fast-forwards to Damen's tenth birthday, a day deemed so special it's marked by treats and sweets and a late-afternoon visit to his father's workshop. The two of them sharing more than wavy dark hair, smooth olive skin, and a nicely squared jaw, but also a passion for perfecting the alchemical brew that promises not only to turn lead into gold but also to prolong life for an indefinite time—the perfect philosopher's stone.

They settle into their work, their established routine, with Damen grinding individual herbs with the mortar and pestle, before carefully measuring the salts, oils, colored liquids, and ores, which his father then adds to the bubbling flasks. Pausing before each step to announce what he's doing, and lecturing his son on their task:

"Transmutation is what we are after. Changing from sickness to health, from old age to youth, from lead to gold, and quite possibly, immortality too. Everything is born of one fundamental element, and if we can reduce it to its core, then we can create anything from there!"

Damen listens, rapt, hanging on to his father's every word even though he's heard the exact same speech many times before. And though they speak in Italian, a language I've never studied, somehow I understand every word.

He names each ingredient before adding it in, then deciding, just for today, to withhold the last one. Convinced that this final component, this odd-looking herb, will create even more magic if added to an elixir that's sat for three days.

After pouring the opalescent red brew into a smaller glass flask, Damen covers it carefully, then places it into a well-hidden cupboard. And they've just finished cleaning the last of their mess, when his mother—a creamy-skinned beauty in a plain watered-silk dress, her golden hair crimped at the sides and confined by a small cap at the back—stops by to call them to lunch. And her love is so apparent, so tremendously clear, illustrated in the smile she reserves for her husband, and the look she gives Damen, their dark soulful eyes a perfect mirror of each other.

And just as they're preparing to head home for lunch, three swarthy men storm through the door. Overpowering Damen's father and demanding the elixir, as his mother thrusts her son into the cupboard where it's stored—warning him to stay put, to not make a sound, until it's safe to come out.

He cowers in that dark, dank space, peering through a small knot in the wood. Watching as his father's workshop—his life's work—is destroyed by the men in their search. But even though his father turns over his notes, it's not enough to save them. And Damen trembles, watching helplessly, as both of his parents are murdered.

I sit on the white marble bench, my mind reeling, my stomach churning, feeling everything Damen feels, his swirling emotions, his deepest despair—my vision blurred by his tears, my breath hot, jagged, indistinguishable from his. We are one now. The two of us joined in unimaginable grief.

Both of us knowing the same kind of loss.

Both of us believing we were somehow at fault.

He washes their wounds and cares for their bodies, convinced that when three days have passed, he can add the final ingredient, that odd-looking herb, and bring them both back. Only to be awak-ened on that third and final day by a group of neighbors alerted by the smell, finding him curled up beside the bodies, the bottle of elixir clutched in his hand.

He struggles against them, retrieving the herb and desperately shoving it in. Determined to get it to his parents, to make them both drink, but overpowered by his neighbors long before he can.

Because they're convinced that he's practicing some sort of sor-cery, he's declared a ward of the church, where devastated by loss and pulled from everything he knows and loves, he's abused by priests determined to rid him of the devil inside.

He suffers in silence, suffers for years—until Drina arrives. And Damen, now a strong and handsome man of fourteen, is transfixed by the sight of her flaming red hair, her emerald green eyes, her ala-baster skin—her beauty so startling it's hard not to stare.

I watch them together, barely able to breathe as they form a bond so caring, so protective, I regret ever asking to see this. I was brash, impulsive, and reckless—I didn't take the time to think it all through. Because even though she's now dead and is no threat to me, watching him fall under her spell is more than I can bear.

He tends to the wounds she suffered at the hands of the priests, handling her with great reverence and care, denying his undeni-able attraction, determined only to protect her, save her, to aid her escape—the day arriving much sooner than expected when the plague sweeps through Florence—the dreaded Black Death that killed millions of people, rendering them all into a bloated, pus-ridden, suffering mess.

He watches helplessly as many of his fellow orphans grow ill and die, but it's not until Drina is stricken that he returns to his father's life's work. Re-creating the elixir he'd sworn off all these years—associating it with the loss of everything he held dear. But now, left with no other choice, and unwilling to lose her, he makes Drina drink. Sparing enough for himself and the remaining orphans, hoping only to shield them from disease, having no idea it would grant immortality too.

Infused with a power they can't understand and immune to the agonized cries of the sick and dying priests, the orphans disband. Heading back to the streets of Florence where they loot from the dead, while Damen, with Drina by his side, is intent on only one thing: seeking revenge on the trio of men who murdered his parents, ultimately tracking them down only to find that without the aid of the final ingredient, they've succumbed to the plague.

He waits for their death, taunting them with the promise of a cure he never intends to fulfill. Surprised by the hollowness of the victory when their bodies finally do yield, he turns to Drina, looking for comfort in her loving embrace . . .

I shut my eyes, determined to block it all out but knowing it's burned there forever, no matter how hard I try. Because while knowing they were lovers off and on for nearly six hundred years is one thing.

Having to watch it unfold—is another.

And even though I hate to admit it, I can't help but notice how the old Damen with his cruelty, greed, and abundance of vanity—has an awful lot in common with the new Damen—the one who ditched me for Stacia.

And after watching over a century of the two of them bonded by a never-ending supply of lust and greed, I'm no longer interested in getting to the part where we meet. No longer interested in seeing the previous versions of me. If it means having to view another hundred years of this, then it just isn't worth it.

And just as I close my eyes and plead—*Just get me to the end! Please! I can't stand to see another moment of this!*—the crystal flickers and flares as a blur of images race past, fast-forwarding with such speed and intensity I can barely distinguish one image from the

next. Getting only the briefest flash of Damen, Drina, and me in my
many incarnations—a brunette, a redhead, a blonde—all of it whirl-
ing right past me—the face and body unrecognizable, though the
eyes are always familiar.

Even when I change my mind and ask for it to slow down, the
images continue to whir. Culminating in a picture of Roman—his
lips curled back, his eyes filled with glee—as he gazes upon a very
aged, very *dead* Damen.

And then—

And then—nothing.

The crystal goes blank.

"No!" I shout, my voice bouncing off the walls of the tall empty
room and echoing right back at me. *"Please!"* I beg. "Come back! I'll
do better. Really! I promise not to get jealous or upset. I'll watch *the
whole entire thing* if you'll only just rewind!"

But no matter how much I beg, no matter how much I plead to
view it again, the crystal is gone, vanished from sight.

I gaze all around, searching for someone to help, some sort of
akashic record reference librarian, even though I'm the only one
here. Dropping my head in my hands, wondering how I could've
been so stupid as to allow my petty jealousies and insecurities to take
over again.

I mean, it's not like I didn't know about Drina and Damen. It's
not like I didn't know what I was going to see. And now, since I was
too big of a wuss to just suck it up and deal with the info before me,
I've no idea how to save him. No idea of how we possibly could've
gone from such a wonderful A to such a horrible Z.

All I know is that Roman's responsible. A pathetic confirmation
of what I already guessed. Somehow he's weakening Damen, reversing his immortality. And if I've any hope of saving him, I need to
learn *how* if not *why*.

Because one thing I know for sure is that Damen does *not* age. He's been around for over six hundred years and still looks like a teen.

I drop my head in my hands, hating myself for being so petty, so small, so foolish—so heinously pathetic, that I robbed myself of the answers I came here to know. Wishing I could rewind this whole session and start over—wishing I could go back—

"You can't go back."

I turn, hearing Romy's voice sneak up from behind me, and wondering how she found her way into this room. But when I look around, I realize I'm no longer in that beautiful circular space, I'm back in the hall. A few tables away from where the monks, priests, shamans, and rabbis once were.

"And you should never fast-forward into the future. Because every time you do, you rob yourself of the journey, the present moment, which, in the end, is all there really is."

I turn, wondering if she's referring to my crystal tablet debacle or life in general.

But she just smiles. "You okay?"

I shrug and look away. I mean, why bother explaining? She probably already knows anyway.

"Nope." She leans against the table and shakes her head. "I don't know a thing. Whatever happens in here is yours and yours to keep. I just heard your cry of distress so I thought I'd check in. That's all. Nothing more, nothing less."

"And where's your evil twin?" I ask, gazing around, wondering if she's hiding somewhere.

But Romy just smiles and motions for me to follow. "She's outside, keeping an eye on your friend."

"Ava's here?" I ask, surprised by how relieved that makes me feel. Especially considering how I'm still annoyed with her for ditching me like that.

But Romy just waves again, leading me through the front door and out to the steps where Ava is waiting.

"Where've you been?" I ask, my question sounding more like an accusation.

"I got a little sidetracked." She shrugs. "This place is so amazing, I—" She looks at me, hoping I'll lighten up and cut her a break, and averting her gaze when it's clear that I won't.

"How'd you end up here? Did Romy and Rayne—" But when I turn, I realize they're gone.

Ava squints, her fingers playing with the newly manifested gold hoops at her ear. "I desired to find you, so I ended up here. But I can't seem to get inside." She frowns at the door. "So is this it? Is this the hall you were looking for?"

I nod, taking in her expensive shoes and designer handbag, and growing more annoyed by the second. Here I take her to Summerland so she can help me save someone's life, and all she wants to do is go shopping.

"I *know*," she says, responding to the thoughts in my head. "I got carried away, and I'm sorry. But I'm ready to help if you still need it. Or did you get all the answers you sought?"

I press my lips together and gaze down at the ground, shaking my head when I say, "I um—I ran into some trouble." A flood of shame washes right over me, especially when I remember how the *trouble* was pretty much of my making. "And I'm afraid I'm right back where I started," I add, feeling like the world's biggest loser.

"Maybe I can help?" She smiles, squeezing my arm so I'll know she's sincere.

But I just shrug, doubting she can do much of anything at this point.

"Don't give up so easily," she says. "After all, this is Summerland, anything is possible here!"

I glance at her, knowing it's true but also knowing I've got some serious work to do back home on the earth plane. Work that's going to require all of my attention and focus, no distractions allowed.

So as I lead her down the stairs, I look at her and say, "Well, there's one thing you can do."

twenty-seven

Even though Ava wanted to stay, I pretty much grabbed hold of her hand and forced her to leave, knowing we'd both wasted plenty of time in Summerland already and I had other places to be.

"Damn!" She squints at her fingers just after we land on the floor cushions in her small purple room. "I was hoping they'd keep."

I nod, noticing how the jewel-encrusted gold rings she'd manifested have returned to her usual silver, while the designer shoes and handbag didn't survive the trip either.

"I was wondering about that," I say, rising to my feet. "But you know you can do that here, right? You can manifest anything you want, you just have to be patient." I smile, wishing to leave things on a positive note by repeating the exact same pep talk Damen gave me back when my lessons first began. Lessons I wished I'd paid a lot more attention to now, having assumed that being immortal meant we had nothing but time. Besides, I'm starting to feel guilty for being so hard on her. I mean, who wouldn't get a little carried away on their first visit to that place?

"So what now?" she calls, following me to the front door. "When do we go back? I mean, you won't return without me—will you?"

I turn, my eyes meeting hers, seeing how consumed she is with her visit and wondering if I'd made a mistake by taking her there.

Avoiding her eyes as I head for my car, calling over my shoulder to say, "I'll give you a call."

The next morning I pull into the parking lot and head for class. Merging into the usual swarm of students just like any other day, except this time I don't strive to keep my distance and maintain my personal space. Instead, I just go with the flow. Not reacting in the slightest when random people brush up against me, despite the fact that I left my iPod, hoodie, and sunglasses at home.

But that's because I'm no longer reliant on those old accessories that never worked all that well anyway. Now I carry my quantum remote wherever I go.

Yesterday, just as Ava and I were about to leave Summerland, I asked her to help me build a better shield. Knowing I could just go back into the hall while she waited outside and receive the answer on my own, but since she wanted to help, and figuring she might learn something too, we lingered at the bottom of the steps, both of us focusing our energy on *desiring* a shield that would allow us (well, me mostly, since Ava doesn't hear thoughts and get life stories by touch) to tune in and out at will. And the next thing you know, we both looked at each other and at the exact same second said, *"A quantum remote!"*

So now, whenever I want to hear someone's thoughts I just surf over to their energy field and hit *select*. And if I don't want to be bothered, I hit *mute*. Just like the remote I have at home. Only this one is invisible so I can pretty much take it everywhere I go.

I head into English, arriving early so I can observe all the action from start to finish. Not wanting to miss a single second of my planned surveillance. Because even though I have visual proof that Roman's responsible for what's happening to Damen—it gets me only so far. And now that the *who* part of the equation is solved, it's time to move on to the *how* and *why*.

I just hope it doesn't take too long. I mean, for one thing, I miss Damen. And for another, I'm so low on immortal juice I'm already forced to ration it. And since Damen never got around to giving me the recipe, I've no idea how to replace it, much less what will happen without it. Though I'm sure it's not good.

Originally, Damen thought he could just drink the elixir once and be cured of all ills. And while that worked for the first one hundred and fifty years, when he started to see subtle signs of aging he decided to drink it again. And then again. Until he ultimately became totally dependent.

He also didn't realize that an immortal could be killed until after I took down his ex-wife, Drina. And while both of us were sure that targeting the weakest chakra was the only method (the heart chakra in Drina's case), and while I'm still sure that we're the only ones who know that—according to what I saw yesterday in the akashic records, Roman's discovered another way. Which means if I have any hope of saving Damen, I need to learn what Roman knows, before it's too late.

When the door finally opens, I lift my gaze as a horde of students burst in. And even though it's not the first time I've seen it, it's still hard to watch them all laughing and joking and getting along, when just last week they barely acknowledged each other. And even though it's pretty much the kind of scene anyone would dream of seeing in their school, under the circumstances, it's not giving me the thrill that it should.

And not just because I'm stuck on the outside looking in, but because it's creepy, unnatural, and weird. I mean, high schools don't operate like this. Heck, *people* don't operate like this. Like will always seek like and that's just the way it is. It's just one of those unspoken rules. Besides, this isn't something they've *chosen* to do. Because little do they realize that all of that hugging, laughing, and ridiculous high-fiving is not because of their newfound love for each other—it's because of Roman.

Like a master puppeteer controlling his subjects for his own amusement—Roman is responsible. And while I don't know *how* or *why* he's doing it, and while I can't prove that he actually *is* doing it, I just know in my heart that it's true. It's as clear as the ping in my gut or the chill that blankets my skin whenever he's near.

I watch as Damen slides onto his seat as Stacia leans on his desk, her heavily padded pushed-up chest looming close to his face as she swings her hair over her shoulder and laughs at her own stupid wit. And even though I can't *hear* the joke since I purposely tuned her out in order to better hear Damen, the fact that he thinks it's stupid, is good enough for me.

It also gives me a small burst of hope.

A burst of hope that soon ends the second his attention returns to her cleavage.

I mean, he's so banal, so juvenile, and to be honest—completely embarrassing. And if I thought my feelings were hurt yesterday, when I was forced to watch him make out with Drina, well, in retrospect, that was nothing compared to *this*.

Because Drina was *then*, nothing more than a beautiful, empty, shallow image on a rock.

But Stacia is *now*.

And even though she's beautiful, empty, and shallow too—she happens to be standing right before me in all of her three-dimensional glory.

I listen to Damen's diluted brain wax all rhapsodic over the virtues and abundance of Stacia's heavily padded chest, and I can't help but wonder if this is his *real* taste in women.

If these bratty, greedy, vain girls are the kind of females he *truly* prefers.

And if I'm just some weird anomaly, some quirky odd fluke, that kept getting in the way the last four hundred years.

I keep my eye on him all through class, watching from my lone seat in the back. Automatically answering Mr. Robins's questions without even thinking, just repeating the answer I *see* in his head. My mind never straying from Damen, reminding myself, again and again, of who he *really* is: That despite all appearances, he's good, kind, caring, and loyal—the undisputed love of my numerous lives. And that this version sitting before me is *not* the real deal—no matter how much it may mirror some of the behaviors revealed yesterday—it's not who he is.

And when the bell finally rings, I follow him. Keeping tabs on him all through second period P.E. (mostly because I don't go), choosing to linger outside his classroom when I'm supposed to be running track. Slipping out of sight the moment I sense the hall monitors about to stroll by, then returning as soon as they've passed. Peering at him through the window and eavesdropping on all of his thoughts, just like the stalker he's accused me of being. Not knowing whether to feel disturbed or relieved when I discover that his attentions aren't strictly relegated to Stacia—that they're pretty much available for whoever's semi–good-looking and sitting nearby—unless, of course, that someone is *me*.

And while third period is also spent spying on Damen, by fourth, I switch my focus to Roman. Looking him right in the eye as I head for my desk, swiveling around and acknowledging him whenever I sense that he's focused on me. And even though his thoughts about me are as banal and embarrassing as Damen's thoughts about Stacia, I refuse to blush or react. I just keep smiling and nodding, determined to grin and bear it, because if I'm going to find out who this guy *really is,* then avoiding him like the Black Plague will no longer do.

So when the bell rings, I decide to break free from this outcast pariah *spaz* role I'm unwillingly cast in, and head straight for the long line of tables. Ignoring the ping in my gut that gets worse with each step, determined to land myself a spot and sit with the rest of my class.

And when Roman nods as I make my approach, I can't help but feel disappointed that he's not nearly as surprised as I'd assumed he would be.

"Ever!" He smiles, patting the narrow space right next to him. "So it wasn't just my imagination. We really did share a moment in class."

I smile tightly and squeeze in beside him, my gaze instinctively switching to Damen, but only for a moment before I force myself to look away. Reminding myself that I need to stay focused on Roman, that it's imperative not to get sidetracked.

"I knew you'd come around eventually. I just wish it 'adn't taken so long. We've so much lost time to make up for." He leans in, his face looming so close I can see the individual flecks of color in his eyes, brilliant points of violet that would be so easy to get lost in—

"This is *nice*. Isn't this *nice*? Everyone together like this—all joined as one. And all this time you were the missing link. But now that you're 'ere, my mission's complete. And you thought it couldn't be done." He tilts his head back and laughs—eyes closed, teeth exposed, as his tousled golden hair catches the glint of the sun. And even though I hate to admit it, the truth is, he's mesmerizing.

Not in the same way as Damen, in fact, not even close. Roman's good looking in a way that reminds me of my old life, having just the right amount of superficial charm and well-calculated hotness that I would've fallen for before. Back when I accepted things at face value and rarely, if ever, looked past the surface.

I watch as he takes a bite of his Mars bar, then I switch my gaze back to Damen. Taking in his gorgeous dark profile as my heart fills with such overwhelming longing I can hardly bear it. Watching his hands flail about as he amuses Stacia with some stupid story, though

I'm far less interested in the anecdote than the hands themselves, remembering how wonderful they once felt on my skin—

". . . so, as nice as it is to have you join us, I can't help but wonder what this is *really* about," Roman says, his eyes still on me.

But I'm still looking at Damen. Watching as he presses his lips against Stacia's cheek, before working their way around her ear and down the length of her neck . . .

"Because as much as I'd like to pretend you were overcome by my undeniable good looks and charm, I know better. So tell me, Ever, what gives?"

I can hear Roman talking, his voice droning on and on in the background like a vague incessant hum that's easy to ignore, but my gaze stays on Damen—the love of my life, my eternal soul mate who's completely unaware of the fact that I even exist. My stomach twisting as his lips brush over her collarbone before heading back to her ear, his mouth moving softly as he whispers to her, trying to coax her into ditching the rest of their classes so they can head back to his house . . .

Wait—coax her? He's trying to convince *her? Does that mean she's not ready and willing?*

Am I the only one around here who just assumed they'd already jumped each other's bones?

But just as I'm about to tune in to Stacia and see what she could possibly be up to by playing hard to get, Roman taps me on the arm and says, "Aw, come on, Ever. Don't be shy. Tell me what you're doing here. Tell me just exactly what it is that put you over the edge."

And before I can even reply, Stacia looks at me and says, "Jeez, Spaz, *stare much?*"

I don't respond. I just pretend I didn't hear while I focus on Damen. Refusing to acknowledge her presence, even though they're so entwined they're practically fused. Wishing he'd just turn around and *see* me—really *see* me—in the way that he used to.

But when he does finally look, his gaze goes right through me, as though I'm not worth the bother, as though I'm invisible now.

And seeing him glance through me like that leaves me numb, breathless, frozen, unable to move—

"Um, hel-*lo*?" Stacia shouts, loud enough for everyone to hear. "I mean, seriously. Can we *help* you? Can *anyone* help you?"

I glance at Miles and Haven sitting just a few feet away, watching as they shake their heads, both of them wishing they'd never had anything to do with me. Then I swallow hard and remind myself that they're not in control—that Roman's the writer, producer, director, and creator of this God-awful show.

I meet Roman's gaze, my stomach twisting, pinging, as I peer into the thoughts in his head. Determined to dig past the superficial layer of the usual inane stuff, curious to see if there's anything more than the horny, annoying, sugar-addicted teen he portrays himself to be. Because the fact is, I'm not buying it. The image I saw on that crystal, with the evil grin of victory spread wide across his face, hints at a much darker side. And as his smile grows wider and his gaze narrows on mine—everything dims.

Everything except Roman and me.

I'm hurtling through a tunnel, pulled faster and faster by a force beyond my control. Slipping uncontrollably into the dark abyss of his mind, as Roman carefully selects the scenes he wants me to see—Damen throwing a party in our suite at the Montage, a party that includes Stacia, Honor, Craig, and all the other kids who never talked to us before, a party that lasts several days, until he's finally kicked out for trashing the place. Forcing me to view all manner of unsavory acts, stuff I'd rather not see—culminating on the final image I saw on the crystal that day—the very last scene.

I fall back from my seat, landing on the ground in a tangle of limbs, still caught in his grip. Finally coming around just as the entire school breaks into a shrill mocking chorus of *"Spaz!"* And watching in horror as my spilled red elixir races across the tabletop and drips down the sides.

"You *all right?*" Roman asks, gazing at me as I struggle to stand. "I know it's tough to watch. Believe me, Ever, I've been there. But it's all for the best, really it is. And I'm afraid you'll just have to trust me on that."

"I *knew* it was you," I whisper, standing before him, shaking with rage. "I knew it all along."

"So you did." He smiles. "So you did. Score one for you. Though I should warn you, I'm still a good ten points ahead."

"You won't get away with this," I say, watching in horror as he dips his middle finger into the puddle of my spilled red drink, allowing the drops to fall onto his tongue in such a deliberate, measured way, it's like he's trying to tell me something, give me a nudge.

But just as an idea begins to form in my head, he licks his lips and says, "But see, that's where you're wrong." Turning his head in a way that displays the mark on his neck, the finely detailed Ouroboros tattoo now flashing in and out of view. "I've already gotten away with it, Ever." He smiles. "I've already won."

twenty-eight

I didn't go to art. I left right after lunch.

No, scratch that. Because the truth is I left in the *middle* of lunch. Seconds after my horrible encounter with Roman, I sprinted for the parking lot (chased by a never-ending chorus of *Spaz!*), where I jumped in my car and sped away long before the bell was scheduled to ring.

I needed to get away from Roman. To put some distance between me and his creepy tattoo—the intricate Ouroboros design that flashed in and out of view just like the one on Drina's wrist used to do.

The undeniable symbol marking Roman as a rogue immortal— just as I'd thought all along.

And even though Damen failed to warn me of them, didn't even know they existed until Drina went bad, I still can't believe it took me so long to get it. I mean, even though he eats and drinks, even though his aura is visible and his thoughts are available to read (well, for me anyway), I realize now it was all a façade. Like those buildings on Hollywood back lots that are carefully crafted to look like something they're not. And that's what Roman did—he purposely projected this happy-go-lucky, jolly young lad from England veneer, with his bright shiny aura, and happy, horny thoughts, when all the while, deep down inside, he's anything but.

The real Roman is dark.

And sinister.

And evil.

And everything else that adds up to *bad*. But even worse is the fact that he's out to kill my boyfriend, and I still don't know why.

Because motive was the one thing in my brief but disturbing visit to the inner recesses of his mind that I failed to see.

And motive will prove very important if I'm ever forced to kill him, since it's imperative to hit just the right chakra to be rid of him for good. And not knowing the motive means I could fail.

I mean, would I go for the first chakra—or root chakra, as it's sometimes called—the center for anger, violence, and greed? Or maybe the navel chakra, or sacral center, which is where envy and jealousy live. But with no idea of what's driving him, it'd be far too easy to hit the wrong one. Which would not only serve in *not* killing him but would probably make him incredibly angry as well. Leaving me with six more chakras to choose from, and at that point, I'm afraid he'd catch on.

Besides, killing Roman too soon will only hurt me—ensuring he takes his secret of whatever he's done to Damen and the rest of the school along with him. And that's one risk I just can't afford. Not to mention that I'm really not all that big on killing people anyway. The only times I've ever gotten physical in the past are when I was left with no choice but to fight or die. And as soon as I realized what I'd done to Drina, I hoped I'd never have to do it again. Because even though she killed me many times before, even though she admitted to killing my entire family—including my dog—that doesn't do much to alleviate the guilt. I mean, knowing I'm solely responsible for her ultimate exit makes me feel awful.

And since I'm pretty much right back where I started, I decide to head back to the beginning. Turning right on Coast Highway and heading for Damen's, figuring I'll use the next couple hours while they're all still at school to break into his house and take a good look around.

I pull up to the guard post, wave at Sheila, and continue toward the gate. Naturally assuming it would open before me, and having to slam on my brakes to avoid major front-end damage when it stays put.

"Excuse me. *Excuse me!*" Sheila shouts, storming toward my car as though I'm some kind of intruder, as though she's never seen me before. When the truth is, up until last week, I was pretty much here every day.

"Hey, Sheila." I smile in a nice, friendly, nonthreatening way. "I'm just heading up to Damen's, so if you could just open the gate, I'll be on my way and—"

She looks at me, her eyes narrowed, her lips pressed together in a thin grim line. "I'm going to have to ask you to leave."

"What? But *why?*"

"You're off the list," she says, hands planted firmly on hips, her face betraying not even the slightest trace of remorse after all those months of smiling and waving.

I sit there, lips pressed together, allowing the words to sink in.

I'm off the list. I'm off the permanent list. Blackballed or blacklisted or whatever it's called when you're denied access to a glorious gated community for an indefinite time.

Which would be bad enough on its own, but having to hear the official breakup message delivered by Big Sheila instead of my boyfriend—makes it even worse.

I gaze down at my lap, gripping the gearshift so hard it threatens to pop off in my hand. Then I swallow hard and look at her when I say, "Well, as you've obviously been made aware, Damen and I broke up. But I was just hoping to drop in real quick and retrieve a few of my things, because as you can see—" I unzip my bag and quickly shove my hand inside. "I still have the key."

I raise it up high, watching as the noonday sun catches and reflects the gold shiny metal, too caught up in my own mortification to foresee that she'd reach out and snatch it.

"Now, I'm asking you nicely to vacate the premises," she says, shoving the key deep into her pocket, its shape visible as the fabric strains over her mammoth-sized breasts. Barely giving me enough time to switch my foot from the brake to the gas before adding, "Go on now. Back up. Don't you make me ask twice."

twenty-nine

This time when I arrive in Summerland, I skip the usual landing in that vast fragrant field, choosing instead to touch down smack in the middle of what I now like to think of as the main drag. Then I pick myself up and brush myself off, amazed to see everyone around me just carrying on with their normal business, as though seeing someone drop right out of the sky and onto the street is a normal, everyday occurrence. Though I guess in these parts it is.

I make my way past karaoke bars and hair salons, retracing the steps Romy and Rayne showed me, knowing I can probably just *desire* to be there instead, but still anxious to learn my own way around. And after a quick pass through the alley and a sudden turn onto the boulevard, I run up those steep marble steps and stand before those massive front doors, watching as they swing open for me.

I step into the great marble hall, noticing how it's much more crowded than the last time I was here. Reviewing the questions in my head, unsure if I need the akashic records or if I can just get my answers right here. Wondering if questions like *Exactly who is Roman and what has he done to Damen?* and: *How can I stop him and spare Damen's life?* require that kind of secured access.

But then, feeling like I need to simplify and sum it all up in one tidy sentence, I close my eyes and think: *Basically, what I want to know is: How can I return everything back to the way it was before?*

And as soon as the thought is complete, a doorway opens before me, its warm inviting light beckoning me in as I enter a solid white room, that same sort of rainbow white as before, only this time, rather than a white marble bench, there's a worn leather recliner instead.

I move toward it, plopping onto the seat, extending the leg rest, and settling in. Unaware that I'm lounging on an exact replica of my dad's favorite chair until I see the initials R.B. and E.B. scratched onto its arm. Gasping when I recognize it as the exact same markings I convinced Riley to make with her Girl Scout camping knife. The exact same markings that not only proved we were the culprits but also earned us a week's worth of restriction.

Or at least until mine got extended to ten days when my parents realized I'd coached her into doing it—a fact that, in their eyes, made me the pre-calculating perpetrator who clearly deserved extra time.

I run my fingers over the gouged leather, my nails digging into the stuffing where the curve of her *R* went too deep. Choking back a sob as I remember that day. *All* of those days. Every single one of those deliciously wonderful days that I once took for granted but now find myself missing so much I can barely stand it.

I'd do *anything* to go back. *Anything* if it meant I could return and put it all back to the way it once was—

And no sooner is the thought complete, when the formerly empty space begins to transform. Rearranging itself from a nearly empty room with a lone recliner to an exact replica of our old den in Oregon.

The air infused with the scent of my mom's famous brownies, as the walls morph from pearlescent white to the soft beige-like hue she referred to as *driftwood pearl*. And when the three-colors-of-blue

afghan my grandma knit suddenly covers my knees, I gaze toward
the door, seeing Buttercup's leash hanging on the knob, and Riley's
old sneakers lying next to my dad's. Watching as all the pieces fill in,
until every photo, book, and knickknack are present and accounted
for. And I can't help but wonder if this is because of my question,
because I asked for everything to return to the way it was before.

Because the truth is, I was actually referring to Damen and me.

Wasn't I?

I mean, is it really possible to *go back in time?*

Or is this lifelike replica, this Bloom family diorama, the closest
I'll ever get?

But just as I'm questioning my surroundings and the true meaning of what I actually meant, the TV turns on, and a flash of colors
race across the screen—a screen made of crystal, just like the crystal
I viewed the other day.

I pull the afghan tighter around me, tucking it snugly under my
knees, as the words L'HEURE BLEUE fill up the screen. And just as
I'm wondering what it could possibly mean, a definition scripted in
the most beautiful calligraphy appears, stating:

A French expression, l'heure bleue, *or "blue hour" refers to the
hour experienced between daylight and darkness. A time revered
for its quality of light, and also when the scent of flowers is at
its strongest.*

I squint at the screen, watching as the words fade and a picture
of the moon takes its place—a full and glorious moon—shimmering
the most beautiful shade of blue—a hue that nearly matches the
sky . . .

And then—and then I see *me*—up on that very same screen.
Dressed in jeans and a black sweater, my hair hanging loose, gazing
out a window at that same blue moon—glancing at my watch as

though I'm waiting for something—something that's soon to arrive. And despite the fuzzy, dreamlike state of watching a me that's not *really* me, I can still feel what she's feeling, hear what she's thinking. She's going somewhere, somewhere she once thought was off limits. Anxiously waiting for the moment when the sky turns the same shade as the moon, a wonderful deep dark blue with no trace of the sun—knowing it heralds her only chance to find her way back to this room and return to a place she once thought was lost.

I watch, my gaze glued to the screen, gasping as she raises her hand, presses her finger to the crystal, and is pulled back in time.

thirty

I tear out of the hall and sprint down the steps. My vision so blurred, my heart pounding so fast, I'm completely unaware of Romy and Rayne until it's too late, and Rayne is crumpled beneath me.

"Omigod, I'm so sorry, I—"

I bend down, my hand outstretched, waiting for her to grab hold of it so I can help her to her feet, asking repeatedly if she's all right, and wincing with embarrassment when she ignores my gesture and struggles to stand. Straightening her skirt and pulling up her kneesocks as I watch in amazement as her skinned knees instantly heal—never having considered the possibility that they might be like me.

"Are—are you—"

But before I can even get to the word, Rayne shakes her head and says, "We are most certainly *not*." Making sure her kneesocks are of exact equal height. "We are *nothing* like *you*," she mumbles, straightening her blue blazer and plaid skirt, then glancing at her much nicer sister who's shaking her head.

"Rayne, please. Remember your manners." Romy frowns.

But even though Rayne continues to glare, her voice loses some of its steam when she says, "Well, we're *not*."

"So—so you know about me?" I ask, hearing Rayne think: *Well, duh!* As Romy nods her head solemnly. "And you think that I'm *bad?*"

Rayne rolls her eyes, while Romy smiles gently, saying, "Please, ignore my sister. We think nothing of the sort. We are in no position to judge."

I glance between them, taking in their pale skin, huge dark eyes, razor-slashed bangs, and thin lips, their features so exaggerated they're like Manga characters come to life. And I can't help but think how strange it is for two people to be so identical on the outside and yet so opposite inside.

"So, tell us what you've learned," Romy says, smiling as she heads down the street, assuming we'll all just follow along—which we do. "Did you find all the answers you seek?"

And more.

I've been wide-eyed and speechless ever since that crystal went blank. Having no idea what to make of the knowledge I've been given, but well aware of the fact that it holds the potential to change not only my life but quite possibly the world. And while I have to admit that it's pretty amazing to have access to such powerful wisdom, the responsibility that goes with it is undeniably huge.

I mean, what am I expected to *do* with it now that I know? Was I shown the information for a reason? Some kind of big global reason? Is there some new expectation of me of which I'm not even aware? And if not, then what's the point?

Seriously—*why me?*

Surely I'm not the first person to ask that sort of question.

Am I?

And the only plausible answer I can seem to come up with is: Maybe I'm meant to go back. Maybe I'm meant to return.

Not to halt assassinations, stop wars, and basically change the course of history—I just don't think I'm the right girl for that job.

Though I do think I've been shown this information for a reason—one that leads right back to what I've been thinking all along: That this whole scenario of the accident, my psychic powers, and Damen making me an immortal has all been a terrible mistake. And that if I can just pop back in time and stop the accident from ever happening—then I can put it all back to the way it was before. I can go back to Oregon and re-enter my old life like my new life never even occurred. Which is what I've wished for all along.

But where does that leave Damen? Does he go back too?

And if so, will he still be with Drina until she manages to kill me, and everything happens all over again?

Will I just be delaying the inevitable?

Or does everything stay the same except me? Does he die at Roman's hands while I'm back in Oregon, completely unaware he exists?

And if that's the case, then how can I let that happen?

How can I turn my back on the one and only person I've ever truly loved?

I shake my head, noticing Romy and Rayne still looking at me, waiting for an answer, though I've no idea what to say. So, instead, I just stand there, my mouth hanging open like a ginormous dork. Thinking how even in Summerland, a place of absolute love and perfection, I'm still a total dweeb.

Romy smiles, closing her eyes as her arms fill with red tulips— beautiful red tulips she promptly offers to me.

But I refuse to take them. I just narrow my eyes and start backing away. "What are you doing?" I glance between them, my voice tenuous, fragile, noticing how they look just as confused as I am.

"I'm sorry," Romy says, trying to ease my alarm. "I'm not sure why I did it. The thought just popped into my head, and so—"

I watch as the tulips dissolve from her fingers, going back to wherever they came from. But having them gone doesn't make the least bit of difference, and all I want now is for them to go too.

"Isn't *anything* private around here?" I shout, knowing I'm over-reacting but unable to stop. Because if those tulips were some kind of message, if she was listening in on my thoughts and trying to persuade me to give up the past and stay put, well, it's just none of her business. They may know all about Summerland, but they know *nothing* about me, and they've no right to butt in. They've never had to make a decision like this. They've no idea how it feels to lose every single person you've ever loved.

I take another step back, seeing Rayne furrow her brow as Romy shakes her head, saying, "We didn't hear a thing. Honest. We can't read *all* of your thoughts, Ever. Only the ones we're permitted to see. Whatever you see in the akashic records is yours and yours to keep. We are merely concerned by your distress. That is all. Nothing more, nothing less."

I narrow my eyes, not trusting her for a second. They've probably been snooping in my thoughts all along. I mean, why else give me the tulips? Why else manifest such a thing?

"I wasn't even visiting the akashic records," I say. "This room was—" I pause, swallowing hard as I remember the smell of my mom's brownies, the feel of my grandma's blanket, and knowing I can have it all again. All I have to do is wait for the right day and time and I can return to my family and friends. I shake my head and shrug. "This room was *different*."

"The Akashic Hall has many faces." Romy nods. "It becomes whatever you need it to be." She looks at me, her eyes roaming over my face as she says, "We only showed up to help, not to upset or confuse you."

"So, what? You're like my guardian angels or spirit guides? Two private-school-uniform-wearing fairy godmothers?"

"Not quite." Romy laughs.

"Then who are you? And what're you doing here? And how come you always manage to find me?"

Rayne glares and pulls on her sister's sleeve, urging her to leave. But Romy stays put, looking me in the eye when she says, "We are only here to aid and assist. That is all you need to know."

I look at her for a moment, glance at her sister, then shake my head and walk away. They're deliberately mysterious and way beyond weird, and I've a pretty good hunch their intentions aren't good.

Even as Romy calls out from behind me, I keep going. Eager to put some distance between us as I head for an auburn-haired woman waiting just outside the theater, the one who, from behind anyway, looks exactly like Ava.

thirty-one

The huge disappointment I felt when I tapped that auburn-haired woman on the shoulder only to discover she wasn't Ava, made me realize just how badly I need to talk to her. So I exit Summerland and land back in my car, plopping onto the driver's seat right in front of the Trader Joe's in the Crystal Cove Promenade parking lot, and startling an unsuspecting shopper so badly she drops both her bags, scattering numerous cans of coffee and soup under a whole row of cars. And I promise myself that from now on, I'll make sure my exits and entries are a bit more discreet.

When I get to Ava's, she's in the middle of a reading, so I wait in her bright sunny kitchen while she finishes up. And even though I know it's none of my business, even though I know I shouldn't be snooping, I go right for my quantum remote and access their session, amazed by the amount of accuracy and detail Ava provides.

"Impressive," I say, after her client is gone and she comes into the kitchen to join me. "*Very* impressive. Seriously, I had no idea." I smile, watching as she goes through her usual ritual of filling the teapot to boil, then placing some cookies onto a plate and pushing it my way.

"That's quite a compliment coming from you." She smiles, taking the seat just across from me. "Though if I remember right, I gave you a pretty accurate reading once too."

I reach for a cookie, knowing it's expected. And when I lick the little bits of sugar from the top, I can't help but feel sad that it no longer holds the allure that it used to.

"You remember that reading? On Halloween night?" She watches me closely.

I nod. I remember it well. That's the night I discovered she could see Riley. Up until then I'd been sure I was the only one who could communicate with my dead little sister, and I wasn't too happy to learn that was no longer the case.

"Did you tell your client she's dating a loser?" I break the cookie in half. "That he's cheating on her with someone she thinks is a friend and that she should dump them both ASAP?" I ask, removing some crumbs that fell onto my lap.

"In so many words," she says, getting up to fetch our tea the moment the pot starts to whistle. "Though I can only hope you'll learn to soften the message if you ever decide to give readings."

I pause, overcome by a sudden pang of sadness when I realize just how long it's been since I last thought about my future, about what I might want to be when I grow up. I went through so many phases—wanting to be a park ranger, a teacher, an astronaut, a supermodel, a pop star—the list was endless. But now that I'm immortal, now that I'm in a position to try out *all* of those things over the course of the next thousand-plus years—I no longer feel that ambitious.

Lately, all I've been thinking about is how to get Damen back.

And now, after this last trip to Summerland, all I can think about is getting the old me back.

I mean, having the entire world at my feet is not so enticing when there's no one to share it with.

"I—I'm still not sure what I want to do. I haven't really thought about it," I lie, wondering if it will be easy for me to slip back into my old life—if I decide to return to it, that is. And if I'll still want to be a pop star like I used to, or if the changes I've experienced here will follow me there.

But when I look at Ava, watching as she lifts her cup to her lips and blows twice before sipping, I remember that I didn't come here to discuss my future. I came to discuss my past. Deciding to bring her into my confidence and share some of my biggest secrets. Convinced not only that I can trust her but that she'll be able to help me as well.

Because the truth is, I need someone I can count on. There's just no way I can go it alone. And it's not about helping me decide whether I should stay or go, because I'm beginning to realize I really don't have much of a choice. I mean, the thought of leaving Damen—the thought of never seeing him again—is almost more painful than I can bear. But when I think about my family, and how they unwittingly sacrificed their lives for me—either because of a stupid blue sweatshirt I insisted my dad return for, which ultimately caused the accident that killed everyone—or because Drina intentionally made the deer run in front of our car so she could be rid of me and have Damen to herself—I feel I have to do something to make it all right.

Because either way you look at it, it leads back to *me*. It's my fault they're no longer living their lives, it's my fault their bright shiny futures were cut so tragically short. If I hadn't gotten in the way, none of this ever would've happened. And even though Riley insisted it all turned out the way it was meant to, the fact that I'm being given the choice just proves that I need to sacrifice my future with Damen so they can have theirs.

It's the right thing to do.

It's the *only* thing to do.

And with the way things are going, with my social exile from school, Ava's pretty much my only friend left. Which means I'll need her to pick up any stray pieces I might leave behind.

I bring my teacup to my lips, then set it back down without drinking. Tracing my fingers around the curve of the handle as I take a deep breath and say, "I think someone's poisoning Damen." Seeing her eyes bug out as she gapes. "I—I think someone's tampering with his—" *Elixir* "—favorite drink. And it's making him act—" *Mortal* "—normal, but not in a good way." I press my lips together and rise from my seat, barely giving her a chance to catch her breath when I say, "And since I'm banned from the gate, I'm gonna need you to help me break in."

thirty-two

"Okay, we're here. Just act cool," I say, crouching down in the back as Ava approaches the gate. "Just nod and smile and give her the name I told you."

I pull my legs in, trying to make myself smaller, less obtrusive, a task that would've been a heck of a lot easier just two weeks ago, before I was faced with this ridiculous growth spurt. Crouching down even farther and pulling the blanket tighter around me as Ava lowers her window and smiles at Sheila, giving her the name of Stacia Miller (my replacement on Damen's list of welcomed guests), who I hope hasn't come around quite enough yet for Sheila to recognize her.

And the moment the gate swings open and we're headed for Damen's, I toss the blanket aside and climb onto the seat, seeing Ava gaze around the neighborhood with obvious envy, shaking her head and muttering, "Swanky."

I shrug and glance around too, never having given it much notice before. Always viewing this place as a blur of phony Tuscan farmhouses and upscale Spanish haciendas with well-landscaped yards and subterranean garages one has to pass in order to reach Damen's faux French chateau.

"I have no idea how he affords it, but it sure is nice," she says, glancing at me.

"He plays the ponies," I mumble, concentrating on the garage door as she pulls into his drive, taking note of its most minute details before closing my eyes and *willing* for it to open.

Seeing it rise and lift in my mind, then opening my eyes just in time to watch it sputter and spurt before dropping back down with a very loud *thud*. An unmistakable sign that I'm still a long way from mastering psychokinesis—or the art of moving anything heavier than a Prada bag.

"Um, I think we should just go around back like I usually do," I say, feeling embarrassed for failing so miserably.

But Ava won't hear of it, grabbing my bag and heading for the front door. And even when I scramble behind, telling her it's no use, that it's locked and we can't possibly enter that way, she just keeps going, claiming we'll just have to unlock it then.

"It's not as easy as you think," I tell her. "Believe me, I've tried it before and it didn't work." Glancing at the extra door I accidentally manifested the last time I was here—the one that's still leaning against the far wall, which is exactly where I left it since apparently Damen's too busy acting cool and chasing Stacia to take the time to get rid of it.

But the moment I think that, I wish I could erase it. The thought leaves me sad, empty, and feeling far more desperate than I care to admit.

"Well, this time you have *me* to help." She smiles. "And I think we've already proved just how well we work together."

And the way she looks at me, with such anticipation, such optimism, I can't see the point in refusing to try. So I close my eyes as we both join hands, envisioning the door springing open before us. And just seconds after hearing the dead bolt slide back, the door opens wide, allowing us in.

"After you." Ava nods, glancing at her watch and scrunching her brow as she says, "Tell me again, exactly how much time do we have here?"

I gaze at my wrist, seeing the crystal horseshoe bracelet Damen gave me that day at the track, the one that makes my heart swell with longing every time I see it. Yet I refuse to remove it. I mean, I just can't. It's my only physical reminder of what we once had.

"Hey? You okay?" she asks, her face creased with concern.

I swallow hard and nod. "We should be okay on time. Though I should warn you, Damen has a bad habit of cutting class and coming home early."

"Then we best get started." Ava smiles, slipping into the foyer and looking all around, her eyes moving from the huge chandelier in the entry to the elaborate wrought-iron banister that leads up the stairs. Turning to me with a gleam in her eye when she says, "This guy is seventeen?"

I move toward the kitchen, not bothering to answer since she already knows that he is. Besides, I've got much bigger things at stake than square footage and the seeming implausibility of a seventeen-year-old who's neither a pop star nor a member of a hit TV show owning such a place.

"Hey—hold up," she says, reaching for my arm and stopping me in my tracks. "What's upstairs?"

"Nothing." And the second it's out I know I totally blew it, answering far too quickly to ever be believed. Still, the last thing I need is for Ava to go snooping around and barging into his "special" room.

"Come on," she says, smiling like a rebellious teen whose parents are gone for the weekend. "School gets out at what? Two fifty?"

I nod, just barely, but it's still enough to encourage her.

"And then it takes, what? Ten minutes to drive home from there?"

"More like two." I shake my head. "No, scratch that. More like thirty seconds. You have no idea how fast Damen drives."

She checks her watch again, then looks at me. A smile playing at the corner of her lips when she says, "Well, that still leaves us plenty of time to take a quick look around, switch out the drinks, and be on our way."

And when I look at her, all I can hear is the voice in my head shouting: *Say no! Say no! Just. Say. No!* A voice I should heed.

A voice that's immediately canceled by hers when she says, "Come on, Ever. It's not every day I get to tour a house like this. Besides, we might find something useful, did you ever consider that?"

I press my lips together and nod like it pains me. Reluctantly following behind as she races ahead like an excited schoolgirl about to see her crush's cool room, when the fact is she's got over a decade on me. Heading straight for the first open door she sees, which just happens to be his bedroom. And as I follow her inside I'm not sure if I'm more surprised or relieved to find it just like I left it.

Only messier.

Way messier.

And I refuse to even think about how *that* might've happened.

Still, the sheets, the furniture, even the paint on the walls—none of it—I'm happy to report—have been changed. It's all the same stuff I helped him pick out a few weeks ago when I refused to spend another minute hanging out in that creepy mausoleum of his, where, believe it or not, he used to sleep. I mean, making out among all those dusty old memories really started to skeeve me out.

Never mind the fact that, technically speaking, I'm one of those dusty old memories too.

But even after all the new furniture was put into place, I still preferred to hang out at my house. I guess it just felt—I don't know—*safer*? Like the threat of Sabine coming home any minute would keep me from doing something I wasn't sure I was ready to do. Which now, after all that's happened, seems more than a little ridiculous.

"Wow, check out this master bath," Ava says, eyeing the Roman shower with the mosaic design and enough showerheads to bathe twenty. "I could get used to living like this!" She perches on the edge of the Jacuzzi tub and plays with the taps. "I've always wanted one of these! Have you used this?"

I look away, but not before she catches a glimpse of the color that flushes my cheeks. I mean, just because I spilled a few secrets and allowed her to come up here doesn't mean she gets an all-access pass to my private life too.

"I have one at home," I finally say, hoping that'll suffice so we can end this tour and be on our way. I need to get back downstairs so I can switch Damen's elixir with mine. And if she stays up here alone, I'm afraid she'll never leave.

I tap my watch, reminding her of just who's in charge around here.

"All right," she says, practically dragging her feet as I lead her out of the bedroom and into the hall. Only to stop just a few doors down and say, "But real quick, what's in here?"

And before I can stop her, she's entered *the room*—Damen's sacred space. His private sanctuary. His creepy mausoleum.

Only it's changed.

And I mean, drastically and dramatically changed.

Every last trace of Damen's personal time warp completely vanished—with not a Picasso, Van Gogh, or velvet settee in sight.

All of it replaced by a red felt pool table, a well-stocked black marble bar with shiny chrome stools, and a long row of recliners facing a wall covered with a ginormous flat screen TV. And I can't help but wonder what became of his old stuff—those priceless artifacts that used to get on my nerves, but now that they've been replaced with such slick modern designs, seem like lost symbols of much better times.

I miss the old Damen. I miss my bright, handsome, chivalrous boyfriend who clung so tightly to his Renaissance past.

This sleek, new-millennium Damen is a stranger to me. And as I look around this room once more, I wonder if it's too late to save him.

"What's wrong?" Ava squints. "Your face has gone white."

I grab hold of her arm and pull her down the stairs. "We need to hurry," I tell her. "Before it's too late!"

thirty-three

I flee down the stairs and into the kitchen, yelling, "Grab the bag by the door and bring it to me!"

I race for the fridge, eager to empty its contents and exchange them with mine, needing to wrap it all up before Damen can come home and catch us.

But when I open his oversized Sub-Zero fridge, just like the room upstairs, it's not at all what I expected. For one thing, it's filled with food.

And I mean lots and lots of food—like he's planning a really huge party—one that will last for three days.

I'm talking sides of beef, slabs of steak, huge wedges of cheese, half a chicken, two large pizzas, ketchup, mayonnaise, assorted takeout containers—the works! Not to mention several six packs of beer all lined up along the bottom shelf.

And even though it appears to be totally normal, here's the thing: Damen's *not* normal. He hasn't really eaten in six hundred *years*.

He also doesn't drink *beer*.

Immortal juice, water, the occasional glass of champagne—yes.

Heineken and Corona—not so much.

"What is it?" Ava asks, dropping the bag on the floor and peering over my shoulder, trying to figure out what I'm so worked up about, and opening the freezer only to find it fully stocked with vodka, frozen pizzas, and several tubs of Ben & Jerry's. "Okay . . . so he's been to the supermarket recently . . . is there some cause for alarm I don't get? Do you two normally just manifest all of your food whenever you're hungry?"

I shake my head, knowing I can't tell her that Damen and I never *get* hungry. Just because she knows we're psychic with the ability to manifest stuff both here and in Summerland, doesn't mean she needs to know the other part of the story, the—*Oh, yeah, did I mention we're both immortal*—part too.

All she knows is what I told her—that I've a very strong suspicion that Damen is being poisoned. What I didn't tell her is that he's being poisoned in a way that's breaking down all of his psychic abilities, his enhanced physical strength, his vast intelligence, his carefully honed talents and skills, even his long-term memories of what went before—all of it's being slowly erased, as he returns to mortal form.

But while he may appear to be just your average high school junior—well, one with screamin' good looks, fistfuls of money, and his own parent-free, multimillion-dollar pad—it's just a matter of time before he begins to age.

And then deteriorate.

And then—ultimately—*die*, like I saw on that screen.

And that's exactly why I need to switch out these drinks. I need to get him back on the good juice so he can start building up his strength and hopefully repair some of the damage that's already been done. While I try to figure out an antidote that'll hopefully save him and return him to the way he once was.

And if his messy house, remodeled room, and well-stocked fridge are any indication, Damen's progressing much more quickly than I assumed.

"I don't even see these bottles you're talking about," Ava says, peering over my shoulder and squinting into the refrigerator light. "Are you sure this is where he keeps them?"

"Trust me, they're there." I rummage through the world's largest condiment collection, before spotting the elixir. Sliding my fingers around the necks of several bottles, which I then hand to Ava. "Just as I thought." I nod, finally making some headway.

Ava looks at me, her brow raised as she says, "Don't you think it's weird he's still drinking it? Because if it really is poisoned, don't you think the flavor must've changed?"

And just like *that,* I begin to doubt.

I mean, what if I'm wrong?

What if this isn't it at all?

What if Damen just grew tired of me, if *everyone* just grew tired of me, and Roman has nothing to do with it?

I grab a bottle and bring it to my lips, stopping only when Ava cries, "You're not going to drink that, are you?"

But I just shrug and take a sip, figuring there's only one way to know for sure if it's poisoned, and hoping one tiny taste won't do any harm. Knowing the second I taste it why Damen didn't notice a difference—because there isn't one. At least not until the aftertaste makes itself known.

"Water!" I gasp, rushing toward the sink and sticking my head under the faucet, gulping all the tap water I can until that awful taste is diluted.

"That bad?"

I nod, wiping my mouth with my sleeve. "Worse. But if you've ever seen Damen drink it, you'd know why he didn't notice. He gulps that stuff like—" I start to say *like a dying man,* but it hits too close to home. So I swallow hard and say, "Like someone who's very thirsty."

Then I hand Ava the remaining bottles so she can set them beside the sink, positioning the poisoned ones along the edge, after pushing all the dirty dishes aside to make room. Both of us working in such smooth seamless tandem I've barely given the last bottle to her, when I'm already bending down to retrieve the "safe" bottles from my bag. Knowing they're safe since Damen last supplied me a few weeks ago, long before Roman appeared. Intending to place them right where the others once were, so Damen will never suspect I was here.

"So what should I do with these old ones?" Ava asks. "Throw them out? Or save them for evidence?"

And just as I look up to answer, Damen walks through the side door and says, "What the hell are you doing in my kitchen?"

thirty-four

I freeze. Two bottles of untainted brew dangling halfway between the fridge and me. Realizing I'd been so preoccupied with thinking *about* Damen that I forgot to tune in and sense if he was anywhere near.

Ava gapes, her face displaying the same wide-eyed, openmouthed mask of sheer panic I'm trying to hide. Then I look at Damen and clear my throat before saying, "It's not what you think!"

Which is pretty much the lamest, most ridiculous thing I could've said since it's *exactly* what he thinks. Ava and I broke into his house so we could tamper with his food supply. Pure and simple.

He drops his bag and moves toward me, his eyes focused on mine. "You have no idea what I'm thinking."

Oh, but I do. Wincing at the horrible thoughts scrolling through his head, his mental accusation of: *Stalker! Freak!* And things far worse than that.

"And how the hell did you even get in here?" he asks, glancing between us.

"Um, Sheila let me in," I say, not quite sure what to do with the bottle I still hold in my hand.

A vein throbs in his temple as he shakes his head and clenches his fists, and I realize I've never seen him this angry before, didn't even know he was capable of it, and feel pretty cruddy to know I inspired it.

"I'll deal with Sheila," he says, his temper barely in check. "What I meant was, what are you doing in *here*? In my *house*? Messing around in my fridge—" His eyes narrow. "What the hell do you think you're up to?"

I glance at Ava, embarrassed to have her witness my one true love talking to me in this way.

"And what's up with her?" He points at Ava. "You bring your party psychic along to cast some kind of spell?"

"You remember that?" I lower the bottle to my side. I'd been wondering what he might've retained from our past, and even though it's dumb, the fact that he remembers meeting Ava fills me with hope. "You remember Halloween night?" I whisper, recalling the first time we kissed, out by the pool, both of us dressed in perfectly matching costumes of Marie Antoinette and her lover, Count Fersen, without having planned it.

"Yeah, I remember." He shakes his head. "And I hate to break it to you, but it was a moment of weakness that'll *never* happen again. One you took far too seriously. And believe me, if I'd known what a freak you'd turn out to be, I wouldn't have bothered. It wasn't worth it."

I swallow hard and blink back the tears. Feeling empty, hollowed out, my insides excavated and tossed aside, as any chance of reclaiming our love—the only thing that makes this particular life worth living—slips out of reach. And even though I remind myself that those are Roman's words not his—that the real Damen isn't capable of treating *anyone* like this—it doesn't make it hurt any less.

"Damen, *please*," I finally manage. "I know it looks bad. Really, I do. But I can explain. You see, we're only trying to *help* you."

He looks at me, his gaze so derisive it fills me with shame. But I force myself to continue, knowing I at least have to try. "*Someone* is trying to poison you." I swallow, meeting his eyes. "Someone you know."

He shakes his head, not buying a word of it. Convinced that I'm stark raving mental and should be locked up immediately.

"And this *person* responsible for poisoning me, this *person* I happen to know, would that, by any chance, be *you*?" He takes another step toward me. "Because *you're* the one breaking into my home. *You're* the one getting all up in my fridge and messing with my drinks. I think the evidence speaks for itself."

I shake my head, talking past the searing heat in my throat when I say, "I know how it looks, but you've *got* to believe me! It's all true, I'm not making it up!"

He takes another step closer, advancing on me in a way so intentional, so slow and deliberate, it's like he's stalking his prey. So I decide to just go for it, to let it all out. I mean, I've got nothing to lose anyway.

"It's Roman, okay?" I suck in my breath, watching his expression change from accusatory to outraged. "Your new friend Roman is—" I glance at Ava, knowing I can't say what Roman *actually* is—an immortal rogue set on killing Damen for some reason I've yet to determine. But it's not like it matters anyway. Damen has no memory of Drina or being immortal, he's so far gone he'd never understand.

"Get out," he says, the look in his eyes so cold it chills me more than the air flowing from his fridge.

"Get the hell out before I call the police."

I peer at Ava, seeing her pour the tampered contents down the drain the second he makes the threat. Then I gaze at Damen, grasping his phone, his index finger already pressing the nine, followed by the one, and then—

I have to stop him. There's no way I can allow him to complete that call. No way I can risk getting the police involved. So I stare into his eyes, even though he refuses to look at me. I just focus all of my energy on him, my thoughts reaching out to him, attempting to meld and influence. Showering him with the most compassionate loving white light along with a bouquet of telepathic red tulips. All the while whispering, "No need for trouble." I slowly back away. "You don't need to call anyone, we're leaving right now." Holding my breath as he stares at the phone, not understanding why he can't seem to press the last *one*.

He lifts his gaze, and for the briefest moment, just a flicker really, the old Damen's returned. Looking at me in the way that he used to—sending a delicious warm tingle all over my skin. And even though it's gone just as soon as it appeared—I'll happily settle for whatever I get.

He tosses his phone onto the counter and shakes his head. And knowing we'd better move fast before my influence ends, I grab my bag and head for the door. Turning just as he empties his cupboards and fridge of every last bottle of juice. Removing their caps and pouring their contents right down the drain, convinced they're not safe for consumption, now that I've tampered with them.

thirty-five

"What will happen now that he no longer has the drink? Will he get better or worse?"

That's the question Ava asked as soon as we got in my car. And the truth is, I had no idea how to answer. I still don't. So I didn't say anything. I just shrugged.

"I'm so sorry," she said, clasping her hands in her lap, looking at me in a way that proved her sincerity. "I feel responsible."

But I just shook my head. Because even though it *was* kind of her fault for wasting so much time when she insisted on touring his house, I'm the one who came up with the brilliant idea of breaking in. I'm the one who got so caught up in the task at hand I forgot to keep my eye on the door. So if anyone's to blame, I am.

But even worse than getting caught is knowing that in Damen's eyes, I've gone from being some weird freaky stalker chick, to a pathetic, delusional loser. Fully convinced I tried to spike his red brew with some crazy, black magic, voodoo concoction in hopes that he'd like me again.

Because that's exactly what Stacia convinced him of just after he relayed the story.

And that's exactly what he's chosen to believe.

In fact, it's what the whole school believes. Including a few of my teachers.

Which makes going to school an even more miserable experience than it was before. Because now, not only must I suffer through endless taunts of *Spaz! Loo-ser!* and *Witch!* but I've also been asked to stay after class by not one but now two of my teachers.

Though I can't say Mr. Robins's request came as much of a surprise. I mean, since we'd already had a little talk about my supposed inability to move on and build a life for myself post-Damen, I can't say I was all that shocked when he kept me after class in order to discuss the *incident*.

What did surprise me was the way I reacted. How quickly I resorted to doing the one thing I thought I'd never do—I lawyered up.

"Excuse me," I said, cutting him off before he could finish. Not interested in any well-meaning though ultimately boundary-crossing "relationship advice" my newly divorced, semi-alcoholic English teacher was prepared to dish out. "But the last time I checked this was all just a *rumor*. An *alleged* event with no evidence to support it." I looked at him, meeting his eyes despite the fact I'd just lied. I mean, while Ava and I were pretty much caught red-handed, it's not like Damen took a picture. It's not like there's yet another video of me making the YouTube circuit. "So unless I'm officially charged and tried—" I paused to clear my throat, partly for dramatic effect and partly because I couldn't believe what I was about to say next. "I shall remain innocent until proven guilty." He balked, preparing to speak, but I wasn't finished. "So unless you need to discuss my behavior in this class, which you and I both know is exemplary, or my grades, which happen to be more than exemplary, unless you're interested in discussing either one of those things—I'm thinking we're pretty much done here."

Fortunately, Mr. Munoz is a little easier. Though that's probably because I'm the one who approaches *him*. Thinking my Renaissance-obsessed history teacher is just the man to help me track down the name of a particular herb I need to make the elixir.

Last night, when I tried to research it on Google, I realized I had no idea what to put in the search box. And with Sabine still watching me like a hawk even though I eat and drink and act as normal as I can, slipping off to Summerland, even for a few minutes, was out of the question.

Which makes Mr. Munoz my last hope—or at least my most immediate hope. Because yesterday, when Damen tossed all of those bottles down the drain, there went half of my already meager supply. Which means I need to make more. Lots more. Not only to keep up my strength between now and the time when I leave, but I also need plenty left over for Damen's recovery.

And since he never got around to giving me the recipe, all I have to go on is what I saw on that crystal when I watched his father prepare the brew, naming all of the ingredients out loud, before stopping to whisper the very last one in his son's ear, speaking so softly there was no way I could hear.

But Mr. Munoz turns out to be no help at all. And after futzing around with a bunch of old books and coming up with zilch, he looks at me and says, "Ever, I'm afraid I can't find the answer to this, but since you're already here—"

I raise my hand, blocking his words from going any further than they already have. And even though I'm not proud of the way I handled Mr. Robins, if Munoz doesn't back off, he'll get the same speech as well.

"Trust me, I know where you're going." I nod, my eyes right on his. "But you've got it all wrong. It's not what you think—" I stop, realizing that as far as denials go, this one is turning out to be incredibly lame. I mean, I just alluded to the fact that while it *might've* occurred—it didn't occur in the *way* that he thinks. Which basically amounts to me pleading guilty—but with extenuating circumstances.

I shake my head, inwardly rolling my eyes at myself, thinking: *Good one, Ever. Keep it up and you will need Sabine to represent you.*

And then he looks at me, and I look at him, and we both shake our heads, mutually agreeing to leave it at that.

But just as I grab my bag and start to leave, he reaches toward me, his hand touching my sleeve, when he says, "Hang in there. It'll all be okay."

And that's all it takes. That simple gesture is all I need to *see* that Sabine has been frequenting Starbucks, just about every single day. The two of them enjoying a tentative flirtation that, while it (thankfully) hasn't moved past a smile, Munoz is definitely anticipating the day when it will. And even though I know I have to do whatever I can to stop them from, God forbid, *dating,* at the moment, I don't have time to deal with it.

I shake off his energy and head out the door, barely making it into the hall before Roman approaches, adjusting his stride so it's timed right to mine. Leering at me when he says, "Was Munoz any help?"

I keep going, wincing when his cool breath hits my cheek.

"You're running out of time," he says, his voice as soft and soothing as a lover's embrace. "It's all moving rather quickly now, wouldn't you agree? And before you know it, it'll all be over. And then—well—then there's just you and me."

I shrug, knowing that's not exactly true. I viewed the past. I saw what happened in that Florentine church. And if I'm not mistaken, there are six immortal orphans quite possibly still roaming the earth. Six little urchins who could be just about anywhere by now—providing they made it. But if Roman's unaware of that fact, well, it's hardly my place to inform him.

So I gaze into his eyes, resisting the lure of those deep navy blues, when I say, "How lucky for me."

"And *me*." He smiles. "You're going to need someone to help mend your broken heart. Someone who understands you. Someone who knows just *what* you really are." He trails his finger down the length of my arm, his touch so shockingly cold, even through the cotton of my sleeve, I quickly pull away.

"You know *nothing* about me," I say, my eyes raking his face. "You've underestimated me. If I were you, I'd be a little more cautious about celebrating so soon. You're a long way from winning this one."

And even though I meant it as a threat, my voice is far too shaky to be taken seriously. So I pick up the pace, leaving his mocking laughter behind as I head for my lunch table where Miles and Haven are waiting.

I slide onto the bench, smiling as I glance between them. It feels like so long since we last hung out, the sight of them sitting here now makes me ridiculously happy.

"Hey you guys," I say, unable to keep the grin off my face, watching as they glance first at me, then at each other, nodding their heads in perfect unison as though this moment was rehearsed.

Miles sips his soda, a drink he never would've gone near before. His bright pink nails tapping the sides of the can as my stomach fills with dread. Debating whether or not to tune in to their thoughts, knowing it'll prepare me for whatever reason they're here, but deciding against it since I'd rather not hear it twice.

"We need to talk," Miles says. "It's about Damen."

"No," Haven cuts in, shooting Miles a look before retrieving her bag of carrot sticks from her purse, the zero-calorie signature lunch of the girls of the A-list. "It's about Damen and *you*."

"What's there to talk about? I mean, he's with Stacia, and I'm— dealing."

They glance at each other, exchanging a look that's loaded but brief. "But *are* you dealing?" Miles asks. "Because seriously, Ever, breaking into his house and messing with his food supply is pretty twisted. Not exactly the actions of someone who's moving on with their life—"

"So, what? You guys just believe every rumor you hear? All those months of friendship, all those times you hung at my house, and you think I'm capable of that—" I roll my eyes and shake my head, refusing to go any further. I mean, if all I managed to get out of Damen was the most fleeting moment of recognition before it was replaced with disdain, when we have a bond that dates back centuries—what can I hope to accomplish with Miles and Haven whom I've known for less than a year?

"Well, I really don't see why Damen would make all that up," Haven says, her eyes on mine, her gaze so harsh and judgmental I realize she didn't actually come here to help. Because while she may act as though she's got only my best interests at heart, the truth is, she's enjoying my fall. After losing Damen to me, after seeing how Roman continues to chase me even after she's made her interest clear, she's happy to see me knocked down. And the only reason she's deigning to sit by me now is so she can look me in the eye while she gloats.

I gaze down at the table, surprised by how much it hurts. But I try not to judge or hold it against her. I know all too well what it's like to feel jealous, and there's nothing rational about it.

"You need to let it go," Miles says, sipping his drink, though his eyes never leave mine. "You need to let go and move on."

"*Everyone* knows you're stalking him," Haven says, covering her mouth with nails painted the color of ballet slippers as opposed to her usual black. "*Everyone* knows you broke into his house—*twice*—that we know of. Seriously, you're out of control, you're acting insane."

I gaze down at the table, wondering how much longer the assault will continue.

"Anyway, as your friends, we just want to convince you that you need to let go. You need to back off and move on. Because the truth is, your behavior is creepy, not to mention . . ."

Haven drones on, hitting all the bullet points I'm sure they agreed upon before they approached me. But I stopped listening after she said *as your friends*. Wanting to hang on to that and reject all the rest, even though it's no longer true.

I shake my head and look up, seeing Roman sitting at the lunch table with his gaze fixed on mine. Tapping his watch, then pointing at Damen in a way so ominous, so threatening, I spring from my seat. Leaving Haven's voice fading behind me like a distant hum as I race for my car, chastising myself for wasting my time with this stuff when there are far more important things to be done.

thirty-six

I'm through with school. Done with subjecting myself to that un-bearable gauntlet of torture each day. I mean, what's the point of going when I'm getting nowhere with Damen, taunted by Roman, and lectured by teachers and pseudo well-meaning ex-friends? Be-sides, if things work out in the way that I hope, then I'll soon be back at my old school in Oregon, living my life as though this never existed. So there's really no point in putting myself through that again.

I head down Broadway, weaving my way through pedestrian traffic before moving on to the canyon, hoping to go someplace quiet where I can make the portal appear without scaring any un-suspecting shoppers. Not remembering until I've already parked that this is the same place where my first showdown with Drina occurred—a showdown that resulted in my first visit to Summer-land when Damen provided the way.

I hunker down in my seat, imagining that golden veil of light hovering before me and landing right in front of the Great Hall of Learning. Barely taking the time to notice its magnificent ever-changing façade before rushing into the grand marble hall with my thoughts focused on two things:

Is there an antidote to save Damen?

And how do I locate the secret herb, the final ingredient needed to pre-pare the elixir?

Repeating the questions again and again as I wait for the door-way to the akashic records to appear—

But getting nothing.

No globes. No crystal sheets. No white circular rooms or hybrid TVs.

Nothing. Nada. Nien.

Just a soft voice behind me saying, "It's too late."

I turn, expecting to see Romy but finding Rayne there instead. Following behind as I roll my eyes and make for the door, eager to put some distance between us as she echoes those same words again.

I don't have time for this. I don't have time to decipher a bunch of cryptic nonsense from the world's creepiest twin. Because even though there's no concept of time in Summerland where every-thing happens in a constant state of *now*, I know for a fact that the time I spend here will be duly noted back home. Which means I need to keep going, keep moving forward, heading down the street as fast as I can until her voice turns to a whisper. Knowing I need to save Damen before I turn back time and go home. And if the an-swers aren't here—then I'll look somewhere else.

I start running. Turning into the alleyway just as I'm overcome by such sudden excruciating pain, I crumple to the ground. My fin-gers clamped to my temples, my head aching as though it's being stabbed from all sides, as a swirl of images unfold in my mind. A series of sketches, one turning into the next like pages in a book, followed by a detailed description of what it includes. And I've just made it to the third page when I realize these are instructions for making the antidote to save Damen, including herbs planted during the new moon, rare crystals and minerals I've never heard of, silk pouches embroidered by Tibetan monks—all of it needing to be carefully assembled in a series of very precise steps before soaking up the energy of the next full moon.

And just after I'm shown the exact herb needed to complete the immortal elixir, my head clears as though it never happened. So I reach for my bag, fumbling for a scrap of paper and a pen, jotting down the final step when Ava appears.

"I made the portal!" she says, her face lighting up as her eyes meet mine. "I didn't think I could do it, but this morning when I sat down for my usual meditation, I thought: What could it hurt to give it a try? And the next thing I knew—"

"You've been here since *morning*?" I say, taking in her beautiful dress, designer shoes, heavy gold bracelets, and jewel-adorned fingers.

"There's no time in Summerland," she scolds.

"Maybe so, but back home it's past noon," I tell her, watching as she shakes her head and frowns, refusing to get bogged down in the tedious rules of the earth plane.

"Who cares? What could I possibly be missing? A long line of clients wanting me to tell them they're about to become extremely rich and famous despite all evidence to the contrary?" She closes her eyes and sighs. "I'm tired of it, Ever. Tired of the grind. But here, everything's so wonderful, I think I might stay!"

"You can't," I say, quickly, automatically, though I'm not sure it's true.

"Why not?" She shrugs, lifting her arms to the sky and twirling around and around. "Why can't I stay here? Give me one good reason."

"Because—" I start, wishing I could just leave it at that, but since she's not a child I'm forced to come up with something better. "Because it's not right," I finish, hoping she'll hear me. "You have work to do. We all have work to do. And hiding out here is like— *cheating.*"

"Says who?" She squints. "You telling me *all* of these people are dead?"

I gaze around, taking in the crowded sidewalks, the long line for the movie theaters and karaoke bars, realizing I have no idea how to answer. I mean, just how many of them are like Ava—tired, fed-up, disillusioned souls who've found their way here and decided to drop out from the earth plane and never return? And how many of them have died and refused to cross over like Riley once did?

I look at Ava again, knowing I've no right to tell her what to do with her life, especially when I remember what I've chosen to do with mine.

Then I reach for her hand and smile when I say, "Well, at the moment, *I* need you. Tell me everything you know about astrology."

thirty-seven

"So?" I lean toward Ava, elbows pressed against the tabletop, trying to keep her focused on me as opposed to the sights and sounds of Saint-Germain.

"I know that I'm an Aries." She shrugs, her eyes preferring the River Seine, the Pont Neuf, the Eiffel Tower, the Arc de Triomphe, and the Notre Dame cathedral (which, in this version of Paris, are all lined up in a row), to me.

"Is that it?" I stir my cappuccino, wondering why I even bothered to order it from the cartoonlike *garçon* with the curlicue mustache, white shirt, and black vest, since it's not like I have any intention of drinking it.

She sighs, turning to look at me when she says, "Ever, can't you just relax and enjoy the view? When was the last time you were in Paris anyway?"

"Never," I say, rolling my eyes in a way she can't miss. "I've never been to Paris. And I hate to break it to you, Ava, but *this*—" I take a moment to gesture around, pointing at the Louvre, which is placed right next to Printemps department store, which is next to the Musée d'Orsay, "—is *not* Paris. *This* is like some cranked up Disney version of Paris. Like, you've taken a pile of travel brochures and French postcards, and scenes from that adorable cartoon movie *Ratatouille*, mixed them all together and *voilà*, created *this*. I mean, did you *see* the waiter? Did you notice how his tray kept tipping and twirling but never once fell? I doubt the *real* Paris has waiters like that."

But even though I'm acting like the biggest party pooper ever, Ava just laughs. Swinging her wavy auburn hair over her shoulder as she says, "Well, for your information, this is *exactly* as I remember it. Maybe these monuments weren't all lined up in a row, but it's so much nicer like this. I did attend the Sorbonne you know. In fact, did I ever mention the time when I—"

"That's great, Ava. Really," I say. "And I'd love to hear all about it if I wasn't *running out of time!* So, what I meant to ask was, what do you know about astrology or astronomy or whatever it is that involves the various moon cycles?"

She breaks off a piece of baguette and butters the side, saying, "Can you be more specific?"

I reach into my pocket and retrieve the folded-up paper I scribbled on right after my vision, squinting at her as I say, "Okay, what exactly is a new moon and when does it occur?"

She blows on her coffee, peering at me when she says, "The new moon occurs when both the sun and moon are in conjunction. Meaning that when you're looking at it from the earth plane, they both seem to occupy the same part of the sky. And because of that, the moon doesn't reflect the light of the sun, which also means it can't be seen because its dark side is facing the earth."

"But what does it *mean*? Is it symbolic of something?"

She nods, breaking off another piece of baguette when she says, "It's a symbol for new beginnings. You know, rejuvenation, renewal, hope—stuff like that. It's also a good time to make changes, drop bad habits—or even bad relationships." She gives me a pointed look.

But I just ignore that and move on, knowing she's referring to Damen and me, having no idea that I'm not just planning to end it,

I'm planning to *erase* it. Because as much as I love him, as much as I can't imagine a future without him, I truly believe it's the best thing for everyone. None of this ever should've happened. *We* never should've happened. It's unnatural, not right, and now it's my job to put it all back.

"So when does that happen in relation to the full moon?" I ask, watching as she covers her mouth when she chews.

"The full moon occurs around two weeks after the new moon. It's when the moon reflects the maximum amount of light from the sun, which, from the earth plane, makes it appear full. When in reality, it's always full since it's not like it goes anywhere. Oh, and as far as symbols go? You want to know that right?" She smiles. "The full moon is all about abundance, completeness, a sort of ripening of things into their full powers. And since the moon's energy is strongest at this point, it's also full of magick power."

I nod, trying to digest everything she just said, and forming the smallest inkling of understanding for why these phases are so important for my plan.

"All the moon's phases are symbolic of something." Ava shrugs. "The moon plays a powerful role in ancient lore and is said to control the tides. And since our bodies are mostly made up of water, some say it controls us too. Did you know that the word *lunatic* comes from the Latin word for moon, which is *luna*? Oh, and don't forget the werewolf legend—it's all about the full moon!"

Inwardly, I roll my eyes. There are no such things as werewolves, vampires, or demons—only immortals, and the immortal rogues who are determined to kill them.

"Can I ask why you're asking all this?" she says, draining the last of her espresso and pushing the cup aside.

"In a minute," I say, my words clipped, terse, far less conversational than hers. But unlike her, I'm not vacationing in Paris, I'm merely tolerating the view to get to the answers I need. "One last thing, what's so special about a full moon during *l'heure bleue*, or blue hour as it's called?"

She looks at me, her eyes wide, her voice breathless when she says, "Do you mean the blue moon?"

I shrug, remembering how the moon was so blue in the image it practically blended with the sky. Then figuring it was somehow symbolic of an actual blue moon with the way its color pulsated and shimmered, I say, "Yeah. But the blue moon specifically during the blue hour, what do you know about that?"

She takes a deep breath, gazing into the distance as she says, "The mainstream thought is that the second full moon in a month constitutes a blue moon. But there's another, more esoteric school of thought that says the *true* blue moon occurs when there are two full moons occurring not necessarily within the same month, but within the same *astrological sign*. It's regarded as a very holy day, one when the connection between the dimensions is very potent, making it an ideal time for meditation, prayer, and mystical journeys. It's said that if you harness the blue moon energy during *l'heure bleue*, then all sorts of magick can occur. The only limitations, as usual, are your own."

She looks at me, wondering what I'm up to, but I'm not ready to share that just yet. Then she shakes her head and says, "But just so you know, a genuine blue moon is very rare, only coming around every three to five years."

My stomach twists as my hands grip the sides of my chair. "And do you know when the next blue moon will occur?" While thinking: *Please let it be soon, please let it be soon!*

Feeling like I'm about to puke *and* keel over simultaneously when she shakes her head and says, "I have no idea."

But of course! The most important thing I need to know—is the one thing she doesn't know.

"Though I know how we can find out." She smiles.

I shake my head, just about to inform her that as far as I can tell, my access to the akashic records has just been revoked, when she closes her eyes and a moment later a silver iMac appears.

"Google, anyone?" She laughs, pushing it toward me.

thirty-eight

Even though I felt like an idiot the second Ava manifested that laptop (I mean, *duh*, why didn't I think of that?), we did get our answer fairly quick.

Though unfortunately, it wasn't the good news I was hoping for.

In fact, it was anything but.

Just when everything was coming together, seeming like it was destined to be—it all fell apart the second I learned that the blue moon, that rarest of full moons that only comes around every three to five years, which also just so happens to be my one and only window for time travel, has its next scheduled appearance—*tomorrow*.

"I still can't believe it," I say, climbing out of my car while Ava feeds the meter from a neat stack of quarters cupped in the palm of her hand. "I thought it was just another full moon, I didn't know there was a difference, or that they're so rare. I mean, what am I supposed to *do*?"

She snaps her wallet shut and looks at me. "Well, from what I can see, you have three choices."

I press my lips together, not sure I want to hear any of them.

"You can do nothing at all and just sit back and watch while everything you love and care about completely falls apart, you can choose to handle just one thing at the cost of all the others, *or* you can tell me just exactly what is going on here so I can see if I can help."

I take a deep breath and look at her standing before me, back in her usual outfit of faded jeans, silver rings, a white cotton tunic, and brown leather flip-flops. Always there, always available, always willing to help me, even when I don't realize I need it.

Even back when I was being dismissive (and if I'm gonna be honest—more than a little mean), Ava was right there, waiting for me to come around, never once holding my bad attitude against me, never once turning her back or shunning me in the way I shunned her. It's like she's been standing by all this time, waiting to step in as my psychic big sister. And now, she's pretty much the only one I have left—the only one I can count on—the only one who comes close to knowing the *real* me—including *most* of my secrets.

And in light of everything I just learned, I've no choice but to tell her. There's no way I can go it alone like I'd hoped.

"Okay." I nod, convincing myself it's not just the right thing to do, but the *only* thing to do. "Here's what I need you to do."

And as we head down the street, I tell her what I saw that day on the crystal. Managing to explain as much as I can while avoiding the *I* word—honoring my promise to Damen that I'll never divulge our immortality. Telling Ava that Damen will need the antidote so that he can get better, followed by his "special red energy drink" so he can rebuild his strength. Explaining that I'm faced with a choice between being with the love of my life, or saving four lives that were never meant to end.

So by the time we're standing outside the shop where she works, the shop I've passed many times before but swore I'd never enter— she looks at me, her mouth opening as if to say something, before clamping shut again. Repeating this scenario a few more times until she's finally able to mumble, "But *tomorrow!* Ever, can you leave that soon?"

I shrug, my stomach sinking when I hear it spoken out loud. But knowing I can't wait another three to five years, I nod with more assurance than I feel when I look at her and say, "And that's exactly why I need you to help me with the antidote, then find a way to get it to him along with the elix—" I pause, hoping I haven't aroused her suspicions, trying to recover when I say, "—*that red energy drink*— so that he can get better. I mean, now that you know how to get inside his house, I'm thinking you can find a way to, I don't know, spike his drink or something," I say, knowing it sounds like the worst plan *ever*, but determined to see that it works. "And then, when he's better—when the old Damen returns—you can explain everything that's happened, and give him the—the red drink."

She looks at me with an expression so conflicted I'm not sure how to read it, so I forge straight ahead. "I know it probably seems like I'm choosing against him—but I'm not. *Really* I'm not. In fact, there's a good chance that none of this will even be necessary. There's a good chance that when I go back to how I was, everything else will go back too."

"Is that what you saw?" she asks, her voice soft, gentle.

I shake my head. "No, it's just a theory, though I think it makes sense. I mean, I can't imagine it any other way. So all of this stuff I'm telling you now is just a precaution since it won't even be necessary. Which means you won't remember this conversation since it will be like it never occurred. In fact, you won't have any recollection of having known me. But just in case I'm wrong—which I'm pretty sure I'm not—but just in case I am, I need to have a plan in place— you know, just in case," I mumble, wondering who I'm trying to convince, me or her.

She grabs hold of my hand, her eyes full of compassion when she says, "You're doing the right thing. And you're lucky. Not many people get the chance to go back."

I look at her, my lips curving into a grin. "Not *many*?"

"Well, no one I can think of offhand." She smiles.

But even though we both laugh, when I look at her again my voice is serious when I say, "Seriously, Ava, I can't bear for anything to happen to him. I mean, I'd—I'd just *die* if I somehow found out that it did—and that it was my fault . . ."

She squeezes my hand and opens the shop door, leading me inside as she whispers, "Don't worry. You can trust me."

I follow her past shelves crowded with books, a wall of CDs, and an entire corner dedicated to angel figurines, before passing a machine that claims to photograph auras as we head for a counter where an older woman with a long gray braid is reading a book.

"I didn't realize you were on the schedule today?" She sets down her novel and glances between us.

"I'm not." Ava smiles. "But my friend Ever here—" She nods her head toward me. "She needs the back room."

The woman studies me, obviously trying to glimpse my aura and get a feel for my energy, then shooting Ava a questioning look when she comes away empty.

But Ava just smiles and nods in consent, signaling that I'm worthy of access to the "back room," whatever that is.

"Ever?" the woman says, her fingers creeping toward her neck, worrying the turquoise pendant that hangs at her collarbone.

A stone that, as I recently learned in my brief study of minerals and crystals on the iMac in Summerland, has been used for amulets meant to heal and protect for hundreds of years. And with the way she just said my name, and by the suspicious look on her face, it's not like I need to access her mind to know that she's wondering if she might need protection from me.

She hesitates, glancing between Ava and me, then focusing solely on me as she says, "I'm Lina."

That's it. No handshake, no welcoming hug. She just states her name and then makes for the door, flipping the sign that hangs there from *OPEN!* to *BE BACK IN 10!* Then motioning for us to follow her down a short hall with a shiny purple door at the end.

"Can I ask what this is about?" She rummages in her pocket for a set of keys, still undecided as to whether or not she'll be letting us in.

Ava nods at me, signaling that it's my turn to take it from here. So I clear my throat and cram my hand into the pocket of my recently manifested jeans whose hems, thankfully, still reach the floor. Retrieving the crumpled-up piece of paper as I say, "I um, I need a few things." Wincing when Lina snatches it out of my hand and looks it over. Stopping to lift a brow, grunt something unintelligible under her breath, and scrutinize me some more.

And just when it seems she's about to turn me away, she thrusts the list back into my hand, unlocks the door, and waves us both into a room that I didn't expect.

I mean, when Ava told me this was the place that would have what I need, I was more than a little nervous. I was sure I'd be thrust into some creepy hidden basement filled with all manner of strange, scary, ritualistic stuff, like vials of cat blood, severed bat wings, shrunken heads, Voodoo dolls—stuff like you see in movies or on TV. But this room is nothing like that. In fact, it pretty much looks like your average, more or less well-organized storage closet. Well, except for the bright violet walls punctuated by hand-carved totems and masks. Oh, and the goddess paintings propped against the overstuffed shelves sagging with heavy old tomes and stone deities. But the file cabinet is pretty standard issue. And when she unlocks a cupboard and starts rummaging around, I try to peek over her shoulder, but I can't see a thing until she's handing me a stone that seems wrong in every way.

"Moonstone," she says, noting the confusion on my face.

I stare at it, knowing it doesn't look like it should, and even though I can't explain it, something about it feels off. And not wanting to offend her since I've no doubt she wouldn't hesitate to evict me, I swallow hard, screw up my courage, and say, "Um, I need one that's raw and unpolished, in its absolute purest form—this one just seems a little too smooth and shiny for my needs."

She nods, almost imperceptibly, but still it's there. Just the briefest tilt of her head and curl of her lips before she replaces it with the stone that I asked for.

"That's it," I say, knowing I just passed her test. Gazing at a moonstone that's not nearly as shiny or pretty but will hopefully do what it's intended to, which is aid in new beginnings. "And then I'm gonna need a quartz crystal bowl, one that's been tuned to the seventh chakra, a red silk pouch embroidered by Tibetan monks, four polished rose quartz crystals, one small star—no, staur-o-lite? Is that how you say it?" I look at her just in time to see her nod. "Oh, and the biggest raw zoisite you've got."

And when Lina just stands there with her hands on her hips, I know she's wondering how all of these seemingly random items can possibly fit together.

"Oh, and a chunk of turquoise, probably like the size of the one you're wearing," I say, motioning toward her neck.

She looks me over, giving me a crisp, perfunctory nod, before turning her back and gathering the crystals. Wrapping them up so casually you'd think she was bagging groceries at Whole Foods.

"Oh, and here's a list of herbs," I say, reaching into my other pocket and retrieving a crumpled sheet of paper, which I then hand to her. "Preferably planted during the new moon and tended by blind nuns in India," I add, amazed when she just takes the list and nods without flinching.

"Can I ask what this is for?" she asks, her eyes on mine.

But I just shake my head. I was barely able to tell Ava, and she's a good friend. So there's no way I'm telling this lady, no matter how grandmotherly she may seem.

"Um, I'd rather not say." I shrug, hoping she'll respect that and get on with it since manifesting these items won't work, it's imperative they spring from their original source.

We look at each other, our gazes fixed, unwavering. And even though I plan to stand my ground for as long as it takes, it's not long before she breaks away and starts riffling through the filing cabinet, her fingers flipping past hundreds of packets as I say, "Oh, and one more thing."

Searching through my backpack for my sketch of the rare, hard-to-find herb that was oft used in Renaissance Florence. The final ingredient needed to bring the elixir to life. Handing it to her as I ask, "Does this look familiar?"

thirty-nine

With all of our ingredients gathered—well, everything but the spring water, extra-virgin olive oil, long white tapered candles (which, oddly, Lina was out of, considering they were pretty much the most normal thing I requested), orange peel, and the photo of Damen I didn't expect her to have—we return to my car.

And I'm just unlocking the door when Ava says, "I think I'll walk home from here since I'm just around the corner."

"You sure?"

She spreads her arms wide as though embracing the night. Her lips curving into a grin as she says, "It's so nice out, I just want to enjoy it."

"As beautiful as Summerland?" I ask, wondering what's brought on this sudden fit of happiness, considering how serious she was in Lina's back room.

She laughs, her head thrown back, her pale neck exposed, leveling her gaze on mine when she says, "Don't worry. I've no plans to drop out of society and move there full time. It's just nice to have the access when I need a little escape."

"Just be careful not to visit too much," I tell her, echoing the same warning Damen once gave to me. "Summerland's addictive," I add, watching as she hugs her arms to her body and shrugs, knowing

I've wasted my words since it's obvious she'll be back as soon and as often as she can.

"So, you've got everything you need?"

I nod and lean against the car door. "And the rest I'll pick up on my way home."

"And you're sure you're ready?" She looks at me, her face drawn and serious again. "You know, leaving all of this? *Leaving Damen?*"

I swallow hard, preferring not to think about that. I'd rather keep busy, focus on one task at a time, until tomorrow comes around and it's time to say good-bye.

"Because once something's done, it can't be undone."

I shrug, meeting her gaze as I say, "Apparently that's not true." Watching as she tilts her head to the side, her auburn hair blowing into her face before she captures the strands and tucks them back behind her ear.

"But what you're returning to—well, you realize you'll be normal again. You won't have access to such knowledge, you'll be completely unaware—are you sure you want to return to all that?"

I gaze down at the ground, kicking a small rock instead of looking at her. "Listen, I'm not gonna lie. All of this is happening so much quicker than I expected—and I hoped to have more time to—to finalize things. But ultimately—yeah, I think I'm ready." I pause, replaying the words I just said and knowing they didn't convey what I meant. "I mean, I *know* I'm ready. In fact, I'm *definitely* ready. Because putting everything back in its place and returning it to the way it should be—well—it feels like the right thing to do, you know?"

And even though I didn't mean for it to happen, my voice rose at the end, making it sound more like a question than the statement I intended it to be. So I shake my head and say, "What I meant was, it's absolutely, positively, one hundred percent the right thing to do." Adding, "I mean, why else was I granted access to those records?"

Ava looks at me, her gaze steady, unwavering.

"Besides, do you have any idea how excited I am to be with my family again?"

She reaches for me, hugging me tightly to her chest, whispering, "I'm so happy for you. Really I am. And even though I'm going to miss you, I'm honored to know you trust me enough to finish the job."

"I've no idea how to thank you," I murmur, my throat feeling tight.

But she just smooths her hand over my hair when she says, "Believe me, you already have."

I pull away and gaze all around, taking in this glorious night in this charming beach town, hardly believing I'm about to walk away from it all. Turning my back on Sabine, Miles, Haven, Ava—Damen—all of it—everything—as though it never existed.

"You okay?" she asks, her voice gentle and smooth as she reads my expression.

I nod, clearing my throat and motioning toward the small purple paper bag at her foot, the shop's name of MYSTICS & MOONBEAMS printed in gold. "You sure you've got it all clear, about how to handle the herbs? You need to keep them in a cool dark place, and you don't crush them or add them to the—*red juice*—until the very last day—the *third* day."

"Don't worry." She laughs. "What's not in here," she picks up the bag and clutches it to her chest, "is in here." She points at her temple and smiles.

I nod, blinking back tears I refuse to indulge, knowing this is only the beginning of a series of good-byes. "I'll stop by your house tomorrow and drop off the rest," I say. "Just in case you end up needing it, though I doubt that you will." Then I slide into my car, start the engine, and pull away. Heading down Ocean without waving good-bye, without once looking back. Knowing my only choice now is to look toward the future and focus on that.

• • •

After stopping by the store to pick up the rest of the items, I haul the bags up to my room and dump their contents onto my desk. Riffling through piles of oils and herbs and candles, eager to get to the crystals since they're going to require the most work. All of them needing to be individually programmed according to type, before being placed in the embroidered silk pouch and set outside where they can absorb as much moonlight as possible, while I manifest a mortar and pestle (which I forgot to pick up at the store, but since it's only a *tool* and not an actual *ingredient*, I figure it should be okay to just manifest one), so I can pulverize some of those herbs and get them all boiling in some (also manifested) beakers, before mixing in all of the other irons and minerals and colorful powders that Lina poured into small glass jars which she carefully labeled. All of this needing to be completed in seven precise steps that commence with the ringing of the crystal bowl that's been specifically tuned to vibrate to the seventh chakra so it may provide inspiration, perception beyond space and time, and a whole host of other things that connect with the divine. And as I look at the heap of ingredients piled high before me, I can't help but feel a small surge of excitement, knowing it's finally all coming together after loads of false starts.

To say I was worried about being able to find this stuff all in one place is putting it mildly. It was such an odd and varied list, I wasn't even sure if those items existed, which kind of made me feel doomed before I'd started. But Ava assured me not only that Lina could deliver but that she could also be trusted. And while I'm still not so sure about that last part, it's not like I had anywhere else to turn.

But the way Lina kept squinting at me, her gaze narrowing on mine as she gathered the powders and herbs, started to set me on edge. And when she held up the sketch I'd drawn and said, "What exactly are you practicing here? Is this some sort of alchemy?" I was sure I'd made a colossal mistake.

Ava glanced at me and was just about to step in when I shook my head and forced a laugh as I said, "Well, if you mean alchemy in its truest sense of mastering nature, averting chaos, and extending life for an indeterminate amount of time"—a definition I'd recently memorized after researching the term—"then no, I'm afraid my intentions aren't anywhere near that grand. I'm just trying out a little white magick—hoping to cast a spell that will get me through finals, get me a date for prom, and maybe even clear up my allergies, which are about to go haywire since it's nearly spring and I don't want my nose to be all red and drippy for prom pictures, you know?"

And when I saw how that failed to convince her, especially the part about the allergies, I added, "Which is why I need all that rose quartz, since, as you know, it's supposed to bring love, oh and then the turquoise—" I pointed at the pendant she wore. "Well, you know how it's famous for healing, and . . ." And even though I was prepared to go on and on, reciting the full list of things I'd learned merely an hour before, I decided to cut it right there and end with a shrug.

I unwrap the crystals, taking great care as I cradle them each in the palm of my hand, closing my fingers around them, and picturing a brilliant white light permeating straight through to their core, performing the all-important "cleansing and purifying" step, which, according to what I read online, is merely the first stage in programming the stones. The second is to ask them (out loud!) to soak up the moon's powerful energy so they can provide the service nature intended them for.

"Turquoise," I whisper, glancing at the door, making sure that it's closed all the way, imagining how embarrassing it would be for Sabine to barge in and catch me cooing to a pile of rocks. "I ask that you heal, purify, and help balance the chakras as nature intended you to do." Then I take a deep breath and infuse the stone with the energy of my intentions before slipping it into the bag and reaching for the next, feeling ridiculous and more than a little hokey, but knowing I've no choice but to continue.

I move on to the polished rose quartz, picking them up individually and infusing them with white light, before repeating four separate times, "May you bring unconditional love and infinite peace." Dropping them each into the red silk bag, watching as they settle around the turquoise before reaching for the staurolite—a beautiful stone believed to be formed from the tears of fairies, and asking it to provide ancient wisdom, good luck, and to help connect to the other dimensions, before moving on to the large chunk of zoisite, and holding it in both of my hands. After cleansing it with white light, I close my eyes and whisper, "May you transmute all negative energies to positive ones, may you aid in connecting to the mystical realms, and may you—"

"Ever? Can I come in?"

I glance at the door, knowing there's just an inch and a half of wood separating me from Sabine. Then I gaze at the pile of herbs, oils, candles, and powders, along with the rock I'm talking to in my hand.

"And please aid in recovery, illness, and whatever else it is that you do!" I whisper, barely getting the words out before I'm shoving it in the bag.

Only it won't fit.

"Ever?"

I shove it again, trying to jam it in there, but the opening's so small and the stone's so big it's not going to happen without ripping the seams.

Sabine knocks again, three firm raps meant to inform me that she knows I'm in here, knows I'm up to something, and that her patience is nearing its end. And even though I don't have time to chat, I'm left with no choice but to say, "Um, just a sec!" Forcing the stone inside as I run out to my balcony and drop it on a small table with the best view of the moon, before rushing back in and going into a full-blown meltdown when Sabine knocks again and I take in the state of my room—looking at it as she might see it, and knowing there's no time to change it.

"Ever? Are you okay?" she calls, with equal parts annoyance and concern.

"*Yeah*—I just—" I grab hold of the hem of my T-shirt and yank it over my head, turning my back toward the door as I say, "Um, you can come in now—I'm just—" And the moment she enters, I slide it back on. Faking a sudden bout of modesty, as though I can't bear for her to see me changing when I've never cared much before. "I'm—I was just changing," I mumble, seeing her brows merge as she looks me over, sniffing the air for the remnants of pot, alcohol, clove cigarettes, or whatever her latest teen-rearing book has warned her against.

"You got something on your—" She motions toward the front of my shirt. "Something—red that—well—that probably won't come out."

She twists her mouth to the side as I gaze down at the front of my T-shirt, seeing it marked by a big streak of red and immediately recognizing it as the powder I need for the elixir. Knowing its bag must have leaked when I see how it's spilled all over my desk as well as the floor underneath.

Great. Way to appear as though you were just changing into a clean shirt! I think, mentally rolling my eyes as she approaches my bed, perches herself on the edge and crosses her legs, her cell phone in hand. And all it takes is one look at the hazy reddish gray glow of her aura to know that the concerned look on her face has less to do with my apparent lack of clean clothes and more to do with me—my strange behavior, my growing secrecy, my food issues—all of which she's convinced lead to something more sinister.

And I'm so focused on how I might go about explaining those things that I fail to see it coming when she says, "Ever, did you ditch school today?"

I freeze, watching as she stares at my desk, taking in the mess of herbs and candles and oils and minerals and all kinds of other weird stuff she's not used to seeing—or at least not all grouped together like that—like they have a purpose—like the arrangement is far less random than it seems.

"Um, yeah. I had a headache. But it's no big deal." I plop onto my desk chair and swivel back and forth, hoping to distract her from the view.

She glances between the great alchemical experiment and me, and is just about to speak when I say, "Well, I mean, it's no big deal now that it's *gone*. Though believe me, it was at the time. I got one of my migraines. You know how I get those sometimes?"

I feel like the world's worst niece—an ungrateful liar—an insincere babbler of nonsense. She has no idea how lucky she is to be rid of me soon.

"Maybe it's because you're not eating enough." She sighs, kicking off her shoes and studying me closely as she says, "And yet, in spite of that, you seem to be growing like a weed. You're even taller than you were a few days ago!"

I gaze down at my ankles, shocked to see that my newly manifested jeans have crept up an inch since this morning.

"Why didn't you go to the nurse's office if you weren't feeling well? You know you're not allowed to just run off like that."

I gaze at her, wishing I could tell her not to sweat it, to not waste another second worrying about it since it'll be over with soon. Because as much as I'm going to miss her, there's no doubt her life will improve. She deserves better than *this*. Deserves better than *me*. And it's nice to know she'll soon have some peace.

"She's kind of a quack," I say. "A real aspirin pusher, and you know how that never works for me. I just needed to come home and lie down for a while. It's the only thing that ever works. So, I just—left."

"And did you?" She leans toward me. "Come home I mean?" And the moment our eyes meet, I know it's a challenge. I know it's a test.

"No." I sigh, staring down at the carpet as I wave my white flag. "I drove down to the canyon and just—"

She watches me, waiting.

"And I just got lost for a while." I take a deep breath and swallow hard, knowing that's as close to the truth as I can get.

"Ever, is this about Damen?"

And the moment my eyes meet hers, I can't hold back, I just burst into tears.

"Oh dear," she murmurs, her arms opening wide as I spring from my chair and tumble right in. Still so unused to my long gangly limbs, I'm clumsy and awkward and nearly knock her to the floor.

"Sorry," I say. "I—" But I'm unable to finish. A new rush of tears overtakes me, and I'm sobbing again.

She strokes my hair as I continue to cry, murmuring, "I know how much you miss him. I know how hard this must be."

But the second she says it, I pull away. Feeling guilty for acting as though this is just about Damen when the truth is it's only partly about him. It's also about missing my friends—in Laguna and in Oregon. And about missing my life—the one I've built here and the one I'm about to return to. Because even though it's obvious that they'll be better off without me, and I mean *everyone*, including Damen, that still doesn't make it any easier.

But it has to be done. There's really no choice.

And when I think of it like that, well, it does make it easier. Because the truth is, whatever the reason, I've been given an amazing, once in a lifetime opportunity.

And now it's time to go home.

I just wish I had a little more time for good-byes.

And when the thought of that brings a new rush of tears, Sabine holds me tighter, whispering words of encouragement, as I cling to her, held in the cocoon of her arms where everything feels safe—and warm—and right—and secure.

Like it's all going to work out just fine.

And as I burrow closer, my eyes closed, my face buried in the place where her shoulder meets her neck, my lips move softly, silently, saying good-bye.

forty

I wake up early. I guess since it's the last day of my life, or at least the last day of the life I've built here, I'm eager to make the most of it. And even though I'm sure I'll be greeted with a full-on chorus of the usual *Spaz! Loo-ser!* and the more recent *Witch!*, knowing it's the last time I'll be subjected to that makes all the difference.

At Hillcrest High (the school I'm returning to), I've got tons of friends. Which makes showing up Monday through Friday a lot more appealing, if not fun. And I don't remember ever once being tempted to ditch (like I am pretty much all the time here), and I wasn't depressed about not fitting in.

And to be honest, I think that's why I'm so eager to return. Because other than the obvious thrill of being with my family again, having a good group of friends who both love and accept me, and who I can be myself with—makes the decision that much easier.

A decision I wouldn't even stop to think twice about if it weren't for Damen.

But even though I can't quite wrap my mind around the fact that I'll never see him again—will never know the touch of his skin, the heat of his gaze, or the feel of his lips upon mine—I'm still willing to give it all up.

If it means reclaiming the old me and returning to my family—then there's really no choice.

I mean, Drina killed me so she could have Damen to herself. And Damen brought me back so he could have me to himself. And as much as I love him, as much as my whole heart aches at the thought of never seeing him again, I know now that the moment he returned me to life, he messed with the natural order of things. Turning me into something I was never meant to be.

And now it's my job to put it all back.

I stand before my closet and reach for my newest jeans, a black V-neck sweater, and my newish ballet flats—just like I wore in the vision I saw. Then I run my fingers through my hair, swipe on some lip gloss, insert the tiny diamond stud earrings my parents bought me for my sixteenth birthday (since they'll definitely notice if they're missing), along with the crystal horseshoe bracelet Damen gave me that has no place in the life I'm returning to, but there's no way I'm removing it.

Then I grab my bag, gaze around my ridiculously big room one last time, and head out the door. Eager to get one final peek at a life I didn't always enjoy and most likely won't even remember, but still needing to say some good-byes and set a few things straight before I'm gone for good.

The second I pull into the school parking lot, I start scanning for Damen. Searching for him, his car, anything, any little nugget, whatever I can get. Wanting to see as much of him as I can, while I can. And feeling disappointed when I don't find him.

I park my car and head to class, guarding against freaking out, jumping to conclusions, and overreacting just because he's not here yet. Because even though he's becoming increasingly normal as the poison slowly chips away at the progress of hundreds of years, from the way he looked yesterday—still gorgeous, still sexy, and not at all beginning to age—I'm guessing rock bottom is still days away.

Besides, I know he'll show up eventually. I mean, why wouldn't he? He's the undisputed star of this school. The best looking, the wealthiest, the one who throws the most amazing parties—or at least that's what I hear. He practically gets a standing ovation just for showing up. And tell me, who could resist that?

I move among the students, gazing at all the people I never even spoke to, and who barely spoke to me other than to yell something mean. And while I'm sure they won't miss me, I can't help but wonder if they'll even notice I'm gone. Or, if it'll all turn out like I think—I go back, they go back, and the time I spent here amounts to less than a blip on their screen.

I take a deep breath and head into English, bracing myself to see Damen with Stacia, but finding her sitting alone instead. I mean, she's gossiping with Honor and Craig as usual, but Damen's nowhere in sight. And as I pass her on the way to my seat, ready for just about anything she might toss in my path, I'm met only by silence, a stolid refusal to even acknowledge me, much less try to trip me, which fills me with dread and unease.

And after taking my seat and settling in, I spend the next fifty minutes glancing between the clock and the door, my anxiety growing with each passing moment. Imagining all manner of horrible scenarios until the bell finally rings and I bolt for the hall. And by fourth period when he still hasn't shown, I'm headed for a full-blown panic attack when I walk into history class and find Roman gone too.

"Ever," Mr. Munoz says, as I stand beside him, gaping at Roman's empty seat as my stomach fills with dread.

"You've got a lot of catching up to do."

I glance at him, knowing he wants to discuss my attendance, my missed assignments, and other irrelevant topics I don't need to hear. So I run out the door, racing through the quad and right past the lunch tables before I stop on the curb, gasping in relief when I see him. Or not *him*, but rather his car. The sleek black BMW he used to prize so much, that's now coated in a thick layer of dirt and grime and parked rather awkwardly in the no-parking zone.

Still, despite its filthy state, I gaze at it as though it's the most beautiful thing I've ever seen. Knowing that if his car's here, then he's here. And all is okay.

And just as I'm thinking I should try to move it so it doesn't get towed away, a throat clears from behind me and a deep voice says, "Excuse me, but aren't you supposed to be in class?"

I turn, my gaze meeting Principal Buckley's when I say, "Um, yeah, but first I just have to—" I motion toward Damen's poorly parked Beemer as though I'm doing a favor not just for my friend but for the sake of the school as well.

But Buckley's less concerned with parking violations and more concerned with repeat truancy offenders like me. And still smarting from our last unfortunate encounter when Sabine pleaded my case from expelled to suspended, he squints as he looks me over and says, "You've got two choices. I can call your aunt and ask her to leave work so she can come down here, *or*—" He pauses, trying to kill me with suspense even though you don't have to be psychic to know where this is going. "Or I can escort you back to class. Which would you prefer?"

For a moment, I'm tempted to choose option one—just to see what he'd do. But in the end, I follow him back to my class. His shoes pounding the cement as he leads me across the quad and down the hall before depositing me at Mr. Munoz's door where my gaze lands on Roman who's not only occupying his seat but shaking his head and laughing as I slink back toward mine.

And even though Munoz is used to my erratic behavior by now, he still makes a point of calling on me. Asking me to answer all manner of questions regarding historical events including those that we've studied and those that we haven't. And my mind is so preoccupied with Roman and Damen and my upcoming plans that I just answer robotically, *seeing* the answers he holds in his head and repeating them pretty much verbatim.

So when he says, "So tell me, Ever, what did I have for dinner last night?"

I automatically say, "Two pieces of leftover pizza and a glass and a half of Chianti." My mind is so ensconced in my own personal dramas it's a moment before I notice he's gaping.

In fact, everyone's gaping.

Well, everyone but Roman who just shakes his head and laughs even harder.

And just as the bell rings and I try to bolt for the door, Munoz steps before me and says, "How do you do it?"

I press my lips together and shrug as though I've no clue what he's talking about. Though it's clear he's not about to let it go, he's been wondering for weeks.

"How do you—*know stuff*?" he says, his eyes narrowed on mine. "About random historical facts we've never once studied—about *me*?"

I gaze down at the ground and take a deep breath, wondering what it could hurt to throw him a bone. I mean, I'm leaving tonight, and chances are he'll never remember this anyway, so what harm could it do to tell him the truth?

"I don't know." I shrug. "It's not like I *do* anything. Images and information just appear in my head."

He looks at me, struggling with whether or not to believe. And not having the time or desire to try to convince him, but still wanting to leave him with something nice, I say, "For instance, I know you shouldn't give up on your book because it's going to be published someday."

He gapes, his eyes wide, his expression wavering between wild hope and complete disbelief.

And even though it kills me to add it, even though the whole idea makes me want to hurl, I know there's something more that needs to be said, it's the right thing to do. Besides, what could it hurt? I mean, I'm leaving anyway, and Sabine deserves to get out and have a little fun. And other than his penchant for Rolling Stones boxers, Bruce Springsteen songs, and his obsession with Renaissance times—he seems harmless. Not to mention how it's not going to go anywhere anyway since I specifically saw her getting together with a guy who works in her building . . .

"Her name is Sabine," I say, before I have a chance to overthink it and change my mind. Then seeing the confusion in his eyes, I add, "You know, the petite blonde at Starbucks? The one who spilled her latte all over your shirt? The one you can't stop thinking about?"

And when he looks at me, it's clear that he's speechless. And preferring to leave it like that, I gather my stuff and head toward the door, glancing over my shoulder to say, "And you shouldn't be afraid to talk to her. Seriously. Just suck it up and approach her already. You'll find she's really nice."

forty-one

When I exit the room, I half expect to find Roman waiting for me with that same taunting gleam in his eye. But he's not. And when I get to the lunch tables, I know why.

He's performing. Orchestrating everyone around him, directing everything they say and do—like a bandleader, a puppet master, a big-top circus ringleader. And just as the hint of something nudges at the back of my mind, just as an inkling of insight begins to take shape—I see *him*.

Damen.

The love of every single one of my lives, now stumbling toward the lunch table, so unstable, so disheveled and haggard, there's no mistaking that things have progressed at an alarming rate. We are running out of time.

And when Stacia turns, makes a face, and hisses, *"Loo-*scr!" I'm stunned to realize the taunt is not meant for me.

It's directed at Damen.

And in a matter of seconds, the whole school joins in. All of the derision once reserved just for me is now directed at him.

I glance at Miles and Haven, watching as they add their voices to the chorus, then I rush toward Damen, alarmed to find his skin so clammy and cold, those once high cheekbones now alarmingly gaunt, and those deep dark eyes that once held such promise and warmth, now watery and rheumy and barely able to focus. And even though his lips are horribly dry and cracked, I still feel an undeniable longing to press mine against them. Because no matter what he looks like, no matter how much he's changed, he's still Damen. *My Damen.* Young or old, healthy or sick, it doesn't matter. He's the only one I've ever really cared about—the only one I've ever loved—and nothing Roman or anyone else does can ever change that.

"Hey," I whisper, my voice cracking as my eyes fill with tears. Tuning out the shrill taunts that surround us as I focus solely on him. Hating myself for turning my back long enough to allow this to happen, knowing he never would've let this happen to me.

He turns toward me, his eyes struggling to focus, and just when I think I've captured a glimmer of recognition—it's gone so fast I'm sure I imagined it.

"Let's get out of here," I say, tugging on his sleeve, trying to pull him alongside me. "What do you say we ditch?" I smile, hoping to remind him of our usual Friday routine. Just reaching the gate when Roman appears.

"Why do you bother?" he says, his arms folded, head cocked to the side, allowing his Ouroboros tattoo to flash in and out of view.

I grip Damen's arm and narrow my gaze, determined to get past Roman whatever it takes.

"Seriously, Ever." He shakes his head, glancing from Damen to me. "Why waste your time? He's old, feeble, practically decrepit, *and,* I'm sorry to say, but from the looks of things, not long for this earth. Surely you're not planning to waste your sweet young nectar on this dinosaur?"

He looks at me, blue eyes blazing, lips curving, glancing at the lunch table just as the shrill of taunts hits the next level.

And just like that *I know.*

The idea that's been nudging me, poking around the edges, and trying to get my attention, has finally been heard. And even though I'm not sure if I'm right, and knowing I'll have no choice but to slink off in shame if I'm wrong, I take in the crowd, my eyes moving from Miles to Haven to Stacia to Honor to Craig to every single kid who's just going through the motions, following along, doing what everyone else says and does without once stopping to question, without once asking *why*.

Then I take a deep breath, close my eyes, and focus all of my energy on them when I shout:

"WAKE UP!!!"

Then I stand there, far too ashamed to look now that all of their derision has switched from Damen to me. But I can't let that stop me, I *know* Roman's performed some sort of mass hypnosis, putting them into some kind of mindless trance where everyone's doing his bidding.

"Ever, please. Save yourself while you still can." Roman laughs. "Even I can't help you if you insists on continuing."

But I don't listen to him—can't listen. I have to find a way to stop him—to stop *them*! I've got to find a way to wake them all up, get them to snap out of it—

Snap!

That's it! I'll just snap my fingers and—

I take a deep breath, close my eyes, and yell as loud as I can:

"SNAP OUT OF IT!"

Which only results in my classmates going wild, their ridicule hitting the next level as a profusion of soda cans are hurled at my head.

Roman sighs, looking at me when he says, "Ever, *really*. I insist. You've got to stop this madness, *now*! You're making a bloody fool of yourself if you think that'll work! What're you gonna do next, slap all their cheeks?"

I stand there, my breath coming in short shallow gasps, knowing I'm not wrong, despite what he says. I'm sure he's got them spellbound, hijacked their minds by some kind of trance—

And then I remember this old documentary I once saw on TV, where the hypnotist brought the patient back not by slapping or snapping but by clapping on the count of three.

I take a deep breath, watching as my classmates climb on top of the table and benches, the better to pelt me with their uneaten food. And I know it's my last chance, that if this doesn't work—well—I don't know what I will do.

So I close my eyes, and yell:

"WAKE UP!"

Then I count from three to one and clap my hands twice at the end.

And then—

And then—nothing.

The whole school goes silent as they slowly come to.

They rub their eyes, blinking, yawning, and stretching as though awakening from a very long nap. Gazing around in confusion, wondering why they're on top of the table with the very same people they once deemed as freaks.

Craig is the first to react. Finding himself so close to Miles their shoulders practically touch, he bolts for the far end. Reassuring himself with the company of his fellow jocks, reclaiming his manhood with a punch on the arm.

And when Haven stares at her carrot sticks with a look of absolute disgust, I can't help but smile, knowing the big happy family is back to their normal routine of name-calling, eye-rolling, and snubbing each other in favor of their usual cliques, returned to a world where animosity and loathing still rule.

My school is back to normal again.

I turn toward the gate, prepared to take Roman down, but he's already gone. So I grip Damen tighter, easing him across the parking lot and into my car as Miles and Haven, the two best friends I've missed so much and will never see again, follow along.

"You guys know I love you, right?" I glance between them, knowing they'll freak, but it has to be said.

They look at each other, exchanging a look of alarm, both of them wondering what could've possibly happened to the girl they once pegged as the Ice Queen.

"Um, *okay* . . ." Haven says, shaking her head.

But I just smile and grasp them both to me, squeezing them tightly as I whisper to Miles, "Whatever you do don't stop acting or singing, it's going to bring you—" I stop, wondering if I should tell him how I just saw a flash of bright lights and Broadway, but not wanting to rob him of the journey by always looking ahead, I say, "It's going to bring you great happiness."

And before he can even respond, I've moved on to Haven, knowing I have to get this over with quick, so I can get Damen to Ava's, but determined to find a way to urge her to love herself more, to stop losing herself in others, and that Josh is worth hanging on to for however long it lasts. "You have so much value," I tell her. "So much to give—I just wish you could see how bright your star truly does shine."

"Um, gag!" she says, laughing as she untangles herself from my grip. "Are you okay?" She squints between me and Damen. "And what's up with him? Why's he all hunched over like that?"

I shake my head and climb inside, having no more time to waste. And as I back out of my space, I look out my window and say, "Hey, do you guys know where Roman lives?"

forty-two

I never imagined I'd be grateful for my sudden growth spurt and newly bulging biceps, but it's because of my new size and strength (not to mention Damen's emaciated state) that I practically carry him all the way from my car to Ava's front door in just a handful of steps. Supporting his body as I knock on her door, fully prepared to break it down if I have to, but glad when she answers and waves us both in.

I head for the hall as Damen stumbles along with me, pausing just outside the indigo door and gaping at Ava when she hesitates to open it.

"If your room is as sacred and pure as you think it is, then don't you think that will only help Damen? Don't you think he needs all the positive energy he can get?" I say, knowing she's conflicted about admitting the "contaminated" energy of a sick and dying man, which is just so ridiculous I hardly know where to begin.

She looks at me, holding my gaze far longer than my diminishing patience would prefer, and when she finally gives in, I barrel right past her, getting Damen settled on the futon in the corner and covering his body with the wool throw she keeps nearby.

"The juice is in my trunk, along with the antidote," I say, tossing her the keys. "The juice won't be any good for another two days, but he should be much better tonight, when the full moon rises and the antidote is ready. And then you can give him the juice later, to help rebuild his strength. Even though he probably won't even need it since it'll all reverse anyway. But still—just in case—" I nod, wishing I felt half as confident as I sound.

"Are you sure this'll work?" she asks, watching as I pull my very last bottle of elixir from my bag.

"It has to." I gaze at Damen, so pale, so weak, so—*old*. And yet, he's still Damen. Traces of his amazing beauty still present, marred only slightly by the acceleration of years resulting in his silver hair, his nearly translucent skin, the fan of wrinkles surrounding his eyes. "It's our only hope," I add, waving her away as I drop to my knees, the door closing behind me as I smooth his hair off his face and gently force him to drink.

At first he fights it, thrashing his head from side to side and keeping his mouth firmly closed. But when it's clear that I'm not about to give up, he gives in. Allowing the liquid to flow down his throat as his skin warms and his color returns. Emptying the bottle and gazing at me with such love and reverence, I'm overcome with joy just to know that he's back.

"I missed you," I murmur, nodding and blinking and swallowing hard, my heart bursting with yearning as I press my lips to his cheek. All the pent-up emotions I've fought so hard to keep in check all this time, now rushing to the surface, bubbling over, as I kiss him again and again. "You're going to be okay," I tell him. "You're going to be back to your old self very soon."

My sudden burst of happiness withering like a popped balloon as his gaze turns dark and sweeps over my face.

"You left me," he whispers.

I shake my head, wanting him to know it's not true. I never left him—he left me—but it wasn't his fault and I forgive him. I forgive him for everything he's ever done—or said—even though it's already too late—even though it doesn't really matter anymore—

But instead I just say, "No. I haven't. You've been ill. *Very* ill. But it's over with now and soon you'll be better. You just have to promise to drink the antidote when—" *When Ava gives it to you*—the words I can't bear to say, *won't* say, not wanting him to know that this is our last moment together—our final good-bye.

"All you need to know is that you're going to be fine. But you need to watch out for Roman. He's not your friend. He's evil. He's trying to kill you. So you must regain your strength so you can take him down."

I press my mouth to his forehead, his cheek, unable to stop until I've covered his entire face with my kiss. Tasting my own salty tears on the curve of his lips, as I breathe him in, hoping to imprint his scent, his taste, the feel of his skin, wanting to carry the memory of him wherever I go.

But even after I tell him I love him—even after I lie down beside him, pull him into my arms, and press his body to mine—even after I remain there for hours, lying right alongside him as he sleeps— even after I close my eyes and concentrate on melding my energy with his, hoping to heal him with my love, my essence, my very being, trying to impress some small part of myself onto him—even after all of that—the moment I move away, he says it again.

An accusation from his dream state, intended only for me.

"You left me."

Not realizing until I've said my final good-bye and closed the door behind me, that he's not referring to the past.

He's prophesying our future.

forty-three

I head down the hall and into the kitchen, my heart heavy, my legs wooden, and every step away from Damen just makes it worse.

"You okay?" Ava asks, standing at the stove, brewing some tea. As though all of those hours didn't just pass.

I shake my head and lean against the wall, unsure how to answer, unable to speak. Because the truth is, *okay* is pretty much the last thing I feel. Empty, hollow, bereft, awful, depressed—yes. But *okay*? Not so much.

But that's because I'm a criminal. A traitor. I'm the worst kind of person you could ever hope to meet. All of the times I tried to imagine that scene, tried to imagine how my last moment with Damen would be, I never once thought it would end like that.

I never once thought I'd stand accused. Even though I clearly deserve to be.

"You don't have much time." She gazes at the clock on her wall, then at me. "Would you like some tea before you leave?"

I shake my head, knowing I've a few things still to tell her, and a few more stops to make before I go for good.

"So you know what to do?" I ask, seeing her nod as she brings her cup to her lips. "Because I'm trusting you, Ava. If this doesn't work out in the way that I think, if the only thing that goes back is me, then you're my only hope." My gaze locks on hers, needing her to understand just exactly how serious this all is. "You've *got* to take care of Damen, he's—he doesn't deserve any of this, and—" My voice cracks as I press my lips together and avert my gaze. Knowing I've got to go on, that there's still more to say, but needing a moment before I can. "And watch out for Roman. He's good-looking and charming, but it's all a façade. Inside, he's evil, he tried to kill Damen, he's responsible for what he's become."

"Don't worry." She moves toward me. "Don't worry about a thing. I got the stuff out of your trunk, the antidote is in the cupboard, the juice is—fermenting, and I'll add the herb on the third day like you said. Not that we'll even need it, since I'm sure everything will go exactly as planned."

I look at her, seeing the sincerity in her eyes, relieved that at least I'm able to leave things in her capable hands.

"So you just get yourself over to Summerland, and I'll take care of the rest," she says, pulling me into her arms and hugging me tightly to her chest. "And who knows? Maybe someday you'll find yourself in Laguna Beach and we'll meet all over again?"

She laughs when she says it and I wish I could laugh along with her, but I can't. The weird thing about saying good-bye is that it never gets any easier.

I pull away, nodding in place of words, knowing that to say anything more will make me break down completely. Barely managing to eek out a "Thanks," before I'm already at the door.

"You've nothing to be thanking me for," she says, following behind. "But, Ever, are you sure you don't want to peek in on Damen, just one last time?"

I turn, my hand on the doorknob, considering, but only for a moment before I take a deep breath and shake my head. Knowing there's no use in prolonging the inevitable, and far too afraid to risk seeing the accusation on his face.

"We've already said good-bye," I say, stepping onto the porch and moving toward my car. "Besides, I don't have much time. There's still one last stop I need to make."

forty-four

I turn onto Roman's street, park in his drive, rush toward the door, and kick it right down. Watching the wood crack and splinter as it teeters from its hinges and swings open before me, hoping to catch him off guard, so I can punch all of his chakras and be done with him for good.

I creep inside, my eyes darting around, taking in walls the color of eggshells, ceramic vases filled with silk flowers, poster-sized prints of all the usual suspects—Van Gogh's *The Starry Night*, Gustav Klimt's *The Kiss,* and an oversized rendition of Botticelli's *The Birth of Venus* framed in gold and hanging right over the mantel. All of it appearing so surprisingly normal, I can't help but wonder if I've got the wrong house.

I expected grit, edge, a post-apocalyptic pad with black leather couches, chrome tables, an abundance of mirrors, and confusing art—something sleeker, hipper, anything but this chintz-ridden fuss palace that's nearly impossible to imagine someone like Roman living in.

I tour the house, checking every room, every closet, even under the bed. But when it's clear he's not home, I head straight for his kitchen, find his supply of immortal juice, and pour it straight down the drain. Knowing it's juvenile, useless, and probably won't make the least bit of difference, since the moment I go back everything will reverse itself again. But even if it adds up to no more than a minor inconvenience, at least he'll know that inconvenience came from me.

Then I riffle through his drawers, searching for a piece of scrap paper and a pen, needing to make a list of all the things I can't afford to forget. A simple set of instructions that won't be too confusing for someone who probably won't remember what any of it means, and yet still clear and concise enough to keep me from repeating the same horrible mistakes all over again.

Writing:

1. Don't go back for the sweatshirt!
2. Don't trust Drina!
3. Don't go back for the sweatshirt *no matter what!*

And then, just so I don't completely forget, and hoping it might trigger some sort of memory, I add:

4. Damen ♡

And after checking it over again (and again), making sure it's all there and that nothing's been missed, I fold it into a square, shove it deep in my pocket, and head for the window, gazing at a sky turned a deep sunless blue, with the moon hanging heavy and full just off to the side. Then I take a deep breath and head for the ugly chintz couch, knowing it's time.

I close my eyes and reach toward the light, eager to experience that shimmering glory one final time as I land on those soft blades of grass in that vast fragrant field. Aided by their buoyancy and bounce as I run, skip, and twirl through the meadow, performing cartwheels, back handsprings, and somersaults, my fingertips grazing over those glorious flowers with their pulsating petals and delicious sweet scent as I wind my way through those vibrating trees along the colorful stream. Determined to take it all in, to memorize every last detail, wishing there was some way to capture this wonderful feeling and hold it forever.

And then, because I have a few moments to spare, and because I need to see him one last time, need to be with him in the way that we used to, I close my eyes and manifest Damen.

Seeing him as he first appeared to me in the parking lot at school. Starting with his shiny dark hair that waves around his cheekbones and hits just shy of his shoulders, those almond-shaped eyes so deep, dark, and even, back then, strangely familiar. And those lips! Those ripe inviting lips with their perfect Cupid's bow, followed by the long, lean, muscular body that holds it all up. My memory so potent, so tangible, every nuance, every pore, is present and accounted for.

And when I open my eyes, he's bowing before me, offering his hand in our very last dance. So I place my hand in his as he tucks his arm around my waist, leading me through that glorious field in a series of wide sweeping arcs, our bodies swaying, our feet floating, twirling to a melody heard only by us. And every time he begins to slip from my grasp, I just close my eyes and make him again, resuming our steps without falter. Like Count Fersen and Marie, Albert and Victoria, Antony and Cleopatra, we are all the world's greatest lovers, we are all the couples we've ever been. And I bury my face in the warm sweet hollow of his neck, reluctant to let our song end.

But even though there's no time in Summerland, there is where I'm going. And so I run my fingers along the planes of his face, memorizing the softness of his skin, the curve of his jaw, and the swell of his lips as they press against mine—convincing myself that it's him—*really him!*

Even long after he's faded and gone.

•   •   •

The moment I head out of the field, I find Romy and Rayne waiting right by the edge, and from the looks on their faces I know they've been watching.

"You're running out of time," Rayne says, staring at me with those saucer-sized eyes that never fail to set me on edge.

But I just shake my head and pick up the pace, annoyed to know they've been spying, and tired of the way they keep butting in.

"I've got it all covered," I say, glancing over my shoulder. "So feel free to—" I pause, having no idea what they do when they're not bothering me. So I lift my shoulders and leave it at that, knowing whatever they're up to, it no longer concerns me.

They run alongside me, peering at each other, communicating in their private twin speak before saying, "Something's not right." They stare at me, urging me to listen. "Something feels terribly wrong." Their voices blending together in perfect harmony.

But I just shrug, not the least bit interested in cracking their code, and when I see those marble steps before me, I storm straight ahead, glimpsing the world's most beautiful structures, before rushing right in. The twins' voices silenced by the doors closing behind me as I stand in the grand marble entry, eyes closed tight, hoping I won't be shut out like the last time, hoping I can go back in time. Thinking:

I'm ready. I'm really and truly ready. So please, let me go back. Back to Eugene, Oregon. Back to my mom and dad and Riley and Buttercup. Please just let me return . . . and set everything straight again . . .

And the next thing I know a short hallway appears, leading to a room at the end—a room that's empty except for a stool and a desk. But not just any old desk, this is one of those long metal desks like the kind we had in the chem lab at my old school. And as I slide onto the seat, a large crystal globe levitates before me, flickering and flaring until it settles on an image of me, sitting at this same metal desk, struggling over a science test. And even though it's pretty much the last scene I ever would've chosen to repeat, I know it's the only opportunity I'll ever get to return. So I take a deep breath, press my finger to the screen—and gasp as everything around me goes black.

forty-five

"O—migod. I *totally* flunked that," Rachel groans, tossing her wavy brown hair over her shoulder and rolling her eyes. "I mean, I *barely* even studied last night. Seriously. And then I stayed up late texting—" She looks at me, her eyes wide as she shakes her head. "Anyway. All you need to know is that my life as we know it is over. So take a good look at me now because as soon as those grades are posted and my parents find out, I'll be grounded for life. Which means this is pretty much the last you'll see of me."

"*Please.*" I roll my eyes. "If anyone flunked, we both know it's me. I've been lost in that class all year! And it's not like I'm going to be a scientist or anything. It's not like I'm ever going to *use* the information." I stop just shy of her locker, watching as she unlocks it and tosses a pile of books inside.

"I'm just glad it's over and that grades won't be out until next week. Which means I better live it up while I can. And speaking of—what time should I swing by tonight?" she asks, brows raised so high they're hidden under her bangs.

I shake my head and sigh, realizing I haven't told her yet and knowing she's gonna be mad. "About that . . ." I walk alongside her as we head for the parking lot, tucking my long blond hair behind my ear as I say, "Slight change of plans. My mom and dad are going out and I'm supposed to babysit Riley."

"And how is that a *slight* change of plans?" Rachel stops just short of the lot, her eyes scanning the rows of cars, determined to see who's riding with who.

"Well, I thought maybe after she goes to sleep, you can come over and—" But I stop, not bothering to finish since it's clear she's not listening. The second I mentioned my little sister, I lost her. Rachel's that rare only child who's never once fantasized about having a brother or sister. Sharing the spotlight just isn't her thing.

"Forget it," she says. "Little people have sticky fingers and big ears, you can't trust 'em. How about tomorrow?"

I shake my head. "Can't. It's family day. We're all heading up to the lake."

"See." Rachel nods. "That's exactly the kind of stuff you don't have to deal with when your parents split. In our house, family day is when we all meet in court to fight over the child support check."

"You don't know how lucky you are," I say, regretting the joke the second it's out. Because not only is it a total lie, but something about it leaves me feeling so sad and guilty I wish I could take it right back.

But it's not like Rachel was listening anyway. She's too busy trying to get the attention of the amazing Shayla Sparks, who's pretty much the coolest senior to ever walk the halls of this school. Frantically waving and stopping just short of jumping up and down and screaming like a groupie, hoping to get Shayla's attention as she loads up her sky-blue VW Bug with all her cool friends. Then lowering her hand and pretending to scratch at her ear as though she's not the least bit embarrassed when Shayla fails to acknowledge her.

"Trust me, that car's not so great," I say, checking my watch and gazing around the lot, wondering just where the heck Brandon is since he really should've been here by now. "The Miata drives better."

"Excuse me?" Rachel peers at me, her brows knit together in complete disbelief. "And since when have you driven either one?"

I squint, hearing the words repeat in my head and having no idea why I just said them. "Um, I didn't." I shrug. "I—I guess I must've read it somewhere."

She looks at me, her eyes narrowed as they work their way down my outfit, grazing over my black V-neck sweater and down to my jeans that are dragging on the ground. "And where'd you get *this*?" She grasps my wrist.

"Please. You've seen that like a million times already. I got it last Christmas," I say, trying to break free of her grip as Brandon comes toward me, thinking how cute he is when his hair falls into his eyes.

"Not the watch silly, *this*!" She taps the bracelet that's next to the watch, the one with silver horseshoes encrusted with pink crystal bits—the one that's not the slightest bit familiar though somehow manages to make my stomach go all weird when I look at it.

"I—I don't know," I mumble, wincing when I see her gape at me like I'm losing it. "I mean, I think my aunt might've sent it to me, you know, the one I told you about, the one who lives in Laguna Beach—"

"Who lives in Laguna Beach?" Brandon asks, slipping his arm around me, as Rachel glances between us, rolling her eyes when he leans in to kiss me. But something about the feel of his lips is so strange and unsettling, I quickly turn away.

"My ride's here," Rachel says, rushing toward her mom's SUV and calling over her shoulder to say, "Let me know if anything changes—you know, about tonight?"

Brandon looks at me, pulling me tighter against him until I'm practically fused to his chest, which only makes my stomach go weird again.

"If what changes?" he asks, oblivious to the way I squirm out of his arms, unaware of my sudden lack of interest, which is a total relief since I've no idea how to explain it.

"Oh, she wants to hit Jaden's party, but I'm scheduled to babysit," I tell him, heading toward his Jeep and tossing my bag onto the floor by my feet.

"Want me to stop by?" He smiles. "You know, in case you need help?"

"No!" I say, too forceful, too quick. Knowing I need to backtrack fast when I see the look on his face. "I mean, Riley always stays up late, so it's probably not a good idea."

He looks at me, his eyes grazing over me like he feels it too, the unidentified *big wrong thing* that hovers between us, making everything feel so dang weird. Then he shrugs and turns toward the road. Choosing to drive the rest of the way in silence. Or at least he and I are silent. His stereo is screaming full blast. And even though that usually gets on my nerves, today I'm glad. I'd rather focus on crap music I can't stand, than the fact that I don't want to kiss him.

I look at him, *really* look at him in the way I haven't done since I've gotten used to us being a couple. Taking in the swoop of bangs framing those big green eyes that slant down ever so slightly at the corners making him impossible to resist—except for today. Today it comes easy. And when I remember how just yesterday I was covering my notebook with his name, well, it just doesn't make any sense.

He turns, catching me staring and smiling as he takes my hand. Entwining his fingers with mine and squeezing them in a way that makes my stomach go queasy. But I force myself to return it, both the smile and the squeeze, knowing it's expected, what a good girlfriend does. Then I gaze out the window, holding down the nausea as I stare at the passing landscape, the rain-soaked streets, the clapboard houses and pine trees, glad to be getting home soon.

"So, tonight?" He pulls into my drive, muting the sound as he leans toward me and looks at me in that way that he has.

But I just press my lips together and reach for my bag, holding it against my chest like a shield, a solid defense meant to keep him away. "I'll text you," I mumble, avoiding his eyes as I glance out the window, seeing my neighbor and her daughter playing catch on the lawn, as I reach for the door handle, desperate to get away from him and into my room.

And just as I've opened the door and slipped one leg out, he says, "Aren't you forgetting something?"

I gaze down at my backpack, knowing it's all that I brought, but when I look at him again, I realize he's not referring to that. And knowing there's only one way to get through this without arousing any more suspicions from him or from me, I lean toward him, closing my eyes as I press my lips against his, finding them objectively smooth, pliant, but basically neutral, with none of their usual spark.

"I'll—um, I'll see you later," I mumble, hopping out of his Jeep and wiping my mouth on my sleeve well before I've even reached the front door. Rushing inside and heading straight to the den where I'm blocked by a plastic drum set, a guitar with no strings, and a small black microphone that's going to break if Riley and her friend don't stop fighting over it.

"We already agreed," Riley says, yanking the mic toward her. "I sing all the boy songs, and *you* sing all the girl songs. What's the problem?"

"The problem," her friend whines, pulling it even harder. "Is that there's hardly any girl songs. And you know it."

But Riley just shrugs. "That's not my fault. Take it up with Rock Band, not me."

"I swear, you are so—" Her friend stops when she sees me standing in the doorway, shaking my head.

"You guys need to take turns," I say, giving Riley a pointed look, glad to be presented with a problem I can handle, even though I wasn't consulted. "Emily, you get the next song, and Riley, you get the one after that, and then so on. Think you can handle that?"

Riley rolls her eyes as Emily snatches the mic from her hand.

"Is Mom around?" I ask, ignoring Riley's scowl since I'm pretty much used to it by now.

"She's in her room. Getting ready," she says, watching me leave as she whispers to her friend, "Fine. I get to sing 'Dead on Arrival,' you can sing 'Creep.'"

I pass by my room, drop my bag on the floor, then make my way into my mom's room, leaning against the archway that separates the bedroom from the bathroom and watching as she puts on her makeup, remembering how I used to love to do this back when I was little and thought my mom was the most glamorous woman on the planet. But when I look at her now, I mean, look at her objectively, I realize she actually is kind of glamorous, at least in a suburban mom kind of way.

"How was school?" she asks, turning her head from side to side, making sure her foundation is blended and seamless.

"Fine." I shrug. "We had a test in science, which I probably failed," I tell her, even though I don't really believe it went all that bad, but not knowing how to express what I really want to say— that everything feels strange, and uncertain, like it's off balance, lacking—and hoping for any reaction I can get out of her.

But she just sighs and moves on to her eyes, sweeping her small makeup brush over her lids and across the crease as she says, "I'm sure you didn't fail." She glances at me through the mirror. "I'm sure you did just fine."

I trace my hand over a smudge on the wall, thinking I should leave, go to my room and chill out for a while, listen to some music, read a good book, anything to take my mind off of me.

"Sorry this is so last minute," she says, pumping her mascara wand in and out of its tube. "I know you probably had plans."

I shrug, twisting my wrist back and forth, watching the way the crystals in my bracelet flicker and flare, glinting in the fluorescent light and trying to remember where it came from. "That's all right," I tell her. "There'll be plenty of other Friday nights."

My mom squints, mascara in hand, pausing in midstroke as she says, "Ever? Is that you?" She laughs. "Is something going on that I should know about? Because that hardly sounds like my daughter."

I take a deep breath and lift my shoulders, wishing I could tell her how something is most definitely going on, something I can't quite place, something that leaves me feeling so—unlike me.

But I don't. I mean, I can barely explain it to myself, much less her. All I know is that yesterday I felt fine—and today—pretty much the opposite of fine. Alien even—like I no longer fit—like I'm a round girl in a square world.

"You know I'm okay with you inviting a few friends over," she says, moving on to her lips, coating them with a swipe of lipstick before enhancing the color with a touch of gloss. "As long as you keep it to a minimum, no more than three, and as long as you don't ignore your sister."

"Thanks." I nod, forcing a smile so she'll think I'm okay. "But I'm kind of looking forward to having a night off from all that."

I head to my room and plop down on my bed, fully content to just stare at the ceiling, until I realize how pathetic that is and I reach for the book on my nightstand instead. Immersed in the story of a guy and girl so entwined, so perfectly made for each other, their love transcends time. Wishing I could climb inside those pages and live there forever, preferring their story to mine.

"Hey, Ev." My dad pokes his head into my room. "I've come to say both hello and good-bye. We're running late, so we gotta leave soon."

I toss my book aside and race toward him, hugging him so tight he laughs and shakes his head.

"Nice to know you're not too grown up to hug your old man."
He smiles, as I pull away, horrified to find that there are *actual tears*
in my eyes, and busying myself with some books on a shelf until I'm
sure the threat is long past. "Make sure you and your sister are
packed and ready to leave. I want to be on the road nice and early
tomorrow."

I nod, disturbed by the strange hollow feeling invading my gut
as he leaves. Wondering, not for the first time, just what the heck is
going on with me.

forty-six

"Forget it. You're not the boss of me, Ever!" Riley shouts, arms folded, face scowling, refusing to budge.

I mean, who would've guessed that a ninety-pound twelve-year-old could be such a force of nature? But no way am I giving in. Because the second my parents left and Riley was watered and fed, I sent Brandon a text, telling him to come by around ten, which is any minute now so it's imperative I get her to bed.

I shake my head and sigh, wishing she didn't have to be so dang stubborn, but fully prepared to do battle. "Um, I hate to break it to you," I say. "But you're wrong. I *am* the boss of you. From the moment Mom and Dad left until the time they return, I am one hundred percent the boss of you. And you can argue all you want, but it won't change a thing."

"This is so *unfair!*" She glares. "I swear, the second I turn thirteen there's going to be some *equality* around here."

But I just shrug, as eager for that moment as she. "Good, then I won't have to babysit you anymore and I can get my life back," I say, watching as she rolls her eyes and taps her foot against the carpeted floor.

"Please. You think I'm stupid? You think I don't know Brandon's coming over?" She shakes her head. "Big deal. Who even cares? All

I want to do is watch TV—*that's it*. And the only reason you won't let me is because you want to hog the den with your boyfriend so you can make out on the couch. And that's exactly what I'm gonna tell Mom and Dad if you don't let me watch my show."

"Big deal. Who even cares?" I say, delivering a pitch-perfect imitation of her. "Mom said I could have friends over, *so there*." But the moment it's out, I can't help but cringe, wondering who's the child here, her or me?

I shake my head, knowing it's just another empty threat, but not willing to take any chances, I say, "Dad wants to leave early, which means you need to get some sleep so you're not all grumpy and cranky in the morning. And for your information, Brandon's *not* coming over." I smirk, hoping it'll mask the fact that I'm a horrible liar.

"Oh yeah?" She smiles, her eyes lighting up as they focus on mine. "Then why'd his Jeep just pull into the drive?"

I turn, peering out the window, then glancing at her. Sighing under my breath as I say, "Fine. Watch your show. Whatever. See if I care. But if it gives you nightmares again, don't come crying to me."

"C'mon, Ever, what's your deal?" Brandon says, his expression crossing the border from curious to annoyed in a matter of seconds. "I waited over an hour for your little sister to go to bed so we could be together and now you start acting like *this*. What gives?"

"Nothing," I mumble, refusing his gaze as I readjust my top. Peering at him from the corner of my eye as he shakes his head and buttons his jeans—jeans that I never asked to be *unbuttoned* in the first place.

"This is ridiculous," he mutters, shaking his head and fastening his belt. "I drive all the way over here, your parents are gone, and now you're acting like—"

"Like what?" I whisper, wanting him to say it. Hoping he can sum it up in just a few words, define just what it is that I'm going through. Because earlier, when I changed my mind and sent him the text asking him to come over, I thought it would put everything back to normal again. But from the moment I answered the door, my first instinct was to close it again. And no matter how hard I try, I can't figure out why I'm feeling this way.

I mean, when I look at him, it's obvious how lucky I am. He's nice, he's cute, he plays football, he's got a cool car, he's one of the most popular juniors—not to mention that I liked him for so long I could hardly believe it when I learned he liked me. But now everything's different. And it's not like I can force myself to feel things that I don't.

I take a deep breath, fully aware of the weight of his stare as I toy with my bracelet. Turning it around and around, trying to remember just how it got there. Aware of something niggling at the back of my mind, something about—

"Forget it," he says, getting up to leave. "But I'm serious, Ever. You need to decide what you want pretty soon, because this . . ."

I gaze at him, wondering if he'll finish the sentence and wondering why I can't seem to care either way.

But he just looks at me and shakes his head, grabbing his keys as he says, "Whatever. Have fun at the lake."

I watch as the door closes behind him, then I move to my dad's recliner, grab the afghan my grandma knit for us not long before she died, and pull it up to my chin and tuck it under my feet. Remembering how just last week I was telling Rachel I was seriously considering going all the way with Brandon, and now—now I can barely stand for him to touch me.

"Ever?"

I open my eyes. Riley's standing before me, her bottom lip trembling, her blue eyes on mine.

"Is he gone?" She glances around the room.

I nod.

"Will you come sit with me, while I try to fall asleep?" she asks, biting down on her lip, giving me that sad puppy dog look that's impossible to resist.

"I told you that show was too scary for you," I say, my hand on her shoulder as we head down the hall, getting her all tucked and settled before arranging myself right around her. Wishing her the sweetest of dreams and smoothing her hair off her face as I whisper, "Don't worry. Go to sleep. There's no such thing as ghosts."

forty-seven

"Ever, you ready? We need to leave soon! We don't want to hit traffic!"

"Coming!" I shout, even though I'm not. I just continue to stand there, right smack in the middle of my room staring at a crumpled piece of paper I'd found in the front pocket of my jeans. And even though it's written in my hand, I've no idea how it got there, much less what it means. Reading:

1. Don't go back for the sweatshirt!
2. Don't trust Drina!
3. Don't go back for the sweatshirt *no matter what!*
4. Damen ♡

And by the fifth time I read it, I'm still just as confused as the first. I mean, what sweatshirt? And why am I not supposed to go back for it? Not to mention, do I even know a Drina? And who the heck is Damen, and why is there a heart by his name?

I mean, *why* did I ever write such a thing? *When* did I ever write such a thing? And what could it possibly mean?

And when my dad calls again, followed by the sound of his footsteps storming up the stairs, I toss the paper aside, watching it land on my dresser before falling to the floor, figuring I'll sort it all out when we return.

As it turns out, the weekend was good for me. Good to get away from my school, good to get away from my friends (and boyfriend). Good to spend time with my family in a way that we don't get to do all that often. In fact, I feel so much better now, that as soon as we get back to civilization, back to where my cell can access a signal— I'm going to text Brandon. I don't want to leave things the way we had. And I really believe that whatever weird thing I was going through is now past.

I grab my backpack and toss it over my shoulder, ready to leave. But as I glance around our campsite one last time, I can't shake the feeling that I've left something behind. Even though my bag is packed and everything appears to be clear, I continue to stand there, my mom calling my name over and over, until she finally gives up and sends Riley.

"Hey," she says, pulling hard on my sleeve. "C'mon, everyone's waiting."

"In a minute," I mumble. "I just have to—"

"Have to *what*?" She smirks. "You have to stare at the smoldering embers for another hour or two? Seriously, Ever, what's your deal?"

I shrug, toying with the clasp on my bracelet, having no idea what my *deal* is, but unable to shake the feeling that something is wrong. Well, maybe not *wrong* exactly, more like *missing* or *undone*. Like there's something I'm supposed to be doing that I'm not. And I just can't decide what it is.

"Seriously. Mom wants you to hurry, Dad's worried about hitting traffic, even Buttercup wants you to get it together so he can stick his head out the window and let his ears flap in the breeze. Oh, and I'd kind of like to get home before all the good shows are over. So, what do you say we move it, okay?"

But when I don't move it, when I don't do much of anything, she sighs and says, "You forget something? Is that it?" Eyeballing me carefully before glancing over her shoulder toward our parents.

"Maybe." I shake my head. "I'm not sure."

"You got your backpack?"

I nod.

"You got your cell phone?"

I tap my backpack.

"You got your brain?"

I laugh, knowing I'm acting strange and ridiculous and freaky as hell, but then after the last few days you'd think I'd be used to it by now.

"You got your sky-blue Pinecone Lake Cheerleading Camp sweatshirt?" She smiles.

"That's it!" I say, my heart beating frantically. "I left it by the lake! Tell Mom and Dad I'll be right back!"

But just as I turn, Riley grabs hold of my sleeve and pulls me right back. "Chillax." She smiles. "Dad found it and tossed it in the backseat. Seriously. So can we go now?"

I glance around the campsite one last time, then follow Riley to the car. Settling into the back as my dad pulls onto the road and a muffled chime comes from my phone. And I've barely dug it out of my bag, barely even had a chance to read it, before Riley's peering over my shoulder, trying to peek. Forcing me to turn so abruptly, Buttercup shifts, shooting me a look that lets me know she's not happy. But even after all that, Riley still tries to see. So I roll my eyes and do what I always do, I whine, *"Mom!"*

Watching as she flips a page in her magazine without missing a beat, automatically saying, "Stop it you two."

"You didn't even look!" I say. "*I* wasn't doing anything! Riley won't leave me alone."

"That's because she *loves* you," my dad says, meeting my eyes in the rearview mirror. "She loves you *so much* she wants to be around you *all* of the time—she just can't get enough of you!"

Words that send Riley clear to the other side of the car, pressing her body against the door as she shouts, "Gag!" Then swinging her legs to her side as far as she can, upsetting poor Buttercup all over again. Shivering dramatically, as though the thought is just way too disgusting to bear, as my dad catches my eye and both of us laugh.

I flip my phone open, reading the message from Brandon that says: *Sorry. My bad. Call me 2nite.* And I immediately respond with a smiley face, hoping that'll tide us over until I can work up enough emotion to send something more.

And I've just leaned my head against the window and am about to close my eyes when Riley turns to me and says, "You can't go back, Ever. You can't change the past. *It just is.*" I squint, having no idea what she's talking about. But just as I start to ask, she shakes her head and says, "This is *our* destiny. *Not* yours. Did you ever stop and think that maybe you were supposed to survive? That maybe, it wasn't just Damen who saved you?"

I stare at her, my mouth hanging open, trying to make sense of her words. And when I glance around the car, wondering if my parents heard too, I see that everything is frozen. My dad's hands are stuck on the steering wheel, his unblinking eyes staring straight ahead, while the page of my mom's magazine is stuck in midflip, and Buttercup's tail is caught at half-mast. Even when I gaze out the window, I notice how all the birds are caught in midflight, while the other motorists are paused all around us. And when I look at Riley again, her intense gaze on mine as she leans toward me, it's clear we're the only ones moving.

"You have to go back," she says, her voice confident, firm. "You have to find Damen—before it's too late."

"Too late for *what*?" I cry, leaning toward her, desperate to understand. "And who the heck is Damen? Why are you saying that name? What does it even mean—"

But before I can finish, she's already rolling her eyes and pushing me away as though none of it happened.

"Jeez, stalk much?" She shakes her head. "I mean, seriously, Ever. *Boundaries!* Because regardless of what *he* thinks," she points toward our dad, "I have absolutely no interest in *you*."

She rolls her eyes and turns away, singing along to her iPod, her voice raspy, warbled, croaking out a Kelly Clarkson song in a way it was never intended. Oblivious to my mom who smiles and chucks her lightly on the knee, oblivious to my dad, gazing at me through the rearview mirror, our smiles meeting at the exact same moment, sharing a joke meant only for us.

Still holding that smile as a huge logging truck pulls out in front of us, slamming into the side of our car, and making the whole world go black.

forty-eight

The next thing I know I'm sitting on my bed, mouth wide open in a silent scream that never had a chance to be heard. Having lost my family for the second time in a year, left with only the echo of Riley's words:

You have to find Damen—before it's too late!

I spring from my bed and bolt for my den, going straight for the minifridge and finding the elixir and antidote gone. Unsure if it means I'm the only one who went back in time while everyone else stayed the same, or if I'm picking up right where I left off—with Damen in danger and me running away.

I sprint down the stairs, moving so fast they're like a blur under my feet, having no idea what day it is, or even what time, but knowing I've got to make it to Ava's before it's too late.

But just when I hit the landing, Sabine calls out, "Ever? Is that you?"

And I freeze, watching as she comes around the corner, wearing a stained apron with a full plate of brownies in hand.

"Oh, good." She smiles. "I just tried your mom's recipe—you know the ones she always used to bake? And I want you to try one and tell me what you think."

I freeze, unable to do anything but blink. Forcing a patience I don't really have when I say, "I'm sure they're fine. Listen, Sabine, I—"

But she doesn't let me finish. She just cocks her head to the side and says, "Well, aren't you at least going to try one?"

And I know this is not just about seeing me eat, it's also about wanting approval—*my* approval. She's been questioning whether or not she's fit to look after me, wondering if she's in some way responsible for my behavioral problems, thinking that if she'd only handled things better, none of this would've happened. I mean, my brilliant, successful, high-performing aunt, who's never lost a single court case—wants approval from *me*.

"Just one," she insists. "It's not like I'm trying to *poison* you!" And when her eyes meet mine, I can't help but notice her seemingly random choice of words, wondering if it's some sort of message, pushing me to hurry, but knowing I have to get through this first. "I know they're probably not nearly as good as your mom's, because hers were the undisputed best, but it *is* her recipe—and for some reason I woke up early this morning with this overwhelming urge to make them. And so I thought—"

Knowing she's capable of going into a full-on opening argument in her pursuit to convince me, I reach toward the stack of brownies. Going for the smallest square, figuring I'll just eat it and run. But when I see the unmistakable letter *E* carved right in its center—I *know*.

It's my sign.

The one I've been waiting for all along.

Just when I'd given up hope, Riley pulled through. Marking the smallest brownie on the plate with my initial in the exact same way that she used to do.

And when I look for the largest one and see an *R* carved onto it, I definitely know it's from her. The secret message, the sign she promised, right before she left me for good.

But still, not wanting to be some crazy delusional person who finds secret meaning in a plate of baked goods, I glance at Sabine and say, "Did you—" I point at my brownie, the one with my initial carved into its middle. "Did you put that there?"

She squints, first at me, and then at the brownie, then she shakes her head and says, "Listen, Ever, if you don't want to try it, then you certainly don't have to, I just thought—"

But before she can finish, I've already plucked it off the plate and plopped it into my mouth, closing my eyes as I savor its chewy sweetness, immediately immersed in the feeling of *home*. That wonderful place I was lucky enough to revisit, no matter how short a time—finally realizing it's not relegated to just one single place, it's wherever you make it.

Sabine looks at me, her face anxious, awaiting my approval. "I tried them once before, but for some reason they didn't turn out nearly as good as your mom's." She shrugs, gazing at me shyly, eagerly awaiting my verdict. "She used to joke that she used a secret ingredient, but now I wonder if that might've been true."

I swallow hard, wiping the crumbs from my lips, and smiling when I say, "There *was* a secret ingredient." Seeing her expression fall, wondering if that means they're no good. "The secret ingredient was *love*," I tell her. "And you must've used plenty, because these are awesome."

"Really?" Her eyes light up.

"Really." I hug her to me, but only for a moment before I'm pulling away. "Today's Friday, right?"

She looks at me, her brows merged. "Yes, it's Friday. Why? Are you okay?"

But I just nod and flee out the door, knowing I've even less time than I thought.

forty-nine

I pull into Ava's drive, and park my car sloppily—back wheels on the cement, front wheels on the grass, moving toward the door so quickly I barely acknowledge the stairs. But just as I reach it, I take a step back—something feels weird, off, strange in a way I can't quite explain. Like it's too *quiet*, too *still*. Even though the house appears just as I left it—planters on either side of the door, welcome mat in place—it's static in a way that seems eerie. And as I raise my knuckles to knock, I've just barely tapped it when it opens before me.

I head through the living room and into the kitchen, calling out for Ava and noticing how everything is just as I left it—teacup on the counter, cookies on a plate, everything in its usual place. But when I peek in the cupboard and see that the antidote and elixir are missing, I'm not sure what to think. Not knowing if it means that my plan worked and it wasn't needed after all, or if the opposite is true, and that something's gone wrong.

I race toward the indigo door at the end of the hall, eager to see if Damen's still there, but I'm blocked by Roman who stands right before it. His face widening into a a grin as he says, "So nice to have you back, Ever. Though I told Ava you would be. You know what they say—you can't go home again!"

I take in his deliberately tousled hair that perfectly frames the Ouroboros tattoo on his neck—knowing that despite my advances, despite my waking the school, he's still the one in charge around here.

"Where's Damen?" My eyes rake over his face, my gut twisting tight. "And what've you done with Ava?"

"Now, now." He smiles. "Don't you worry 'bout a thing. Damen's right where you left him. Though I must say I can't believe that you left him. I underestimated you. I had no idea. Though I can't help but wonder how Damen would feel if he knew. I bet he underestimated you too."

I swallow hard, remembering Damen's last words: *You left me.* Knowing he didn't underestimate me at all, he knew exactly which path I'd choose.

"And as for Ava." Roman smiles. "You'll be happy to know that I've *done* nothing with her. You should know by now that I only have eyes for *you*," he murmurs, moving so fast I've barely had a chance to blink when his face is mere inches from mine. "Ava left on her own accord. Allowing us our privacy. And now that it's just a matter of—" He pauses to glance at his watch. "Well—seconds really, until you and I can make it official. You know, minus all the nasty guilt you would've felt had we hooked up sooner—before he'd had a chance to *pass*. Not that I would've felt guilty, but you strike me as the sort who likes to think of yourself as good and pure and well intentioned and all that rubbish, which, truth be told, really is a bit too maudlin for my tastes. But I'm sure we'll find a way to work through all that."

I tune out his words as I plan my next move. Trying to determine his weakness, his kryptonite, his most vulnerable chakra. Since he's blocking the very door I need to get through, the door that leads to Damen, I've no choice but to go *through* him. Though I need to be careful with how I proceed. Because when I do make a move, it needs to be swift, unexpected, right on target. Otherwise, I'm in for a battle I may never win.

He lifts his hand to my face and caresses my cheek, and I slap it so hard the crunch of his bones pierces the air as his crumpled fingers wobble and dangle before me.

"*Ouch.*" He smiles, shaking his hand as he flexes his instantly healed digits. "You're a feisty one, aren't you? But you know how that only turns me on, right?" I roll my eyes, feeling his cold breath on my cheek as he says, "Why do you continue to fight me, Ever? Why do you push me away when I'm all you have left?"

"Why are you doing this?" I ask, my stomach twitching as his eyes darken and narrow, displaying a complete absence of color and light. "What did Damen ever do to you?"

He tilts his head back, peering at me when he says, "It's real simple, darlin'." His voice suddenly changing, dropping the British accent and adopting a tone I've never heard from him before. "He killed Drina. So I'm killing him. And then everything's even. Case closed."

And the second he says it, I *know*. I know exactly how I'll take him down and get behind that door. Because along with the *who* and the *how*, I've now got the *why*. The elusive motive I've needed all this time. And now the only thing standing between Damen and me is one solid punch to Roman's navel chakra, or sacral center as it's sometimes called—the center of jealousy, envy, and the irrational desire to possess.

One solid blow and Roman is history.

But still, before I take him down, I've one more thing to do. So I look at him, my gaze fixed and unwavering when I say, "But Damen didn't kill Drina. *I* did."

"Nice try." He laughs. "Pathetic, a bit maudlin like I said, but I'm afraid it won't work. You can't save Damen that way."

"But why not? If you're so interested in justice, an eye for an eye and all that—then you should know that *I'm* the one who did it." I nod, my voice taking on new urgency and strength. "*I'm* the one who killed that bitch." Watching as he sways, ever so slightly, but still enough for me to notice. "She was always hanging around, completely obsessed with Damen. You must've known that, right? That she was totally fixated on him?"

He winces. Neither confirming nor denying, but that wince is all I need to keep going, knowing I've hit the sore spot. "She wanted me out of the way so she could have Damen to herself, and after months of my trying to ignore her and hoping she'd go away, she was dumb enough to show up at my house and try to confront me. And—well—when she refused to back down and went after me instead—I killed her." I shrug, relaying the story with a lot more calm than I felt at the time, making sure to leave out my own ineptitude, cluelessness, and fears. "And it was so *easy*." I smile, shaking my head as though reliving the moment all over again. "Seriously. You should've *seen* her. It's like, one moment she was standing before me all flaming red hair and white skin—and the next—*gone*! And by the way, Damen didn't show up until the deed was already done. So, as you see, if anyone's guilty, it's *me* and not him."

My gaze is on his, my fists ready to strike, moving right into his space when I say, "So, what do you say? You still wanna date me? Or would you rather kill me instead? Either way, I'll understand." I place my hand on his chest and push him hard against the door. Thinking how easy it would be to just lower it a few inches, jab really hard, and be done with all this.

"*You?*" he says, the word more like a question, a crisis of conscience, than the accusation he meant it to be. "You and *not* Damen?"

I nod, my body tensed, poised for fight, knowing nothing will keep me from getting into that room, and raising my fist as he says, "It's not too late! We can still save him!"

I freeze, my fist hovering at the halfway mark, unsure if I'm being played.

Watching as he shakes his head, visibly distressed when he says, "I didn't know—I thought for sure it was him—he gave me *everything*—he gave me *life*—*this life*! And I thought for sure that he—"

He moves around me and flees down the hall, calling, "You go check on him—I'll get the antidote!"

fifty

The first thing I see when I burst through the door is Damen. Still lying on the futon, looking as thin and pale as he did when I left him.

The second thing I see is Rayne. Huddling by his side, pressing a damp cloth to his face. Her eyes growing wide when she sees me, her hand held up before her as she shouts, "Ever, *no*! Don't come any closer! If you want to save Damen, then stop right there—do *not* break the circle!"

I gaze down, seeing some grainy white substance that looks just like salt, formed into a perfect ring that keeps the two of them in and me out. Then I look at her, wondering what she wants, what she could possibly have in mind cowering beside Damen and warning me away. Noticing how she looks even odder outside of Summerland with her ghostly pale face, tiny features, and large coal-black eyes.

But when my gaze shifts to Damen, watching as he fights and struggles for each breath—I know I have to get to him, no matter what she says. It's my fault he's like this. I abandoned him. Left him behind. I was stupid, and selfish, and naïve enough to think that everything would work out okay just because I wanted it to, and that Ava would stick around to pick up the pieces.

I step forward, my toe landing just outside the border as Roman rushes in from behind me and shouts, "What the bloody hell is *she* doing in here?" His eyes wide with shock as he gapes at Rayne, still crouching beside Damen from behind the barrier.

"Don't trust him!" she says, her eyes darting between us. "He knew I was here all along."

"I didn't know any such thing! I've never even seen you before!" He shakes his head. "I mean, sorry darlin', but Catholic schoolgirls just ain't my thing. I prefer my women a little more feisty, like Ever, here." He reaches toward me, trailing his fingers down the length of my back, chilling my skin in a way that makes me want to react— but I don't. I just take a deep breath and try to stay calm. Focusing on his *other* hand—the one that's holding the antidote—the key to saving Damen.

Because in the end, that's the only thing that matters— everything else can wait.

I snatch the bottle and unscrew the top. And I'm just about to penetrate Rayne's circle of protection when Roman puts his hand on my arm and says, "Not so fast."

I pause, glancing between them, Rayne looking me right in the eye when she says, "Don't do it, Ever! Whatever he tells you, do *not* listen. Listen only to me. Ava dumped the antidote and ran off with the elixir not long after you left, but luckily I got here just before *he* did." She gestures toward Roman, her eyes like angry points of the darkest night. "He needs you to break the circle so he can get in, because he can't get to Damen without you. Only the worthy can access the circle, only those with good intent. But if you step in now, Roman will follow, so if you care about Damen, if you truly want to protect him, you have to wait until Romy gets here."

"Romy?"

Rayne nods, glancing between Roman and me. "She's bringing the antidote, it will be ready by nightfall since it needs the full moon's energy to be fully complete."

But Roman just shakes his head, laughing as he says, "What antidote? I'm the only one with the antidote. Hell, I'm the one who made the poison, so what the hell does she know?" And when he sees the confusion on my face, he adds, "I really don't see how you have much of a choice. If you listen to this one"—he flicks his fingers toward Rayne—"Damen *will* die. But if you listen to me, he *won't*. The math's rather simple, don't you think?"

I look at Rayne, watching as she shakes her head and warns me not to listen to him, to hold out for Romy, to wait for nightfall, which is still hours away. But then I gaze at Damen beside her, his breath becoming more labored, the color drained from his face—

"And if you're trying to trick me?" I say, all of my attention now focused on Roman.

Holding my breath as he says, "Then he dies."

I swallow hard and stare at the floor, unsure what to do. Do I trust Roman, the rogue immortal who's responsible for all of this in the first place? Or do I trust Rayne, the creepy twin with her covert double-talk and an agenda that's never been clear? But when I close my eyes and try to concentrate on my gut, knowing that it's rarely wrong, even though I often ignore it, it's frustratingly still.

Then looking at Roman when he says, "But if I'm *not* tricking you, then he *lives*. So I really don't see how you have much of a choice—"

"Don't listen to him," Rayne says. "He's *not* here to help you, *I* am! *I'm* the one who sent you the vision in Summerland that day, *I'm* the one who showed you all the ingredients required to save him. You were shut out of the akashic records because you'd already made your choice. And while we tried to show you the way, while we tried to help you and stop you from leaving, you refused to listen, and now—"

"I thought you didn't know my business?" I narrow my gaze. "I thought you and your creepy sister couldn't access—" I pause, glancing at Roman, knowing I have to tread carefully with what I'm about to say. "I thought you couldn't *see* certain things."

Rayne looks at me, her face stricken, shaking her head as she says, "We never lied to you, Ever. And we never misled you. We *can't* see certain things, that's true. But Romy's an empath and I'm a precog, and together we get feelings and visions. That's how we first found you, and we've been trying to guide you ever since, using the information we sense. Ever since Riley asked us to look after you—"

"*Riley?*" I gape, my stomach swirling with nausea. *How could she be involved in any of this?*

"We met her in Summerland and showed her around. We even went to school together, a private boarding school she manifested, which is why we wear this." She motions to her plaid skirt and blazer, the uniform she and her sister always wear. And I remember how Riley always dreamed of going to boarding school, saying it was so she could get away from me. So it makes sense that she'd manifest one. "Then, when she decided to—" she pauses, glancing at Roman before she continues, "to *cross over*, she asked us to look after you if we ever saw you around."

"I don't believe you," I say, even though I have no reason not to. "Riley would've told me, she would've . . ." But then I remember how she once said something about meeting some people who showed her around, and I wonder if she was referring to the twins.

"We also know Damen—he—he helped us once—a long time ago . . ." And when she looks at me, I'm just about to fold when she says, "But if you could just wait a few more hours until the antidote's complete, then Romy will be here and . . ."

I glance at Damen, his emaciated body, his pale, clammy skin, his eyes appearing sunken, his breath ragged, every inhale and exhale progressively weaker—and I know there's only one choice to make.

So I turn my back on Rayne and look at Roman when I say, "Okay, just tell me what to do."

fifty-one

Roman nods, his eyes on mine as he removes the antidote from my grasp and says, "We'll need something sharp."

I squint, not quite understanding. "What're you talking about? If that's *really* the antidote like you say, then why can't he just drink it? I mean, it's ready, right?" My stomach twisting under the weight of his gaze, so steady and focused on mine.

"It *is* the antidote. It just requires one final ingredient to make it complete."

I suck in my breath, knowing I should've known better, that it couldn't be that easy when Roman's involved. "What is it?" I say, my voice as shaky as I feel inside. "What kind of game are you playing?"

"There, there." He smiles. "Not to worry. It's nothing too complicated—and it certainly won't take *hours*." He shakes his head at Rayne. "All we need to get this show on the road is just a drop or two of your blood. That's it."

I stare at him, not comprehending. I mean, how could that make the slightest bit of difference between life and death?

But Roman just looks at me, answering the question in my head when he says, "In order to save your immortal partner, he must consume an antidote containing a drop of his true love's blood. Believe me, it's the only way."

I swallow hard, far less afraid of shedding blood than being played a fool and losing Damen for good.

"Surely you're not worried that you're not really Damen's one true love—*are you*?" he asks, his lips curving the tiniest bit. "Perhaps I should call Stacia instead?"

I grasp a pair of nearby scissors and aim them toward my wrist, and I'm just about to plunge when Rayne screams, "Ever, *no! Don't* do it! It's a trick! Don't believe him! Don't listen to a word he says!"

I look at Damen, seeing the labored rise and fall of his chest moving so slow and ragged now there's no time to waste. I know in my heart that he has only minutes left, not hours. Then I bring the scissors down hard, watching as their sharp pointy tip penetrates my wrist, nearly splitting it in two. Shooting a geyser of blood straight into the air, before gravity takes over and pushes it down. Hearing Rayne scream, a wail so piercing it cuts through the sound of everything else, as Roman crouches beneath me, collecting my blood.

And other than feeling faint, and the slightest bit dizzy, it's only a matter of seconds before my veins are fused and my skin is all healed. So I grab the bottle, ignore Rayne's protests, and break through the circle, pushing her aside as I drop to my knees, slipping my fingers under Damen's neck as I force him to drink. Watching his breath grow fainter and fainter—until it stops completely.

"*NO!*" I cry. "You *can't* die—you *can't* leave me!" I force the liquid down the length of his throat, determined to bring him back, return him to life, like he once did with me.

I hold him to me, willing him to live. Everything around us completely shut out as I focus on Damen, my one true soul mate, my eternal partner, my only love, refusing to say good-bye, refusing to give up hope. And when the bottle is empty, I collapse onto his chest, pressing my lips against his, filling him with my breath, my being, my *life*. As I murmur the words he once said to me: "Open your eyes and look at me!"

Over and over again—

Until he finally does.

"Damen!" I cry, a flood of tears streaming down my cheeks and onto his face. "Oh, thank God, you're back! I missed you so much—and I love you—and I promise I'll never *ever* leave you again! Just—just please forgive me—please—"

His eyes flicker open as his mouth tries to move, forming words I can't hear. And when I lower my ear to his lips, so grateful to be with him again, our reunion is cut short by a series of claps.

Slow, steady claps coming from Roman who's now standing behind me. Having penetrated the circle as Rayne cowers in a far corner of the room.

"Bravo!" he says, his face mocking, amused, as he glances between Damen and me. "Well done, Ever. I must say, that was all very—*touching.* It's not often one bears witness to such a heartfelt reunion."

I swallow hard, my hands shaking, my stomach beginning to ping, wondering what he could possibly be up to. I mean, Damen's alive, the antidote worked, what else could there be?

I glance at Damen, watching the steady rise and fall of his chest as he falls back to sleep, then I gaze toward Rayne who's looking at me with widened eyes and an expression of disbelief.

But when I look at Roman again, I'm sure he's just enjoying a last chance at fun, a pathetic show of bravado now that Damen is saved. "So, you want to go after me now? Is that it?" I say, fully prepared to take him down if I have to.

But he just shakes his head and laughs. "Now why would I want to do that? Why would I want to rid myself of a whole new brand of fun that's only just begun?"

I freeze, panic building inside me, but trying not to show it.

"I had no idea you'd be so easy, so predictable, but then again, that's love, right? It tends to make one a little bit crazy, a tad bit impulsive, even irrational, don't you think?"

I narrow my eyes, having no idea what he's going on and on about but knowing it can't be good.

"And yet, it's amazing how quickly you fell for it. No sales resistance at all. Seriously, Ever, you just sliced yourself open with virtually no questions asked. Which goes back to my original point, never underestimate the power of love—or, in your case, was it guilt? Only you know for sure."

I stare at him, a horrible understanding growing inside me, knowing I've made a grave mistake—that I've somehow been played.

"You were just *so* desperate to trade your life for his, *so* willing to do anything to save him—that it all went so seamlessly, so much easier than I ever expected. Though truth be told, I know just how you feel. In fact, I would've done the same thing for Drina—if only I'd been given the choice." He glares at me, his lids so narrowed his eyes are like angry slivers of darkness. "But, since we already know how that ended, I suppose you'd like to know how this ends too, right?"

I glance at Damen, ensuring he's still okay, watching him sleep as Roman says, "Yes, he's still alive, don't worry your pretty head about that. And just so you know, he'll most likely remain that way for many, many, *many* years to come. I have no plans to go after him again, so don't you fret. In fact, it was never my intention to kill either one of you, regardless of what you might've thought. Though, in all fairness, I suppose I should warn you that all this happiness does bear a cost."

"What is it?" I whisper, staring at Roman, having no idea what he could want besides Drina who's already gone. Besides, whatever the cost, I'll pay it. If it means getting Damen back, I'll do what it takes.

"I see I've upset you," he coos, shaking his head. "Now I've already told you that Damen will be fine. In fact, more than fine. He'll be raring to go and better than ever. Just look at him, would you?

See how his color's returned, how his form's bulking up? Very soon he'll be right back to that handsome, strapping young lad you've convinced yourself that you love so damn much you'd do *anything* to save him, no questions asked—"

"Get to the point," I say, my eyes on his, annoyed by the way these immortal rogues always insist on making every single moment about *them*.

"Oh no." He shakes his head. "I've waited *years* for this moment, and I will *not* be rushed. You see, Damen and I go way back. Back to the very beginning, in Florence, where we met." And when he sees my expression, he adds, "Yes, I was a fellow orphan, the youngest orphan, and when he spared me from the plague I looked to him like a father."

"Which would make Drina your mother?" I say, watching his gaze harden before relaxing again.

"Hardly." He smiles. "You see, I loved Drina, I'm not afraid to admit it. I loved her with all of my heart. I loved her in the same way you think you love him." He motions toward Damen, who's returned to the way he was when we met. "I loved her with every ounce of my being, I would've done anything for her—and I never would've abandoned her like you did with him."

I swallow hard, knowing I deserve that.

"But it was always about Damen. *Always. About. Damen.* That's all she could focus on. All she could see. Until he met you—the first time—and Drina turned to me." He smiles briefly, but it quickly fades when he says, "For *friendship*," practically spitting the word. "And *companionship*. And a big strong shoulder to cry on." He scowls. "I would've given her anything she wanted—anything in the world—but she already had everything—and all she wanted was the one thing I couldn't give her, *wouldn't* give her—Damen. *Sodding. Auguste.*" He shakes his head. "And unfortunately for Drina, Damen only wanted *you*. And so it began—a love triangle that lasted four hundred years, each of us relentless, driven, never once giving up hope, until I was *forced* to—because *you* killed her. Guaranteeing we'd never be together. Guaranteeing our love would never be known—"

"You knew I killed her?" I gasp, my stomach twisting into a horrible knot. "This *whole* time?"

He rolls his eyes. "Well, *duh!*" He laughs, performing a perfect imitation of Stacia at her brattiest. "I had it all planned, though I must say, you really threw me for a loop when you abandoned him like that. I underestimated you, Ever. I truly did. But even so, I held on to my plans, I told Ava you'd be back."

Ava.

I look at him, my eyes wide, not sure I want to know what happened to the one person I thought I could trust.

"Ah, yes, your good friend Ava. The only one you could count on, right?" He nods. "Well, as it turns out, she gave me a reading once, quite a good one too I might say, and well, we kept in touch. You know she practically fled town the moment you left? Took all the elixir too. Left Damen alone in this room, vulnerable, defenseless, just waiting for me. Didn't even stick around long enough to see if your little theory was true—figuring you were long gone, so, either way, you'd never know the difference. You know, you really should be more careful about who you trust, Ever. You shouldn't be so naïve."

I swallow hard and shrug. There's nothing I can do about it now. I can't take it back, I can't change the past, the only thing I can change now is what happens next.

"Oh, and I loved how you kept peering at my wrist, searching for my Ouroboros tattoo." He laughs. "Little did you realize we wear them wherever we choose, so I chose my neck."

I stand there silently, hoping to hear more. Damen didn't even know there were immortal rogues until Drina went bad.

"I started it." He nods, his right hand over his heart. "I'm the founding father of the Immortal Rogue tribe. While it's true that your friend Damen gave us all the first drink, when the effects began to wear off, he left us to age and wither, refusing to give us more."

I shrug and roll my eyes. Granting someone over a century's worth of living is hardly what I'd call selfish.

"And that's when I started experimenting, learning from the world's greatest alchemists until I'd surpassed Damen's work."

"You call that a triumph? Turning evil? Taking and giving life at will? Playing *God*?"

"I do what I have to." He shrugs, inspecting his nails. "At least I didn't leave the remaining orphans to shrivel. Unlike Damen, I cared enough to track them down and save them. And yeah, every now and then I recruit someone new. Though I assure you there's no harm done to the innocent, only to those who deserve it."

Our eyes meet, but I quickly look away. Damen and I should've seen this coming, shouldn't have assumed Drina was the end.

"So imagine my surprise when I show up here only to find this— little—urchin—huddling with Damen in her little magick circle, while her creepy twin runs around town, trying to piece an antidote together before nightfall." Roman laughs. "Quite a successful search too, I might add. You should've waited, Ever. You shouldn't have broken the circle. Those two deserve far more credit than you were willing to give them, but then, as I said, you do have a tendency to trust the wrong ones. Anyway, meanwhile back at the bungalow, I just kicked around here, waiting for you to show up and break the protective seal, like I knew you would."

"Why?" I gaze at Damen, then over at Rayne, still huddled in the corner, too frightened to move. "What difference does it make?"

"Well, it *is* what killed him." He shrugs. "He could've lived for days had you not broken through like that. Lucky for you I had the antidote on hand to bring him back. And even though there's a price, a huge hefty price, what's done is done, right? And now there's no going back. *No. Going. Back.* You understand that better than any of us now, don't you?"

"Enough," I say, my hands curled into fists. Thinking I should get rid of him now, eliminate him for good. I mean, Damen's safe, Roman's not needed, so what harm could it do?

Except that I can't. It's not right. I mean, Damen *is* safe. And I can't just go *eliminating* people just because I deem them no good. I can't abuse my power that way. Much is expected to those given much, and all that.

I relax my fists, unfolding my fingers as he says, "That's a wise choice. You don't want to do anything too rash, even though soon you'll be tempted. Because you see, Ever, while Damen's going to be fine, perfectly fine and healthy and basically everything you could ever want him to be, I'm afraid that's just going to make it all the more difficult when you realize you can never be together."

I look at him, my fingers shaking, my eyes blazing, refusing to believe him. Damen's going to live—I'm going to live—so what could possibly keep us apart?

"Don't believe me?" He shrugs. "Fine, go ahead, consummate your love and find out. It's not like I care. My loyalties to Damen ended centuries ago. So I'll have absolutely no qualms when you jump his bones and he ends up dead." He smiles, his eyes right on mine, and when he sees the incredulous look on my face, his smile grows into a laugh. A laugh so large it reaches toward the ceiling and shakes the walls of this room, before it settles all around us like a blanket of doom.

"Have I ever lied to you, Ever? Go ahead, think about it. I'll wait. Haven't I been truthful all along? Oh, sure I may have saved a few of the smaller, insignificant details for last, which, though it may be quite naughty of me, really does add to the fun. But now, it seems we've come to the point of full disclosure, so I'd like to make it clear, crystal clear, that the two of you can *never* be together. No DNA exchange whatsoever. And in case you still don't get what that means, then allow me to spell it out by stating that no bodily fluids of any kind may ever be exchanged. And just in case you need a translation of *that,* well, it means you can't kiss, lick, spit into each other's mouths, share each other's elixir—oh, and of course, you also can't do what's yet to be done. Hell, you can't even cry on his shoulder over the fact that you can't do what's yet to be done. In short, you can't do *anything.* Or at least not with each other. Because if you do, Damen will die."

"I don't believe you," I say, my heart racing, my palms slick with sweat. "How is that even possible?"

"Well, I may not be a doctor or scientist by profession, but I did study with some of the greats back in the day. Do Albert Einstein, Max Planck, Sir Isaac Newton, or Galileo mean anything to you?"

I shrug, wishing he'd stop name-dropping and get on with it already.

"So, in the simplest terms, allow me to say that while the antidote alone would've saved him by stopping the receptors from multiplying additional aged and damaged cells, the moment we added your blood, we made sure that any future reintroduction of your DNA will only cause them to go active again, thereby reversing the entire process and killing him. But we don't need to go all Science Channel here, just know that you can never be together again. *Never.* Understood? Because if you do, Damen dies. And now that I've told you—the rest is up to you."

I stare at the ground, wondering what I've done, how I could've been stupid enough to trust him. Barely listening when he says, "And if you don't believe me, then go ahead, hop on board and give it a try. But when he keels over, don't come crying to me."

Our eyes lock, and just like that day at the lunch tables at school, I'm sucked inside the abyss of his mind. Feeling his longing for Drina, her longing for Damen, his longing for me, my longing for home, and knowing it's all resulted in *this*.

I shake my head, wrenching myself from his grip as he says, "Oh, look, he's waking! And looking as gorgeous and hunky as ever. Enjoy your reunion, darlin', but remember, don't enjoy it *too* much!"

I glance over my shoulder, seeing Damen beginning to stir, stretching his body and rubbing his eyes, then I lunge for Roman, wanting to hurt him, destroy him, make him pay for all that he did.

But he just laughs and dances out of my way, heading for the door and smiling as he says, "Trust me, you don't want to do that. You just might need me someday."

I stand before him, shaking with rage, tempted to plunge my fist into his most vulnerable chakra and watch him vanish forever.

"I know you don't believe it now, but why don't you take a moment to think about it. Now that you can no longer cuddle with Damen, you're about to become very lonely, very quickly. And since I pride myself on being the forgiving type, I'd be more than willing to fill your void."

I narrow my eyes and raise my fist.

"And then—there's the small, inconsequential fact that there just may be an antidote to the antidote —"

His eyes meet mine as I suck in my breath.

"And since I created it, only I would know for sure. So, the way I see it, you eliminate me, you eliminate any hope of the two of you ever being together. Is that a risk you're willing to take?"

We stand there, the two of us joined in the most hideous way, our eyes locked, unmoving, until Damen calls my name.

And when I turn, all I see is *him*. Returned to his usual splendor as he rises from the futon and I rush to his arms. Feeling his wonderful warmth as he presses his body to mine, gazing at me in the way that he used to—as though I'm the most important thing in his world.

I bury my face in his chest, his shoulder, his neck, my entire body thrumming with tingle and heat as I whisper his name again and again, my lips moving across the cotton of his shirt, summoning his warmth, his strength, wondering how I'll ever find the words to confess the horrible thing that I've done.

"What happened?" he asks, his eyes on mine as he pulls away. "Are you okay?"

I glance around the room, noticing Roman and Rayne are both gone. Then I peer into his deep dark eyes as I say, "You don't remember?"

He shakes his head.

"None of it?"

He shrugs. "The last thing I remember is Friday night, at the play. And then after—" He squints. "What is this place? Surely this isn't the Montage?"

I lean into his body as we head for the door. Knowing I have to tell him—sooner rather than later—but wanting to put it off for as long as I can. Wanting to enjoy the fact that he's back—that he's alive and well and we're together again. Heading down the steps and unlocking my car as I say, "You were sick. *Very* sick. But now you're better. But it's kind of a long story, so—" I shove the key in the ignition, as he places his hand on my knee.

"So where do we go from here?" he asks, as I shift into reverse.

Feeling his gaze as I take a deep breath and pull onto the street, determined to ignore the much larger question in his question, when I smile and say, "Anywhere we want. The weekend starts now."

Read on for a preview of the next book
in Alyson Noël's Immortals series

Shadowland

Available from St. Martin's Griffin in February 2010

•   •   •

Fate is nothing but the deeds committed in a prior state of existence.
—Ralph Waldo Emerson

one

"Everything is energy."

Damen's dark eyes focus on mine, urging me to listen, really listen this time. "Everything around us—" His arm sweeps before him, tracing a fading horizon that'll soon fade to black. "Everything in this seemingly solid universe of ours isn't solid at all—it's energy— pure vibrating energy. And while our perception may convince us that things are either solid or liquid or gaseous—on the quantum level it's all just particles within particles—it's all just *energy.*"

I press my lips together and nod, his voice overpowered by the one in my head urging: *Tell him! Tell him now! Quit stalling, and just get it over with! Hurry, before he starts talking again!*

But I don't. I don't say a word. I just wait for him to continue so I can delay even further.

"Raise your hand." He nods, his palm facing out, moving toward mine, as I lift my arm slowly, cautiously, determined to avoid any and all physical contact, when he says, "Now tell me, what do you see?"

I squint, unsure what he's after, then shrugging I say, "Well, I see pale skin, long fingers, a freckle or two, nails in serious need of a manicure . . ."

"Exactly." He smiles, as though I just passed the world's easiest test. "But if you could see it as it *really* is, you wouldn't see that at all. Instead, you'd see a swarm of molecules containing protons, neutrons, electrons, and quarks. And within those tiny quarks, down to the most minuscule point, you'd see nothing but pure vibrating energy moving at a slow enough speed that makes it appear solid and dense, and yet quickly enough that it can't be observed for what it truly is."

I narrow my eyes, not sure I believe it. Never mind the fact that he's been studying this stuff for hundreds of years.

"Seriously, Ever. Nothing is separate." He leans toward me, fully warmed up to his subject now. "Everything is one. Items that appear dense, like you, and me, and this sand that we're sitting on, is really just a mass of energy vibrating slowly enough to seem solid, while things like ghosts and spirits vibrate so quickly they're nearly impossible for most humans to see."

"I see Riley," I say, eager to remind him of all the time I used to spend with my ghostly sister. "Or at least I used to, you know, before she crossed the bridge and moved on."

"And that's exactly why you can't see her anymore." He nods. "Her vibration is moving too fast. Though there are those who can see past all of that."

I gaze at the ocean before us, the swells rolling in, one after another. Endless, unceasing, immortal—like us.

"Now raise your hand again and bring it so close to mine we just nearly touch."

I hesitate, filling my palm with sand, unwilling to do it. Unlike him, I know the price, the dire consequences the slightest skin-on-skin contact can bring. Which is why I've been avoiding his touch since last Friday. But when I peer at him again, his palm waiting for mine, I take a deep breath and lift my hand too—gasping when he draws so close the space that divides us is razor thin.

"Feel that?" He smiles. "That tingle and heat? That's our energy connecting." He moves his hand back and forth, manipulating the push and pull of the energy field between us.

"But if we're all connected, like you say, then why doesn't it feel the same?" I whisper, drawn by the undeniable magnetic stream that links us, causing the most wonderful warmth to course through my body.

"We *are* all connected, we're made of the same vibrating source. But while some energy leaves you cold and some leaves you luke-warm, the one that you're destined for?—it feels just like *this*."

I close my eyes and turn away, allowing the tears to stream down my cheeks, no longer able to keep them in check. Knowing I'm barred from the feel of his skin, the touch of his lips, the solid warm comfort of his body on mine. This electric energy field that trembles between us is the closest I'll get, thanks to the horrible decision I made.

"Science is just now catching up with what metaphysicians and the great spiritual teachers have known for centuries. Everything is *energy*. Everything is *one*."

I can hear the smile in his voice as he draws closer, eager to en-twine his fingers with mine. But I move away quickly, catching his eye just long enough to see the look of hurt that crosses his face—the same look he's been giving me since I made him drink the anti-dote that returned him to life. He's wondering why I'm acting so quiet, so distant, so remote—refusing to touch him when only a few weeks before I couldn't get enough. Incorrectly assuming it's because of his hurtful behavior—his flirting with Stacia, his cruelty toward me—when the truth is, it has nothing to do with that. He was under Roman's spell; the entire school was. It wasn't his fault.

What he doesn't know is that while the antidote returned him to life, the moment I added my blood to the mix it also ensured we could never be together.

Never.

Ever.

For all of eternity.

Unless we can find an antidote to the antidote, that is.

"Ever?" he whispers, his voice deep and sincere. But I can't look at him. Can't touch him. And I certainly can't utter the words he deserves to hear:

I messed up—I'm so sorry—Roman tricked me, and I was desperate and dumb enough to fall for his ploy—and now there's no hope for us because if you kiss me, if we exchange our DNA—you'll die—

I can't do it. I'm the worst kind of coward. I'm pathetic and weak. And there's just no way I can find it within me.

"Ever, please, what is it?" he asks, alarmed by my tears. "You've been like this for days. Is it me? Is it something I've done? Because you know I don't remember much of what happened, and the memories that are starting to surface, well, you must know by now that wasn't the real me. I would *never* intentionally hurt you. I would *never* harm you in any way."

I hug myself tightly, scrunching my shoulders and bowing my head. Wishing I could make myself smaller, so small he could no longer see me. Knowing his words are true, that he's incapable of hurting me, only I could do something so hurtful, so rash, so ridiculously impulsive. Only I could be stupid enough to fall for Roman's bait. So eager to prove myself as Damen's one true love—wanting to be the only one who could save him—and now look at the mess that I've made.

He moves toward me, sliding his arm around me, grasping my waist and pulling me near. But I can't risk the closeness, my tears are lethal now, and must be kept far from his skin.

I scramble to my feet and run toward the ocean, curling my toes at its edge and allowing the cold white froth to splash onto my shins. Wishing I could dive under its vastness and be carried by the tide. Anything to avoid saying the words—anything to avoid telling my one true love, my eternal partner, my soul mate for the last four hundred years, that while he may have given me eternity, I've brought us our end.

I remain like that, silent and still, waiting for the sun to sink, until I finally turn to face him. Taking in his dark shadowy outline that is nearly indistinguishable from the night, and speaking past the sting in my throat when I mumble, "Damen . . . baby . . . there's something I need to tell you."